YORK NOTES

THE BLOODY CHAMBER

ANGELA CARTER

Notes by Steve Roberts
Revised by David Grant

Longman
is an imprint of

PEARSON

York Press

The right of Steve Roberts to be identified as the Author of this Work has been asserted by him in accordance with the Copyright, Designs and Patents Act 1988

YORK PRESS
322 Old Brompton Road, London SW5 9JH

PEARSON EDUCATION LIMITED
Edinburgh Gate, Harlow,
Essex CM20 2JE, United Kingdom

Associated companies, branches and representatives throughout the world

© Librairie du Liban *Publishers* 2008, 2012

Quotations from *The Bloody Chamber* by Angela Carter copyright © Angela Carter 1979. Reproduced by permission of the author c/o Rogers, Coleridge & White Ltd., 20 Powis Mews, London W11 1JN

First published 2008
This new and fully revised edition 2012

10 9 8 7 6 5 4 3 2 1

ISBN 978–1–4479–1315–3

Illustration on p. 7 by Neil Gower
Phototypeset by Border Consultants Ltd
Printed in Slovakia by Neografia

© INTERFOTO/Alamy for page 6 / Igor Borodin/Shutterstock.com for page 7 / CHRISTOPHE ROLLAND/Shutterstock.com for page 10 top / © iStockphoto.com/Klubovy for page 10 bottom / © iStockphoto.com/sara_winter for page 11 / © iStockphoto.com/annikishkin for page 12 / gualtiero boffi/Shutterstock.com for page 13 / © iStockphoto.com/eyewave for page 14 / Silvia Antunes/Shutterstock.com for page 16 / © iStockphoto.com/RyanJLane for page 17 / Elnur/Shutterstock.com for page 18 / alike/Shutterstock.com for page 19 / Fedorov Oleksiy/Shutterstock.com for page 21 / © iStockphoto.com/christophriddle for page 22 top / InnaFelker/Shutterstock.com for page 22 bottom / hd connelly/Shutterstock.com for page 23 / Chepko Danil Vitalevich/Shutterstock.com for page 24 / © iStockphoto.com/Hiob for page 26 / © iStockphoto.com/acid_ninja for page 27 / Justin Black/Shutterstock.com for page 28 / Kondrashov Mikhail Evgenevich/Shutterstock.com for page 29 / motorolka/Shutterstock.com for page 30 / SVERDLOVA/Shutterstock.com for page 31 / Smileus/Shutterstock.com for page 32 / © iStockphoto.com/GlobalP for page 33 / Chuck Wagner/Shutterstock.com for page 35 / Sebastian Duda/Shutterstock.com for page 36 / alexptv/Shutterstock.com for page 37 / © iStockphoto.com/teamtime for page 38 / © iStockphoto.com/AnnBaldwin for page 39 / Chris Sargent/Shutterstock.com for page 40 / © iStockphoto.com/topdeq for page 41 / Kotenko Oleksandr/Shutterstock.com for page 42 / Olinchuk/Shutterstock.com for page 43 / Keattikorn/Shutterstock.com for page 44 / © iStockphoto.com/Andrew_Howe for page 45 / © iStockphoto.com/Bliznetsov for page 46 / dundanim/Shutterstock.com for page 48 / Olena Simko/Shutterstock.com for page 49 / © iStockphoto.com/MilosJokic for page 50 / akva/Shutterstock.com for page 51 / nito/Shutterstock.com for page 52 / © iStockphoto.com/Nikada for page 53 top / Jan Sommer/Shutterstock.com for page 53 bottom / JKlingebiel/Shutterstock.com for page 54 / Roland Zihlmann/Shutterstock.com for page 56 / AM-STUDiO/Shutterstock.com for page 57 / Menna/Shutterstock.com for page 58 / Vakhrushev Pavel/Shutterstock.com for page 59 / FWStupidio/Shutterstock.com for page 60 / © iStockphoto.com/caracterdesign for page 61 / © iStockphoto.com/Lisa-Blue for page 62 / alin b./Shutterstock.com for page 63 / © iStockphoto.com/Klubovy for page 64 / Tompet/Shutterstock.com for page 65 / photosync/Shutterstock.com for page 66 / © iStockphoto.com/viki2win for page 67 / © iStockphoto.com/siloto for page 68 top / © iStockphoto.com/GrenouilleFilms for page 68 bottom / © iStockphoto.com/Klubovy for page 70 / Mikael Damkier/Shutterstock.com for page 72 / © iStockphoto.com/BackyardProduction for page 73 / Simon Krzic/Shutterstock.com for page 74 / © iStockphoto.com/largeformat4x5 for page 75 / © iStockphoto.com/gremlin for page 76 / hvoya/Shutterstock.com for page 77 / charles taylor/Shutterstock.com for page 78 / © iStockphoto.com/selimaksan for page 79 / © iStockphoto.com/Wildroze fior page 80 / © iStockphoto.com/Eerik for page 81 / © iStockphoto.com/debibishop for page 82 top / marinini/Shutterstock.com for page 82 middle / chaoss/Shutterstock.com for page 83 / © iStockphoto.com/kai813 for page 84 / terekhov igor/Shutterstock.com for page 88 / Tomas Sereda/Shutterstock.com for page 89 / James Steidl/Shutterstock.com for page 90 / Khram/Shutterstock.com for page 91 / © iStockphoto.com/benedek for page 92 / © iStockphoto.com/erikreis for page 93 / Nataliiap/Shutterstock.com for page 94 / © iStockphoto.com/iofoto for page 95 / © iStockphoto.com/Goldfaery for page 109 / © iStockphoto.com/skynesher for page 111

CONTENTS

PART FOUR: STRUCTURE, FORM AND LANGUAGE

PART FIVE: CONTEXTS AND CRITICAL DEBATES

PART SIX: GRADE BOOSTER

ESSENTIAL STUDY TOOLS

HOW TO STUDY *THE BLOODY CHAMBER*

These Notes can be used in a range of ways to help you read, study and (where relevant) revise for your exam or assessment.

READING THE COLLECTION

Read the collection once, fairly quickly, for pleasure. This will give you a good sense of the over-arching shape of the collection, and a good feel for the highs and lows of the action in different stories, the varying pace and tone of the **narratives**, and the sequence in which information is withheld or revealed in each of them. You could ask yourself:

- How do individual characters change or develop? Are there any characters or character types that appear in more than one story? How do my own responses to them change?
- From whose point of view are the stories told? Is each **narrator** very different or are there similarities between them?
- Are the events in each story presented chronologically, or is the time scheme altered?
- What impression do the locations and settings, such as forests and castles, make on my reading and response to the collection?
- What sort of language, style and form am I aware of in the different stories? Does Carter paint detail precisely, or is there deliberate vagueness or ambiguity – or both? Does she use **imagery**, or recurring **motifs** and **symbols**?

On your second reading, make detailed notes around the key areas highlighted above and in the Assessment Objectives, such as form, language, structure (AO2), links and connections to other texts (AO3) and the context/background for the collection (AO4). These may seem quite demanding, but these Notes will suggest particular elements to explore or jot down.

CHECK THE BOOK **A04**

Sarah Gamble's *Angela Carter: A Literary Life* (2005) examines Carter's life and work in its literary and historical context. Gamble's main problem, that 'most of the facts of Carter's life that have entered the public domain were put there by Carter herself', reveals how difficult it can be to separate fact and fiction in a writer's life.

INTERPRETING OR CRITIQUING THE COLLECTION

Although it's not helpful to think in terms of the collection being 'good' or 'bad', you should consider the different ways it can be read. How have critics responded to it? Do their views match yours – or do you take a different viewpoint? Are there different ways you can interpret specific events, characters or settings? This is a key aspect in AO3, and it can be helpful to keep a log of your responses and the various perspectives which are expressed both by established critics, but also by classmates, your teacher or other readers.

REFERENCES AND SOURCES

You will be expected to draw on critics' comments, or refer to source information from the period or the present. Make sure you make accurate, clear notes of writers or sources you have used, for example noting down titles of works, authors' names, website addresses, dates, etc. You may not have to reference all these things when you respond to a text, but knowing the source of your information will allow you to go back to it, if need be – and to check its accuracy and relevance.

REVISING FOR AND RESPONDING TO AN ASSESSED TASK OR EXAM QUESTION

CONTEXT **A04**

When this collection of stories was published as *The Bloody Chamber* in 1979 by Victor Gollancz, only two tales, 'The Bloody Chamber' and 'The Tiger's Bride', had not been seen or heard before (though, in one sense, all the stories have been seen and heard before by most of us). The other eight are **revisions** of Angela Carter's earlier stories or radio scripts.

The structure and the contents of these Notes are designed to help to give you the relevant information or ideas you need to answer tasks you have been set. First, work out the key words or ideas from the task (for example, 'form', 'Puss-in-Boots', 'patriarch', etc), then read the relevant parts of the Notes that relate to these terms or words, selecting what is useful for revision or a written response. Then, turn to **Part Six: Grade Booster** for help in formulating your actual response.

THE BLOODY CHAMBER IN CONTEXT

ANGELA CARTER

1940 Born Angela Olive Stalker in Eastbourne, Sussex. Evacuated to South Yorkshire where she lives with her maternal grandmother for the first five years of her life.

1958 Begins an apprenticeship as a junior newspaper reporter on the *Croydon Advertiser*.

1960 Marries Paul Carter and moves with him to Bristol. Unable to get work as a journalist, she enrolls as a mature student at Bristol University, studying medieval literature.

1966 Carter's first novel, *Shadow Dance*, is published, the year after she graduates.

1967–8 Carter establishes a reputation as an award-winning writer. *The Magic Toyshop* (1967) wins the John Llewellyn Rhys Prize. *Several Perceptions* (1968) wins the Somerset Maugham Award.

1969 Carter separates from her husband and leaves Europe, via America, for Japan. She returns to England in 1972.

1972–8 The novels *The Infernal Desire Machines of Doctor Hoffman* (1972) and *The Passion of New Eve* (1977) and a collection of short stories, *Fireworks: Nine Profane Pieces* (1974) are published. In 1978 *The Sadeian Woman*, a controversial feminist reappraisal of the life and works of the Marquis de Sade is published.

1979 Publication of *The Bloody Chamber* establishes Carter as an 'extreme' writer, attracting not only **feminist** critics and media reviewers, but a wider general readership.

1984 One of Carter's most acclaimed novels, *Nights at the Circus* is published and the film *The Company of Wolves*, directed by Neil Jordan, is released.

1992 Carter's last novel, *Wise Children*, a feast of carnival magic and comic **realism**, is published only a few months before her death from lung cancer on 16 February.

FAIRY TALES RE-TOLD

The stories in *The Bloody Chamber* take their inspiration from fairy tales, variants of older European folk tales that existed long before they were ever captured in writing. Carter interweaves old and new material into stories that seem familiar and yet strange. This invites the reader to question the purpose of the collection. In turn, this leads us to consider what effect Carter intends the stories to have on us as readers and how she achieves this effect. Helen Simpson, in her introduction to the 2006 Vintage edition of *The Bloody Chamber*, suggests that Carter did not want to present a simplistic feminist **revision** of these fairy tales. Her declared intention, in her own words, was 'to extract the latent content from the traditional stories and to use it as the beginnings of new stories' (pp. vii–viii).

CHECK THE BOOK **AO3**

As early as 1967, in her second novel, *The Magic Toyshop*, it is possible to see Carter's fascination with fairy tales.

CHECK THE BOOK **AO4**

A **magic realism** extravaganza, *Nights at the Circus* stars a trapeze artist called Fevvers, who hatches from an egg and grows wings at puberty.

CHECK THE BOOK **AO3**

Perrault's book of fairy tales, *Histoires ou contes du temps passé* (1697), was translated by Angela Carter as *The Fairy Tales of Charles Perrault* in 1977.

THE STORIES AND THEIR SOURCES

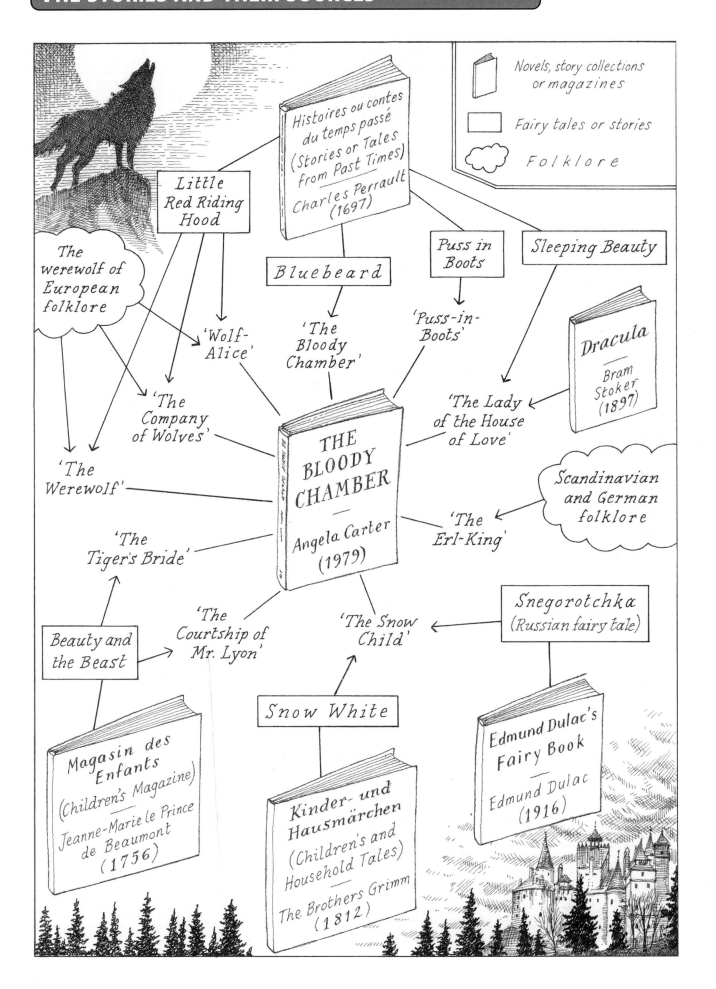

Novels, story collections or magazines

Fairy tales or stories

Folklore

The werewolf of European folklore

Little Red Riding Hood

Histoires ou contes du temps passé (Stories or Tales from Past Times) — Charles Perrault (1697)

Puss in Boots

Sleeping Beauty

Bluebeard

'Wolf-Alice'

'The Bloody Chamber'

'Puss-in-Boots'

Dracula — Bram Stoker (1897)

'The Company of Wolves'

'The Werewolf'

THE BLOODY CHAMBER — Angela Carter (1979)

'The Lady of the House of Love'

Scandinavian and German folklore

'The Tiger's Bride'

'The Erl-King'

Beauty and the Beast

'The Courtship of Mr. Lyon'

'The Snow Child'

Snegorotchka (Russian fairy tale)

Snow White

Magasin des Enfants (Children's Magazine) — Jeanne-Marie le Prince de Beaumont (1756)

Kinder- und Hausmärchen (Children's and Household Tales) — The Brothers Grimm (1812)

Edmund Dulac's Fairy Book — Edmund Dulac (1916)

KEY ISSUES

CHANGE

The tales, singularly and as a collection, revolve around themes of death and love; treachery and cruelty; redemption and salvation; and, above all, the possibility of change. Nearly all the tales are framed in a European winter landscape that signifies the bleakness and hardship of life. But this gloomy tone is relieved by Carter's exuberance and eccentricity, and her determined focus on the powerful possibilities of transformation to bring hope and strength to the women in the tales.

GENDER, CLASS AND POWER

Carter's tales explore female sexuality. They do not present stereotypical feminist views of women as either heroic fighters against, or passive victims of, **patriarchal** dominance. Neither do these tales comment on or describe directly the experience of women in late 1970s Britain, a time when new laws were offering hope of an end to sexual discrimination; medical advances in birth control such as the pill were changing the conventions of sexual conduct; and positions of real political power and influence were being taken by women. The election of Margaret Thatcher as the first female prime minister in 1979 was seen by many as a significant historical moment for women.

Issues of class and power are as present in Carter's stories as they are in the 'traditional' tales from which they are drawn, but not idealised in the same way. Carter's aristocratic male characters are defined by the stereotypes of power, greed and cruelty associated with privilege. Carter's female characters are often their victims. The stories are structured by the resolving of this imbalance of power – but frequently in surprising ways.

SYMBOLISM

One of the problems of deliberate use of **symbolism** in literature and art is the assumption that the reader will 'read' the symbol as the writer intended. It is easy to question the relevance to a modern urban reader's experience of the symbols of, for example, the forest as a place of fearful discovery and **metaphor** for the dangers of the adult world; or, the wolf as sexual predator and metaphor for human appetites. Perhaps the many tellings and retellings of these tales – from Roald Dahl to Walt Disney and beyond – have made the stories so familiar that their power is lost. But Carter's landscapes are landscapes of the psychological. Fear of the unknown, fear of pain, fear of death – and all the other associations which Carter's symbols conjure – are the very fabric of human nature and, as such, retain their power over the reader.

SETTINGS

LONG AGO AND FAR AWAY

All of the tales in the collection are set in a far away time and a far away place. These settings are largely borrowed from the traditional tales that inspired the collection. They create a sense of distance for the reader, putting Carter's characters in a place where anything – even the most fantastical elements of Carter's imagination – are possible. Against this traditional backdrop, the more contemporary elements which Carter has introduced to the tales can stand in the foreground, clearly drawing the reader's attention.

CHECK THE FILM A03

Willy Russell's play *Educating Rita* (1980) was made into a film in 1983 starring Julie Walters and Michael Caine. The play puts a modern **feminist** slant on the idea of men shaping women to their own desires – as explored by George Bernard Shaw in *Pygmalion* (first performed in 1913).

CONTEXT A04

Questions about the place of the female voice in society and the presence or absence of female sexuality in the mainstream media are still raised by texts such as Eve Ensler's *The Vagina Monologues* (first staged in 1996) that present a provocative challenge to the perceived male-dominated culture of the twenty-first century.

CHECK THE POEM A03

Roald Dahl's poems in *Revolting Rhymes* (1982) reinterpret the fairy tales 'Cinderella', 'Jack and the Beanstalk', 'Snow White and the Seven Dwarfs', 'Goldilocks and the Three Bears', 'Little Red Riding Hood' and 'The Three Little Pigs'.

WINTER

A significant number of Carter's tales are set in a cold, harsh winter. Winter is a time when wealth matters. The rich wear furs, eat heartily and warm themselves at the fireside. The poor starve and die. The mystical atmosphere of this perpetual winter variously suggests the emotional coldness of lonely Mr Lyon, the harshness of the peasant life in 'The Werewolf' and provides the very stuff of which a snow child can be made.

THE CASTLE

The castle in literature is often the domain of the rich and powerful, inhabited by a lone male waited upon hand and foot by an army of servants. In Carter's tales, however, the castle or mansion represents not only wealth and power, but a place of imprisonment in which a captive can be held, unable to escape and away from the eyes of the outside world. It is a world of secret places, of secret chambers, towers and tunnels. These sexual metaphors – suggesting the male and female sexual organs – are neither accidental nor masked in the collection.

The Countess in 'The Lady of the House of Love' lives her eternal life in a 'chateau', perhaps ironically suggesting the romance implied in the title but not realised in the story. Her chateau is in the Carpathian mountains, in central eastern Europe, suggesting strong overtones of the vampire myth, familiar from Bram Stoker's novel *Dracula*, and its many adaptations.

THE FOREST

Carter interprets the forest as the essence of nature: wild and unpredictable, it is a place beyond civilisation. A **metaphor** for the most dangerous of journeys, the most dangerous of experiences, the most dangerous of life's events, she suggests that the forest will devour you if you stray from the path – perhaps the path of righteousness or the path of good sense.

THE GOTHIC

The Bloody Chamber can be seen as a **Gothic** text. Works of literature that have been defined or labelled as Gothic share certain features. The supernatural is dominant, whether it be the ghost of Cathy in Emily Brontë's *Wuthering Heights* or the reconstructed monster of Mary Shelley's *Frankenstein*. The Gothic emphasises extremes of emotional and physical sensation, such as Heathcliff and Catherine's all-conquering love in *Wuthering Heights*, and extremes of location, from Bronte's wild Yorkshire moors to the arctic circle across which Dr Frankenstein tracks his monster.

The Gothic tradition in literature was an attempt to warn, in a sensational and entertaining way, about the social and personal consequences of going against the accepted beliefs of the time, whether it be Macbeth's and Doctor Faustus's over-reaching ambition (both early examples of Gothic **protagonists**) or Dr Frankenstein's dabbling in the divine art of creation. The thrills are provided by the sense of going beyond the boundaries of acceptable behaviour. This is usually accompanied by dire consequences for the protagonist.

Though Carter disliked the term being applied to her work, the Gothic tradition is clearly visible in this collection of stories. The **imagery** of blood and passion, the overwhelming forces of nature and supernatural beings, the shuddering anticipation of horrible events, and typically Gothic architecture of castles, towers and secret passages all have their origins in the Gothic tradition.

CHECK THE BOOK **A03**

Bram Stoker's *Dracula* (1897) was originally dismissed as 'an artistic mistake' by a reviewer in the *Manchester Guardian*, though others regarded it favourably in comparison with the works of Edgar Allan Poe (1809–49) and Mary Shelley (1797–1851).

CHECK THE BOOK **A03**

For a short essay on Gothic fiction, see *The Oxford Companion to English Literature* (edited by Margaret Drabble, revised sixth edition, 2006).

CONTEXT **A03**

Frankenstein was written by Mary Shelley in response to a literary challenge from Lord Byron in 1816. The same competition to produce a horrific tale also caused John Polidori, Byron's personal physician, to write 'The Vampyre', the first tale of its kind to be published in the English language (in instalments in the *New Monthly Magazine* in 1819).

PART TWO: STUDYING *THE BLOODY CHAMBER*

THE BLOODY CHAMBER: SYNOPSIS

STUDY FOCUS: A TALE OF SEVEN EPISODES · A02

Carter tells 'The Bloody Chamber', the first and longest story in the collection, through the **narrative** voice of the main female character, who recounts her experiences in seven major episodes. Each episode is marked by a break in the text indicating a pause in the narrative flow. These breaks help to mark the passage of time and add emphasis to significant moments in the story.

THE JOURNEY

The opening of the tale places the young bride on a train travelling to her new husband's castle. It establishes the young bride's relationship with her husband, and the contrast between her former life in the French capital and the opulence of her new circumstances. It becomes clear that the story is taking place at some imprecise time around the end of the nineteenth century.

ARRIVAL

The bride arrives in the matrimonial home in a remote part of Brittany. We focus on her discomfort as she learns more of her husband's taste for pornography, and her fear as her husband takes her to the marital bed. The husband's taste for images of sexual violence is reflected in his treatment of his new wife.

THE KEYS

The husband is called away on business. He entrusts her with the keys to the castle – including the one to his secret room which, he insists, she must promise never to enter. As he leaves, he tells her that he has taken on a piano-tuner.

THE DILEMMA

In her husband's absence the young wife plays the piano, talks to the blind piano-tuner and phones her mother. Her boredom and curiosity, however, soon lead her to search out the true nature of her new husband. She goes through his papers and learns something of his past but is drawn to the secret room she has promised not to enter.

THE CHAMBER

The young wife enters the bloody chamber and discovers its secrets: the remains of her husband's three past wives.

THE RETURN

The girl leaves the chamber, knowing that hers will be the next corpse on display. Comforted by her true companion (the piano-tuner) she faces the consequences of her actions and contemplates escape. Her husband returns to the castle unexpectedly and condemns her to death for her disobedience.

THE END

The resolution of the crisis is provided by her heroic mother, who arrives at the crucial moment to save her daughter from being beheaded and shoots the Marquis dead. This, leaves the wife widowed with rich rewards: wealth, love and happiness as she returns to Paris with the piano-tuner and her mother. These pleasures are handled with care in the **denouement** of the story, which restores the character of the young woman through love and personal fulfilment.

CONTEXT **A04**

The conflict and climax of this story are typical of the folk and fairy tale genre: a helpless young woman naively enters the beast's lair and falls prey to his desires. It is in the resolution or **denouement** of the story that Carter subverts the reader's expectations and the genre's traditional values.

THE BLOODY CHAMBER, pp. 1–14

SUMMARY

- A young bride travels from Paris through the night with her much older husband towards her new home, a large and isolated castle in Brittany.

- She thinks about the first night she and her new husband will spend together. She ponders the age difference between them and realises she does not know him very well. She is aware of his three previous marriages and his wealth; although she feels there might be something strange in the Marquis's desires, she is excited and enthralled by him.

- The couple arrive at the castle for their honeymoon and are greeted without much warmth by the housekeeper.

- The Marquis delays the consummation of their marriage, and the wife is left alone. She tries to play the piano which her husband bought her as a wedding gift and then browses in the Marquis's library. She is shocked by the images in some of the books.

- The Marquis finds her with his books and leads her back to the bedroom to take her virginity.

ANALYSIS

THE OPENING

'The Bloody Chamber' is set in France around the year 1900 during the Third Republic, a time known for its corruption and decadence. The structure of the story is taken from the European fairy tale 'Le Barbe Bleue' ('Bluebeard'), written in 1697 by Charles Perrault.

Bluebeard was written as a moral tale warning against excessive curiosity. Carter, however, frames the story as the 'sexual awakening' of a young woman, deliberately **parodying** a particular type of erotic literature. The first paragraph sets a feverish tone, as the **narrator** recalls the 'delicious ecstasy' of a young woman, just seventeen years old, anticipating her wedding night, with her 'burning cheek' and 'pounding … heart' (p. 1). The parody is most obvious in the **clichéd** phallic **imagery** of the train's 'great pistons ceaselessly thrusting' (p. 1). We get a sense that the narrator sees her younger self as an entirely different person, and this detached **narrative** perspective puts the reader at a distance from the character's experiences. The narrator implies she has been changed by the events of this story, though it is not clear how long ago these events took place.

GROWING UP

The first part of the story is set up as a journey, a **metaphor** for the young girl's emotional and physical journey as she leaves the security of her childhood home and enters the adult world. Her view of her destination, 'the unguessable country of marriage' (p. 1), is reminiscent of Hamlet's description of death as the 'undiscovered country from whose bourne / No traveller returns' (*Hamlet*, Act III Scene 1). Carter's use of this **intertextual** echo seems to suggest a connection between sex, marriage and death; perhaps the death of youth and innocence, perhaps the narrator's death at the hands of her husband.

CONTEXT **A04**

In Perrault's tale Bluebeard, a wealthy aristocrat, marries a local girl. He then goes away, leaving his wife the keys of the chateau. She enters a room that she has been forbidden to visit and discovers her husband's three dead wives. She relocks the door, but the key is blood-stained. Bluebeard returns and threatens to kill her, but her brothers arrive, kill Bluebeard and rescue her. She remarries and shares her wealth with her family.

CRITICAL VIEWPOINT **A03**

It can be argued that the structure of Carter's 'The Bloody Chamber' is close to Perrault's original model, but the intended moral is different.

Marriage is represented in the **symbol** of the wedding ring. Carter's narrator introduces this symbol with a 'pang of loss' for her youth and freedom (p. 1). The female roles of mother, daughter and wife are interwoven in the image of the wedding ring, with the 'gold band' (p. 1) **symbolising** the ownership of the young woman and the price agreed between the mother and the Marquis for her hand in marriage. The act of putting on the ring marks the end of childhood, a severing of the link with her mother, and becoming a mother herself. The theme of maturation, growing up, and an exploration of what it means for a girl to become a woman are embedded in this story.

STUDY FOCUS: MEN AND WOMEN A04

The character of the mother is established early on as 'adventurous' and 'indomitable' (p. 1). We learn that she was capable of dealing with pirates, plague and man-eating tigers as a teenager, but was reduced to poverty by marrying for love and being widowed by war not long after. The narrator's memory of her father is only of the sadness of losing him: 'a legacy of tears that never quite dried' (p. 2). In contrast, the mother is armed and prepared to defend herself against any threat. You need to consider how men and women are portrayed in 'The Bloody Chamber' and to what extent they conform to or contradict stereotypes of 'wife', 'mother', 'father' and 'husband'.

THE MARQUIS

The male character, the aristocratic businessman, is first introduced as a mysterious figure. He gradually takes on more of an identity as the story unfolds. He is associated with symbols of wealth – 'gold' and a 'gigantic box', in which the narrator's 'wedding dress is … wrapped up … like a Christmas gift' (p. 1) – while his physical form is conveyed through a 'kiss' and a 'rasp of beard' (p. 2). The narrator builds his identity through recalling his 'opulent male scent' (p. 3), and Carter places her characters in a mating game: the 'exquisite tact' (p. 2) of his courtship of the girl is linked to the attentiveness of a lion stalking his prey. The explicit reference to his 'dark mane' (p. 3) is the first of many **allusions** to his bestial qualities. His title is revealed when he is introduced as 'my Marquis' (p. 4), but he is given no other name. His identity is not fully revealed; this is emphasised by the description of his face as a 'perfectly smooth' mask (p. 3).

Almost immediately after the Marquis has been introduced as a mysterious enigma, he is explicitly linked to a **symbol** that will recur throughout the story. The **narrator** makes a strange comparison between the man, as 'a sentient vegetable', and a flower commonly associated with 'funereal' matters: the lily (p. 3). The suggestion here is that his cultured manners, calm detachment and composure are the product of an inhuman nature: he has the capacity to think but no real awareness of other people's feelings. There is 'gravity' (p. 4) in his desire for his new wife which she cannot resist, and this seems to be linked somehow to lilies, with their beauty and almost overpowering heavy perfume.

The Marquis remains shapeless and mysterious while the narrator recounts the beauty, talent and tragic demise of his first three wives; and she is clearly flattered by his invitation 'to join this gallery of beautiful women' (p. 5). Carter here **foreshadows** the events of the story in a seemingly innocent remark that also alludes to the original story of Bluebeard. She glimpses, indirectly in his reflection, the way he views her as a piece of meat. The narrator's innocence and naivety attract the Marquis's 'carnal avarice' (p. 6), while the Marquis represents to the narrator the mysterious and appealing danger of the unknown. This appeal is linked to her growing up and explains her willingness to expose herself to the risks involved in becoming an adult.

CONTEXT A04

Gilles de Rais was a fifteenth-century marshal of France and baron of Brittany who fought alongside Joan of Arc. His crimes are said to have inspired the tale of Bluebeard. Found guilty of child abuse and multiple murders, Gilles de Rais was executed in 1440. Whatever the truth of the matter, the folk tale may be interpreted as a warning against the dangers of challenging the power of the aristocracy.

GRADE BOOSTER A02

The key to unlocking Carter's implied viewpoint in *The Bloody Chamber* lies in the rich connotations of her language choices. For example, the Marquis's 'carnal avarice' (p. 6) suggests two seemingly contrasting lusts: the sexual and the financial, physical gratification and the display of wealth. Both of these are satisfied by his bride as they are by his collection of erotic art.

STUDY FOCUS: AN UNSYMPATHETIC CHARACTER **A04**

The Marquis's identity is formed through the details Carter gives of his expensive habits: he goes to the opera; he wears a monocle; he bestows rich gifts to display his wealth and secure the affections of women; he smokes cigars; and trains stop especially for him where there is no station. None of these are attributes likely to make him a sympathetic character to a modern audience. He is the 'richest man in France' (p. 8): what more need be said to define this character or arouse our suspicion? He **symbolises** everything about **patriarchal** society that stops women having control of their own lives. Carter's villain in 'The Bloody Chamber' is a representative of the past, of patriarchy, of a dying social order.

CRITICAL VIEWPOINT A03

Carter questions the gender stereotypes of the typical 'rites of passage' recounting of first sexual experience, both adopting and subverting the genre of erotic literature; how successfully is open to question. This has been a particular focus for feminist critics (see **Part Five: Critical debates**).

CONTEXT A04

Sadism is the term given to a number of sexual practices, associated with the Marquis de Sade, that share the characteristic of deriving pleasure from inflicting pain on someone else.

CONTEXT A04

Donatien Alphonse François de Sade (1740–1814), known as the Marquis de Sade, was condemned to death in 1772 for his cruelty and sexual transgressions. Escaping, he was later imprisoned at Vincennes and in the Bastille, where he wrote works of perversion and fantasy, among them *Les 120 Journées de Sodome* (written in 1784).

IMAGERY AND VIOLENCE

The symbol of the flower is used for a second time as the couple arrive in their bedroom, which is filled with white lilies. There is something sordid and corrupting about the way in which the Marquis strips the bride he has 'acquired' (p. 10). Carter allows her narrator to make a political and social point linking marriage and prostitution – the 'formal disrobing of the bride, a ritual from the brothel' (p. 11) – which can only heighten our sense of unease as the girl is 'stripped' to resemble the erotic art he collects. This is particularly unsettling as, despite her awareness of having been a 'bargain' (p. 11), she admits she is aroused by his treatment of her.

The postponement of his satisfaction, with no regard for her, suggests the Marquis's absolute control. This suggestion of sadism is reinforced by the violent **imagery** in the narrator's description of her husband's erotic art, emphasised by the shocking bluntness of her language. Carter uses more figurative but equally vivid language to describe one of the pictures: 'split fig' and 'scimitar' (p. 13) convey the vulnerability and aggression depicted in the image entitled 'Reproof of curiosity', a 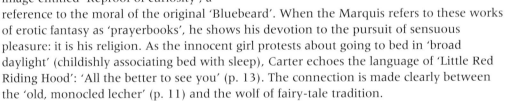reference to the moral of the original 'Bluebeard'. When the Marquis refers to these works of erotic fantasy as 'prayerbooks', he shows his devotion to the pursuit of sensuous pleasure: it is his religion. As the innocent girl protests about going to bed in 'broad daylight' (childishly associating bed with sleep), Carter echoes the language of 'Little Red Riding Hood': 'All the better to see you' (p. 13). The connection is made clearly between the 'old, monocled lecher' (p. 11) and the wolf of fairy-tale tradition.

The connection between sex, violence and death is made clear as she is 'impaled' (p. 14) by him. The physical violence in this verb is particularly striking, but it can also be seen as an **allusion** to vampirism. It recalls the disputed connection between Bram Stoker's Count Dracula and Vlad Tepes, the legendary Vlad the Impaler. In any case, the narrator does not use coy **clichés** or **euphemisms** here. Her sense of detachment as she reports the experience, seen in the bedrooms' multiple mirrors, is chilling.

See **Extended commentary, pp. 8–11** for further discussion of part of this section.

GLOSSARY

1	**wagon-lit** a sleeping car on continental trains in the nineteenth century
	pistons the moving part in a steam engine that provides the thrust or motive force – a cliché of phallic imagery, especially in cinema
	Conservatoire a specialist school of music, particularly reserved for training the most talented musicians in the classical style
2	**junkful** a junk is a kind of ship used in the notoriously pirate-infested waters of China and the East Indies
	reticule a small handbag, often of woven material, used by fashionable ladies of rank in the nineteenth century
	footpads a seventeenth-century term for a thief, particularly someone who ambushed travellers, similar in meaning to the more modern 'mugger'
	egregious similar in meaning originally to 'outstanding' or 'excellent', now mostly used as a criticism of blatant or flagrant conduct or behaviour
	sea-girt a seventeenth-century term, sometimes applied to a peninsula, indicating a piece of land surrounded by sea
	leonine lion-like, a term in use since the sixteenth century
4	**vellum** fine writing material made from the skin of young animals
8	**amniotic** the amnion is the sack in which a foetus develops, suspended in amniotic fluid
	salinity saltiness
	leather-gaitered wearing leather gaiters, protective coverings for the lower leg
	calyx the outer covering of a flower still in bud
	deliquescent dissolving or melting away, sometimes used to suggest decay, rot or the decomposition of things that have died
9	**châtelaine** the mistress of the house, the keeper of the keys
11	**voluptuary's** a voluptuary is a seventeenth-century term for someone chiefly interested in their own pleasure, seeking luxury and delighting in sensation
12	**Eliphas Levy** pen name of Alphonse Louis Constant, nineteenth-century occultist writer who had a strong influence on the spiritualist movement with his writings on magic

KEY QUOTATIONS: THE BLOODY CHAMBER   A01

Key quotation 1: The Marquis had been: 'Married three times within my own brief lifetime to three different graces, now … he had invited me to join this gallery of beautiful women' (p. 5).

Possible interpretations:

- Emphasises the narrator's youth and her husband's experience.
- Foreshadows the Marquis's view of women and the danger he poses to them.
- Links to the wider theme of men and women.

Key quotation 2: The narrator's marital bedroom is filled with lilies: 'The lilies I always associate with him; that are white. And stain you.' (p. 11)

Possible interpretations:

- **Imagery** of the lilies' apparent purity suggests the narrator's innocence and the Marquis's sexual corruption.
- Lilies are traditionally a symbol of chastity and virtue; to the narrator, however, they are 'funereal', associated with death.
- Flowers suggest a link to the fairy-tale context, such as the rose in 'Beauty and the Beast'.

GRADE BOOSTER   A02

In this section of the story – and throughout the collection – Carter's rich use of symbolism adds layers of meaning to the narrative. Identifying its relevance, supported with close and careful analysis of its implications, shows an awareness not only of the writer's craft but of her viewpoint and intention.

EXTENDED COMMENTARY

THE BLOODY CHAMBER, PP. 8–11

From 'Sea; sand; a sky that melts into the sea' to 'And stain you.'

The bride's journey towards the Marquis's castle is carefully crafted into a kind of waking dream. Carter's **simile** for daybreak, 'a cool dream' (p. 8), is reflected in the **narrator's** blurred perception of her surroundings. This helps to create the sense that the moral and physical boundaries and limits of the Marquis's world will be equally unfamiliar. The 'melting' sea and sky are described as if they are the hazy images captured in landscape art using pastel colours. The 'misty' style of such art is often thought to be typically soft, gentle and unfocused. Carter deftly links the liquidity of this image of the landscape to the 'deliquescent harmonies' the bride was playing on the piano at the moment of her first meeting with her husband. Debussy's music is meditative and tranquil, calm and unthreatening. Its **symbolism** of romantic love is an **ironic** reminder of the gap between the bride's romantic 'reverie' (p. 8) and the reality of the Marquis.

Although the bride has arrived at her destination, her journey continues: through the 'mysterious, amphibious' castle (p. 9) and through the interior landscape of the bride's psychological state. Carter narrows the focus from the public lives of the two main characters to the private and intimate bedroom scene, though this is interrupted.

The Marquis remains 'still as a pond iced thickly over' (p. 9), Carter's simile suggesting the coldness of the character's nature. His passivity and blankness of expression give way to a 'weary appetite' when he approaches his 'familiar treat' (p. 11), and he smiles as he examines his wife. Carter's description of the 'rare movement' of his lips makes the Marquis seem incapable of expressing human feeling. He is seen to be an 'old, monocled lecher' controlling this 'Most pornographic of all confrontations' (p. 11).

The narrator discovers her place and position in the new life she is entering. First she encounters the housekeeper who has also been the Marquis's 'foster mother' (p. 9). This, and the housekeeper's 'correct but lifeless' greeting, brings to mind the the wicked stepmother in traditional fairy tales. The bride recognises that this person, her social inferior, is really the one in control of the enormous 'ocean liner' (p. 9) that is the castle, because she knows how to do the work necessary for the place to function. Next she is led to the bedroom and the grand bed with its imposing **Gothic** decoration of gargoyles; its dark colour scheme of blood red; and its black wood adorned with luxurious gold leaf. She realises the extent to which her life has changed when she realises the servants have taken care of things without her noticing. There is some **ambiguity** in the statement 'Henceforth, a maid would deal with everything' (p. 10). Initially, it is most likely to be understood as her recognition that female servants will do all the work. In another sense, it foreshadows the way the female characters must take control of their own lives if they want to avoid becoming mere servants of a patriarchal man.

CONTEXT **A04**

Achille-Claude Debussy (1862–1918) was a French composer inspired by the Symbolist movement. The Symbolists formed an artistic and poetic movement in France and Belgium in the late nineteenth century. Their focus was on spirituality and **metaphor**, as opposed to **realism** and naturalism.

Carter's choice of language emphasises the contrast between the characters' very different attitudes to desire. The bride is 'trembling' (p. 10) and blushing as the blood rushes to her face. These are the **clichés** of honeymoon behaviour. However, at this stage it is not clear whether the bride is blushing with embarrassment or flushed with the excitement of desire.

The Marquis, by contrast, is slow, methodical and teasing as he strips the wrappings of his 'bargain' to reveal her 'scarlet, palpitating core' (p. 11). Carter's **metaphor** is that of an artichoke, a vegetable whose tough outer layers are peeled away to get to the artichoke heart. This very physical image gives some romantic overtone to the unpeeling of the bride's layers. It soon becomes clear, however, that this is not a romantic encounter: the Marquis is interested only in the physical. The **narrator's** statement 'he closed my legs like a book' (p. 11) shocks not just because of the Marquis's disturbing voyeurism, but also because it equates the bride with his collection of pornographic texts. He considers her nothing more than a text to be read or consumed at his pleasure. To him, she is nothing more than an object whose function is his pleasure.

The mirrors and the lilies are powerful **symbols** of the Marquis's control and dominance in this environment. The lilies are associated with funeral rites and therefore with death (see **Part Two: The Bloody Chamber, pp. 14–26** for more on the connection between marriage and death); the mirrors embody the Marquis's objectification of his bride as a living, breathing pornographic image.

The journey into the character of the narrator is interrupted at the point where she experiences a 'strange, impersonal arousal' (p. 11). This conflicting reaction of being aroused and simultaneously repulsed by the Marquis is explored in the image of the lilies whose pollen can 'stain you'. It is a disturbing image that connects desire, sex and death. The ending of the tale will return explicitly to this idea of shame and 'stain' (p. 11) as the indelible result of damaging experience.

THE BLOODY CHAMBER, pp. 14–26

SUMMARY

- The Marquis is called away on business.
- He trusts the narrator with the keys to the entire castle, holding back only one. The narrator greedily demands it from him. He explains that it is the key to his private study, the only key she must not use.
- His wife resents being left alone, but entertains herself by playing the piano, recently tuned by the young blind piano tuner who she now meets, and bossing the servants around. However, she finds herself suddenly weeping when speaking to her mother on the telephone.
- Bored and curious, she searches through the Marquis's papers in his office and finds some intimate souvenirs of his previous wives.
- She is spurred on to find out more of the Marquis's secrets and decides to use the forbidden key. Though she is not afraid, she hesitates before opening the door.

CONTEXT **A04**

Justine ou les malheurs de la vertu (1791) was the first book to be published by the Marquis de Sade. The **protagonist** is Justine, a virtuous woman who recounts the extreme experiences of her life. The main ideas in this classic of erotic literature are that all morals are impositions on the freedom of the individual and that those who impose them are corrupt hypocrites.

ANALYSIS

IDENTITY AND ISOLATION

The narrator uses a cold, detached tone in recalling the moment of their marriage's consummation. The earlier suggestion that she may have been excited by the Marquis's aggressive sexuality gives way to a list of moments revealing a strong sense of isolation and no hint of any pleasure on her part. Their physical relationship is a 'one-sided struggle' (p. 14); she hears rather than participates in the climax; her involvement is described as if she were hardly there at all, but is merely a passive victim of his desire. Her comment 'I had bled' (p. 14) suggests she is wounded both physically and emotionally by his uncontrolled aggression. It is presented entirely without emotion or any sense of her feelings or pleasure. The Marquis takes possession of his property by 'winning' the virginity that she had so eagerly anticipated losing. The detached numbness of the narration here reflects the impact of selfish male desire. It is possible that there is also a connection with the shocked 'out of body' accounts of rape, given by some victims, describing a kind of numbed detachment from the horror and pain of the experience.

She is uncertain whether she knows the true identity of the Marquis or not after this experience. The doubts she has about her husband reveal her disappointment and also hint at something more fearful in her attitude towards him. She realises that his 'deathly composure' is a fragile 'mask' for his true nature, broken at the height of his ecstasy (p. 14). His pleasure, when she hears him 'shriek and blaspheme' (p. 14), is conveyed as something savage, mad and unholy. Carter is playing here with conventions and codes associated with love and marriage. If one takes the Christian view that marriage is a union sanctified by God, then sex may be seen as something sacred: a form of worship. The Marquis, however, seems to be almost demonic in his passion.

STUDY FOCUS: DEATH AND MARRIAGE A02

The 'insolent incense' of the lilies in the Marquis's bedroom turns it into an 'embalming parlour' (p. 14), a place where corpses are prepared for burial. Carter is constructing clues for the reader here in her choice of **symbol**. The link between the marriage bed and death is clearly becoming more prominent at this point in the story. This link can be read at several different levels of meaning. Marriage (where traditionally the woman became the man's property) can be seen **metaphorically** as the death of a woman's freedom, the death of her independent self. It can be interpreted more literally as being the direct or indirect cause of death for many women through domestic drudgery, domestic violence or the dangers of childbirth. The long-held fear of these dangers is embedded in this story and echoes throughout the collection as a whole.

THE PRICE OF LOVE

Carter moves the plot along with the telephone call from the Marquis's agent and we return to the scene of the 'honeymoon' (p. 15) couple after the consummation of their marriage. The emphasis here is placed on the age difference between the man and the 'little girl', adding the unpleasant association of child abuse to our understanding of the relationship. Her realisation that she has been 'bought with a handful of coloured stones and the pelts of dead beasts' echoes the nineteenth-century socialist view that marriage was a form of legalised prostitution. Although the **narrator** refers to her 'wounded vanity' (p. 15), it is clear that the experience for her of this new life of luxury is degrading and that, despite the wealth it has brought her, she feels she has sold herself cheaply. In effect, she realises here that the distinction between the aristocratic wife and the common prostitute is only in their price – and that what she had to sell, her virginity, has been used up in one moment. It was her virgin status, she deduces, that first attracted him to her: the Marquis reveals this to her 'shock of surprise' when he tells her that, 'in these civilized times', the evidence of her changed status will not be publicly displayed to his 'interested tenants' (p. 16).

Carter builds on our earlier knowledge of this man as a connoisseur and collector. The images of the paintings described are powerful depictions of women as victims, but the Marquis is attracted to them as much by the titillating stories behind the images as the images themselves.

At this stage, the narrator is uncertain of her own desire. She fears that the Marquis may know something about her nature that she is reluctant to acknowledge. She refers to this as the 'beastly truth' that her 'innocence' conceals 'a rare talent for corruption' (p. 17), suggesting that her vulnerable innocence is made yet more vulnerable by his predatory sexuality. The way Carter has the Marquis providing her with all the keys except one is an expert mirroring of the relationship in **symbolic** form. His generosity and trust seem impressive, but the reservation of one secret adds to the mystery already built up around this character. The reader comes to know the character of the Marquis through the narrator, but we are not limited by her naivety in our appraisal of his nature.

ALONE AGAIN

The narrator is ambivalent about her attitude to her departed husband, longing for the man who disgusts her. She acknowledges a 'certain queasy craving' for the 'thousand, thousand baroque intersections of flesh upon flesh' (p. 19). It is clear that, despite – or perhaps because of – not being sexually fulfilled by the Marquis, she is still enthralled by the possibility of sexual delight at which he has hinted. It is apparent that she has not understood that when he speaks of sexual pleasure, it is his feelings he is concerned with, not hers.

CONTEXT A04

Friedrich Engels wrote in *Ludwig Feuerbach and the End of Classical German Philosophy* (1886): 'the marriage laws … could all disappear tomorrow without changing in the slightest the practice of love and friendship'.

CONTEXT A04

The exaggerated value the Marquis places on virginity has its roots in the traditions of patriarchal society. While men may 'sow their wild oats' freely, patriarchal societies traditionally demand that the chastity and virtue of young women must be preserved for only one man: their husband. A bride's virgin state was proudly displayed on the morning after the couple's wedding night by hanging the blood-stained bed sheets out of a window.

The **narrator** gives herself a momentary, and **ambiguous**, 'jealous scare' when, with some 'relief' (p. 20), she imagines the Marquis in the arms of a more experienced mistress in New York. However, she is soon distracted when she discovers the piano has now been tuned. This moment is a turning point in the **narrative**, showing the young woman rediscovering herself as she was before she became a wife. She feels 'far more at ease' with herself in her old clothes, playing the piano, than in her new role. It is not at all accidental that Carter has this character relaxing into the 'costume of a student' (p. 20). The connotations of willingness to learn, relative innocence, potential ignorance and dedication to discovery are all relevant to her situation.

CONTEXT A04

Eve's temptation by the serpent in the Garden of Eden is recounted in Chapter 3 of the Book of Genesis.

STUDY FOCUS: A BIBLICAL PARALLEL A03

The way in which the narrator is allowed to possess the key – only on condition that she must not use it – is reminiscent of the biblical tale of Adam and Eve in the Garden of Eden. It is quite easy to see the Marquis as godlike here, providing a kind of paradise on Earth, but with limited freedom to know the truth. It is easy to see the narrator as Eve either succumbing to temptation or resolutely pursuing knowledge, depending on one's point of view. 'The Bloody Chamber' challenges the status of the myth of man's expulsion from paradise as a direct result of woman's behaviour. It becomes clear, whether the phone call to summon the Marquis away is genuine or not, that he is deliberately setting a test for his bride that he really hopes and expects her to fail. The Marquis has enticed his wife to disobey him, but the fact that she has been set up does not absolve her of responsibility: she chooses to disobey him for her own reasons. This is the crux of the matter in which the narrator becomes entangled.

GLOSSARY

14	**stertorously** noisily, from the Latin *stertere* ('to snore')
	somnolent soporific or something that makes a person feel sleepy
16	**satyr** in Greek mythology, part human, part animal beings associated with Dionysus, the god of wine, with a reputation for great sexual energy
	baroque a term used to describe architecture, particularly in the eighteenth century, that made use of odd, irregular shapes and grotesque features
	pellucid clear, shining or transparent
19	**vicuña** very fine silky wool or cloth
	libertine derived from the Latin *libertinus*, 'freedman', it was applied to men, typically, who saw themselves as freethinkers and nonconformists; by the sixteenth century generally used in criticism of promiscuous and amoral conduct
21	**trousseau** a bride's 'wardrobe' or personal collection of clothes and household goods
24	**Liebestod** German for 'Love Death', 'Liebestod' is the title of an aria from Richard Wagner's opera *Tristan und Isolde* (first performed in 1865)
	Grand Guignol a sensational style of theatre, popular in France in the nineteenth century and early twentieth century, similar to **melodrama**
25	**viscera** the internal parts of a body, especially the guts or the bowels

REVISION FOCUS: TASK 1 A02

How far do you agree with the following statements?

● The narrator's simple naivety makes it difficult for the reader to sympathise with her.

● The Marquis is to blame for the narrator's curiosity and disobedience.

Try writing opening paragraphs for essays based on these discussion points. Set out your arguments clearly.

KEY QUOTATIONS: THE BLOODY CHAMBER (A01)

Key quotation 1: The Marquis has taken his bride's virginity: 'I clung to him as though only the one who had inflicted the pain could comfort me for suffering it.' (p. 14)

Possible interpretations:

- Emphasises the narrator's vulnerability and dependence.
- Suggests the Marquis's violent subjugation of his wife.
- Links to the wider theme of men and women.

Key quotation 2: The bride fears the feelings which the Marquis is stirring in her: 'I seemed reborn in his unreflective eyes, reborn in unfamiliar shapes.' (p. 17)

Possible interpretations:

- Suggests the narrator is lost in the unfamiliar territory to which her husband has taken her.
- Implies the narrator is unreliable – or at least naive – and incapable of seeing and understanding what is becoming apparent to the reader.
- A suggestion of the transformations so typical of fairy tales.

Key quotation 3: The narrator hunts for her husband's true nature in his paperwork: 'I had the brief notion that his heart, pressed flat as a flower, crimson and thin as tissue paper, lay in this file.' (pp. 23–24)

Possible interpretations:

- Conveys an image of the Marquis as unfathomable, unemotional, perhaps incapable of emotion.
- Links to the wider theme of the nature of love, particularly the distinction between a husband's love for a wife and a wife's for a husband.
- The image of a flower, pressed and dead, echoes and reflects the earlier image of lilies and its connotations of death.

GRADE BOOSTER (A02)

It can be argued that it is difficult for the reader to sympathise with a character's situation if they do not sympathise with the character. Consider the extent to which Carter creates sympathy for this heroine – and to what extent Carter relies on the stereotypes of the patriarch and his victim to shape the reader's response to her heroines by placing them in the hands of dangerous men.

EXTENDED COMMENTARY

THE BLOODY CHAMBER, PP. 20–6

From 'After my three hours of practice' to 'and the door creaked slowly back.'

The piano-tuner is introduced as a complete opposite to the Marquis. The older man is cruel, voyeuristic and blasphemous; the young man is gentle, blind and trained in his trade by a 'good priest' (p. 20). In the light of the 1970s **feminist** discussion of the notion of the 'male gaze', the question of who can look at whom is significant in this story. The piano-tuner is prevented from looking at the woman in the way that the 'normal' sighted man sees her. His blindness is a symbol of both his weakness and the possibility of a more equal relationship: one not based on selfish – primarily visual – gratification for the man alone.

The narrator's childlike nature is displayed once more in her petty victory over the domestic staff. It is Carter's way of reminding the reader that the narrator is not yet part of the adult world and still sees herself as a giggling schoolgirl. The emptiness of her existence in the absence of her man is heightened by her realisation that her 'new rank' (p. 21) has isolated her from human contact. Carter deftly suggests that pleasure in power and the control of others is not confined to men. The narrator takes great pleasure in making her arbitrary demands for dinner, suggesting that her newfound authority has brought a joy in selfish manipulation, similar to her husband's. Although 'a little comforted' after filling a few moments talking to her mother on the telephone, 'the dead waste of time' weighs heavily on her. Her immediate future is an 'unimaginable desert' (p. 21).

Having reached this climax of boredom, the narrator rediscovers her husband's keys. The maid's reproachful look suggests she is clearly aware, unlike her new mistress, that in this household it is entirely possible that someone might 'set a trap' (p. 22). The **metaphor** of lighting up the castle's darkness goes hand in hand with the 'exhilaration' the young bride feels at the prospect of finding the Marquis's 'true nature' (p. 22).

Finding little to satisfy her curiosity, the narrator begins to suspect that there must be 'a great deal to conceal if he takes such pains to hide it' (p. 23). The narrator's curiosity echoes the reader's own interest in her searches in the private office. We glean some hints that he is ruthless in business and possibly involved in the opium trade. His wife experiences the dubious thrill of unearthing the Marquis's past passions. She finds the mementoes of his former lovers kept in a file marked 'personal'. These macabre keepsakes suggest submissive desire, fascination with death and ghoulish enjoyment of vampirism.

The quotation from Baudelaire's *Journaux intimes* (1887) – 'the supreme and unique pleasure of love is the certainty that one is doing evil' (p. 24) (in the original French: 'la volupté unique et suprême de l'amour gît dans la certitude de faire le mal') – inverts the normal association between goodness and love. Carter's chosen name for the Romanian countess, Carmilla, recalls – in a somewhat contrived manner – an early and notorious literary example of the female vampire. The narrator naively realises her inexperience compared to these 'grown-up games' (p. 24).

As she journeys to the darkest core of the man's castle to discover his inner identity, the narrator is not overwhelmed by fear or any consciousness of betraying her promise to the Marquis. The vivid description of the corridor draws heavily on the **Gothic** tradition: an enclosed, dark space, lit only by flickering flame, creates a shadowy world of half-glimpsed images of abused women. The passage leads down beneath the castle and the notion of being underground creates obvious connotations of the mythological underworld of the dead or being buried alive. If the narrator wants to discover her husband's true nature, the most obvious place to explore is surely his secret place. Yet, Carter makes it appear accidental that the narrator is drawn to the key she has been forbidden to use. This could suggest that Carter is more concerned with exploring ideas than creating plausible characters, or that the narrator must cross lesser boundaries before she invades his darkest secret.

Carter draws out the moment of discovery of the 'subterranean privacy' (p. 26), allowing her narrator the obligatory pause of trepidation before turning the key in the lock. The break in the narrative at this point further prolongs the denial of the moment of discovery for the narrator and the reader. It also causes us to speculate on the nature of this hidden and mysterious room, not only at a surface or literal level of meaning, but also what the room might represent in Carter's inventive and original view of the world.

THE BLOODY CHAMBER, pp. 26–8

SUMMARY

- The narrator opens the door to the forbidden chamber, where she discovers the Marquis's terrible secret. The room has been used for acts of torture and murder.
- First she discovers the naked embalmed body of her husband's first wife. Next she finds the skull of his second wife. Finally, trapped in the 'Iron Maiden' (p. 28), she finds the still bleeding body of his third wife.
- The narrator realises with horror that the Marquis intends to add her to the collection. In her shock she drops the key and it becomes covered in blood. Retrieving the key, she runs away from the 'bloody chamber' (p. 35).

ANALYSIS

LOVE AND DEATH

Carter begins the section on the discovery of the chamber with another quotation from Baudelaire equating love with torture: 'There is a striking resemblance between the act of love and the ministrations of a torturer' (p. 26). The **narrator** refers back to her brief 'honeymoon' (p. 15) experience to confirm the point, reaffirming the connection between love, sex and death. Carter's use of 'mutilation' and 'annihilation' (p. 26) places particular emphasis on the physical horror the narrator has unearthed. While it is unequivocally a picture of the torture and murderous abuse of women, Carter also includes some suggestions that are far more disturbing than mere violence. The narrator is shocked to see evidence that the victims cooperated with the murderer: the way the 'dead lips smiled' (p. 27), suggesting the opera singer enjoyed being strangled, is a particularly disturbing image. The narrator is similarly captivated by the deathly beauty of the celebrated painter's model, recognisable even as a severed skull. The most gruesome discovery is that of the countess, who enjoyed a dangerous flirtation with death, penetrated by multiple spikes. The association with the earlier impaling of his new bride is hard to overlook, even if it is not spelled out by Carter.

SIN AND REDEMPTION

The narrator realises that she is the next addition to this grisly collection. Carter heightens the moment by drawing the narrator's (and the reader's) attention to the opal ring, the symbol of her marriage, 'as if to tell me the eye of God – his eye – was upon me' (p. 28). The connection between the Marquis and God, all knowing and all powerful, captures her vulnerability and her guilt. The section closes with a resonant Gothic touch as she slams the 'door of hell' behind her. In the light of these references to God and hell, it is possible to come to the idea that the narrator now sees herself as a sinner in need of salvation. Though this is not explicitly stated here, the ideas of shame and redemption are significantly highlighted at the end of the story. The narrator's need 'to keep my hands clean' (p. 28) recalls Pontius Pilate, who, as the Roman governor of Judaea, was responsible for the execution of Jesus Christ but, according to the New Testament, **symbolically** washed his hands to rid himself of any personal guilt.

> **CONTEXT** **A03**
>
> Matthew 27:24 states: 'When Pilate saw that he could prevail nothing, but that rather a tumult was made, he took water, and washed his hands before the multitude, saying, I am innocent of the blood of this just person'.

STUDY FOCUS: SYMBOLISM

It becomes possible at this point to examine what the 'bloody chamber' (p. 35) might represent at a symbolic level in this tale. It could be taken, at one level, as the murderous and hostile heart of man, a place where dark desires are entombed, where sex and power bring equal pleasure. It is a logical extension of the argument that men wish to possess women utterly. This idea was prefaced earlier in the note from the Marquis's former wife: 'My darling, I cannot wait for the moment when you may make me yours completely' (p. 24). To take a life is the ultimate act of power over another human being, and the suggestion here is that death is the ultimate form of submission.

At another level, the 'bloody chamber' may be viewed as a symbol of female identity. In entering the chamber, the woman is coming to know her fate as a woman through seeing the fate of other women. The idea of death as a metaphor for marriage has already been established in the story; in the bloody chamber it becomes a frighteningly inevitable reality.

CHECK THE FILM

Angela Carter's Curious Room is a BBC Omnibus programme first broadcast in September 1992. It was filmed in the last months before her death. Carter's life and work are examined in searching for her 'curious room'. For Carter, this is a **metaphorical** space where all the secrets of a person's life are stored before birth; life is the process of trying to find 'the curious room' and rediscover or remember those secrets.

GLOSSARY

26 **sacerdotal** related to the sacred duties of priests, connected with the idea of sacrifice

27 **catafalque** a wooden structure suggesting a tomb or monument, used in funeral ceremonies to support a coffin

bier stretcher that bears the corpse to the grave or where a body rests before burial

28 **rictus** open-mouthed – often implying a fixed or set grimace or grin associated with death

KEY QUOTATIONS: THE BLOODY CHAMBER

Key quotation 1: The bride lights candles in the Marquis's secret chamber: 'Each time I struck a match to light those candles … it seemed a garment of that innocence of mine for which he had lusted fell away from me.' (p. 27)

Possible interpretations:

- Despite the horror of her discovery, still the narrator considers her husband's feelings for her while making no mention of her feelings for him, or how they may have changed with this discovery.
- Echoes earlier descriptions equating physical nakedness with vulnerability.

Key quotation 2: The bride summons all her courage to enter the Marquis's secret chamber: 'Until that moment, this spoiled child did not know she had inherited nerves and a will from the mother who had defied the yellow outlaws of Indo-China' (p. 26)

Possible interpretations:

- A first suggestion that the narrator is no longer, and will never be, her husband's victim.
- A suggestion that nerves and will are every woman's inheritance if they are not crushed by a husband's dominance.

THE BLOODY CHAMBER, pp. 28–42

SUMMARY

GRADE BOOSTER A02

You need to consider not only how Carter presents her characters, but also how the characters themselves interact with and reflect upon each other. For example, consider how the introduction of the gentle piano-tuner might affect the reader's response to the characters of the Marquis and the narrator.

- The **narrator** takes refuge in her music room. She tries to ring her mother – but the telephone has been cut off.

- Dreading the return of the Marquis, she plays the piano for consolation. Jean-Yves, the blind piano-tuner, listens. When they talk she faints. He takes care of her and she reveals her predicament. He tells her of the castle's history of murder.

- The Marquis returns suddenly. The narrator dismisses the piano-tuner and faces the Marquis alone. He demands the keys, and her broken promise to him is revealed. The blood on the key stains her forehead.

- The piano-tuner and the narrator go to the courtyard and are taunted by the Marquis as he prepares to kill them.

- The narrator's head is placed on a stone, the Marquis raises his sword, but the fatal blow is interrupted by the narrator's mother who shoots the Marquis dead.

- The young lovers set up a new home in Paris with her mother, turning the wealth of the Marquis to good use.

ANALYSIS

CONTEXT A04

A pentacle is seen as a symbol of protection in British folklore. Jacqueline Simpson and Steve Roud state that it 'was reinterpreted in Christian terms as an emblem of the Five Wounds of Jesus, guaranteed to put demons to flight' (*A Dictionary of English Folklore*, 2000).

POWER AND MAGIC

As the narrator tries to escape the horrors of the chamber, and her own imminent death, the first thing that she sees is a picture of Saint Cecilia, the Christian martyr and patron saint of musicians and poets. It is Carter's teasing sense of humour that keeps the narrator ignorant of her story: Cecilia was beheaded. The narrator very quickly realises that the Marquis's power may well extend beyond the walls of the castle to prevent her escape. She has not only journeyed far from her Parisian home, but also has **metaphorically** travelled far back in time to an almost medieval or feudal society. Carter introduces the idea of **symbolic** protection from evil here, as the narrator tries to create a 'pentacle' (p. 30) through the magic of her music. A pentacle is a pagan **symbol**, a five-pointed star or pentagram drawn within a circle, used for a variety of purposes in pagan rites. This image recurs in many of the stories. The piece she chooses to play is a symbolic retreat into her childhood: the first part of '*The Well-Tempered Clavier*' (p. 30) by Bach would have been something she learned and practised at an early stage of her musical studies.

THE PIANO-TUNER

In one sense, the charm the narrator weaves in her music does bring her some protection when the young, blind piano-tuner is drawn to the sound of her playing. His gentle manner, the antithesis of the Marquis's cruelty, provokes a far greater reaction in her. In a coyly romantic moment, she faints and regains consciousness in the piano-tuner's arms. Her companion is identified with the natural order of the world; he is a natural man, speaking with the 'rhythms' (p. 31) of the land and the sea. It is a suggestion of a possible harmony between them in keeping with their common love of music. He is the only character in this story to be given a first name: Jean-Yves.

THE TRADITION OF MISOGYNY

The narrator and the piano-tuner share secrets. She tells him of the inner secrets of the castle and he tells her of the secrets of the castle's history. The reader realises the Marquis is re-enacting the murderous traditions of his ancestors. This is Carter's way of making it harder to view the Marquis as some kind of individual madman. This sadist has inherited a long tradition of misogynistic crimes.

THE BLOODSTAIN AS EVIDENCE

The romantic moment shared by the narrator and the piano-tuner is brought to an abrupt end by the sudden appearance of the Marquis's car, **personified** as a beastly monster 'gouging' (p. 32) its way through the pre-dawn mist. The **narrator** tries in vain to remove the evidence of her guilt: the bloodstain on the key. This is a neat inversion of the earlier reference to the medieval tradition of a bloodstain being a sign of virtue and innocence (pp. 15–16). In this instance, blood takes on a more ominous association with guilt and sin as evidence of wrongdoing.

A DECEITFUL CHARADE

The Marquis's presence is again announced by the narrator's sense of smell: his 'pungent aroma' (p. 33) is the first sign of his arrival in the bedroom. The married couple now begin a deceitful charade. The Marquis is merely waiting to find out if she has fallen into the trap he has set; the narrator is trying to prevent him discovering her 'new knowledge' (p. 34). She cannot bear his 'intimate touch' (p. 34), associating it with the tortured wives in the chamber. The Marquis demands the return of his keys, resisting her attempts to seduce him into delay. The narrator realises that she is dealing with a man who is in a state of complete and overwhelming 'despair' (p. 35). However, this does little to help the reader understand why she feels pity for the 'atrocious loneliness of that monster!' (p. 35). When he realises that she has 'sinned' (p. 36), the Marquis shows signs of conflicting emotions – excitement, shame, guilt, joy. Carter's use of the **oxymorons** 'sombre delirium' (p. 35) and 'guilty joy' (p. 36) encapsulates the contradictory shifts and changes in his mood.

Another strange, and more striking, use of 'magic' by Carter has the stain on the key transferring to the woman's forehead in a bizarre ritual where she kneels obediently before the Marquis. The early clues to her fate – the references to the decapitation of aristocrats in the French Revolution, the visual effect of the blood-red ruby choker around her neck, the picture of Saint Cecilia – are all now confirmed as the Marquis instructs her to prepare for the 'last rites' (p. 36).

ADAM AND EVE

The powerless young man stays to comfort her when all the other servants leave. His attitude is rather less than comforting, though: first he tells her she does not deserve her fate; then he reminds her that she disobeyed her husband and that is the reason for her punishment. Despite her plea that 'I only did what he knew I would', the piano-tuner still connects her to the mythological guilty female: 'Like Eve' (p. 38). Yet he does not desert her; he is willing to share her fate. This makes an almost exact **analogy** between Jean-Yves and the biblical Adam, who had to share Eve's punishment.

CONTEXT A04

Androgyny is a term derived from the Greek words for man and woman and is a common theme in literature dealing with gender issues. Jean-Yves is, to some extent, androgynous in that he is a man without the more threatening aspects of typical masculine traits, and exhibits more typically feminine virtues: tolerance, musicality, tenderness, courage and submissiveness.

CHECK THE BOOK A03

Nathaniel Hawthorne's novel *The Scarlet Letter* (1850) makes use of marks of shame in a similarly **ambiguous** and subversive manner. The protagonist, Hester Prynne, must wear a scarlet letter 'A' sewn onto her dress to mark her as an adulterer.

As the Marquis prepares to execute his wife, he is dressed in clothes that epitomise the height of masculine sartorial elegance. The reference to the London tailors and shirt makers shows how Carter can communicate a wealth of information about a character's attitudes and values by name-dropping a luxury item. The sword he intends to use is given an intriguing history: it has been ceremonially presented to Napoleon Bonaparte, 'the little corporal' (p. 39), by one of the Marquis's ancestors. The story is briefly told of his family's defeat, humiliation and suicide. The sword is thus associated with death and military dictatorship. In one sentence, Carter has demonstrated how the economy of the short story leads a writer to communicate more through implication and inference. It is no coincidence that her choice of **simile** for this weapon, 'sharp as childbirth' (p. 39), raises the theme of maternal mortality.

CONTEXT **A04**

Pregnancy and childbirth historically posed high risks to the mother. At the beginning of the twentieth century, one in every hundred mothers would die giving birth to their child. In developed countries today that risk has been reduced to one in every ten thousand.

THE COURTYARD

As the narrator is summoned to the place of execution, the miraculous hope of rescue appears in the distance. The obvious clue to the identity of Carter's ***deus ex machina*** plot device (derived from the tradition of Greek **tragedy** where hopeless situations are resolved by the sudden arrival of the gods) is the fact that she is dressed in 'widow's weeds' (p. 38). The improbable arrival of the narrator's mother in the nick of time is contrived, but is entirely apt for the **narrative** style of the fairy tale. Of course, it is at first uncertain whether this rescuer will arrive in time. The tale is building towards its last climax.

CONTEXT **A03**

The Marquis's stubborn headlong attack on the better armed mother (who literally outguns him) mocks the macho tradition of the tragic hero, as typified by Macbeth's insistence on fighting to the bitter end in Shakespeare's 1606 play *Macbeth*.

The place of execution weirdly echoes the earlier scene of the consummation of the marriage. The Marquis is twisting her hair into a rope and kissing the nape of her neck; she is naked apart from her jewellery. The violence implied in the earlier scene is now brought to the fore in this macabre ritual. But 'the beast' (p. 40) is interrupted. The male loses control in the face of a challenge from the 'wild thing' that is her mother. The 'puppet master', 'the king', is amazed that he is no longer in command. He is frozen as if in 'clockwork tableaux' (p. 40). Carter makes the only direct connection between the Marquis and the fairy-tale villain Bluebeard at this point.

As he makes a 'death or glory' (p. 41) charge at the rebellious objects who have failed to conform to his plan, the mother calmly shoots him dead. In a neat **allusion** to the dangerous and animalistic nature of the Marquis, Carter mentions the mother's ability to dispatch a 'man-eating tiger'. She 'disposed' (p. 41) of the danger in each case, and the mother's attitude is clear: when confronted by deadly beasts, kill without hesitation. The character is a **feminist** reinvention of the hero as a maternal icon.

CONTEXT **A04**

A strong woman who possesses the stereotypical attributes of men is often described as an Amazon. In Greek mythology, the Amazons were a tribe of warrior women said to live without men. The belief that they cut off their right breast in order to be able to use their weapons more effectively may have been introduced later to suggest that adopting supposedly masculine traits disfigures women and makes them 'unnatural'.

HAPPILY EVER AFTER

All that is required now is the epilogue or the 'happily ever after' moment to draw this tale to a satisfying conclusion.

It is not so strange that, after the adventures of their youth, the mother and daughter take to the 'quiet life' (p. 41). It is a model of domestic harmony based on public service, education, cultural endeavour and redistribution of wealth. The term '*maternal telepathy*' (p. 41) is coyly introduced by the narrator to avoid the despised **cliché** of 'female intuition' (though whether the notion of mothers being endowed with psychic powers is any more valid in gender politics is debatable). The story ends with a very downbeat turn of phrase, as the narrator reflects on the mark she still bears of her experience. It is not just that she is ashamed of being tricked or trapped by the Marquis into being his victim; it is that she is aware she was not a completely unwilling victim of his desires.

GLOSSARY

35 **chthonic** something that lives in the ground or beneath it

37 **vassal** an underling, servant or slave

40 **Medusa** in Greek mythology, a monstrous female Gorgon with writhing serpents for hair and a gaze capable of turning a person to stone. She was defeated by Perseus, who cut off her head. In some versions of the myth, Medusa's severed head retains its lethal power

CONTEXT A04

Feminist revisions of the Greek myth of Medusa emphasise the Gorgon's beauty rather than her monstrosity, recasting her as a victim of male aggression.

KEY QUOTATIONS: THE BLOODY CHAMBER A01

Key quotation 1: As she plays the piano to calm herself, there is a knock on the door: 'I saw, not the massive, irredeemable bulk of my husband but the slight, stooping figure of the piano-tuner.' (p. 30)

Possible interpretations:

● Places the piano-tuner in direct contrast with the Marquis.

● Asks the reader to question what might be considered the nature of an ideal man.

Key quotation 2: The key to the Marquis's secret chamber is indelibly stained with blood: 'the more I scrubbed the key, the more vivid grew the stain … I saw the heart-shaped stained had transferred itself to my forehead' (pp. 33 … 36)

Possible interpretations:

● The stain is a symbol of the narrator's unforgiveable disobedience.

● A magical element in the story, typical of fairy tale.

● Links to a suggestion of sin through association with the mark of Cain.

THE COURTSHIP OF MR LYON

SUMMARY

- A girl worries about her father's safe return in bad weather. In fact, her father's car is stuck. He is a ruined man, unable to provide for his daughter.

- He abandons his car and walks through the snow, coming upon a mansion where he finds food and drink but no inhabitants. He then discovers the local garage will repair his car at his unknown host's expense.

- As he leaves, he sees a rose in the garden and, reminded of his promise to bring one back for his daughter, picks it for her.

- A great beast, like a lion but dressed in human clothes, appears and challenges the man over the theft. The man explains it is for his daughter and the Beast's angry mood changes when he sees her photograph.

- The man has little option but to return to the Beast's house with his daughter as instructed. Her father leaves her with the Beast when he goes back to London to take care of his business affairs.

- The Beast and the girl share an odd shyness when in each other's company, but she becomes less afraid of him.

- The girl's father calls her away with news of his good fortune. She promises she will return before the winter is over but soon forgets the Beast.

- Pining for her, the Beast has lost the will to hunt and is starving to death. The Beast's companion, a spaniel, finds the girl and leads her back to the Beast.

- The girl kisses the Beast and he is transformed from a lion into a man. The ending of the story suggests that they grow old together.

CHECK THE FILM A03

Jean Cocteau's *La Belle et la Bête* (1946), a version of 'Beauty and the Beast', made in black and white, achieves many surreal effects and has a magical and enchanting style that influenced later adaptations.

CHECK THE BOOK A03

Alice's Adventures in Wonderland (1865) and its sequel *Through the Looking-Glass and What Alice Found There* (1871) were written by Charles Dodgson (1832–98) under the pseudonym Lewis Carroll. They are considered classics of children's literature.

ANALYSIS

BEAUTY AND THE BEAST

This revision of 'Beauty and the Beast' is the most conventional updating of a traditional tale in the collection. The tale begins with the 'lovely girl' working in the 'mean kitchen' (p. 43), worrying for her father's safety. The winter landscape and the isolation of the girl are gathered into one image as if she were 'made all of snow' that resembles 'bridal satin'. The associations of whiteness, purity and virginity inform us of this character's status. The character retains the name Beauty and her youth is emphasised by the fact that her father regards her as 'his girl-child' (p. 43). The opening of the tale looks ahead and hints at the ending of the story which, as in most fairy-tale happy endings, features the ideal of matrimonial harmony.

MAGIC AND WEALTH

Beauty's father is an incompetent businessman, twice ruined and now bankrupt, blaming his vehicle for being stuck in the snow. His chance discovery of a magical mansion that provides for all his needs does not alarm him. He aspires to this level of wealth and understands that one of the privileges of this wealth is the 'suspension of reality' (p. 44): in this magical house there are none of the mundane concerns of ordinary life. Carter is making a political point here: the rich are not bound by the 'laws of the world' (p. 44); these apply to the less fortunate. The labels on the food and drink provided, in anticipation of visitors, are taken directly from Lewis Carroll's *Alice's Adventures in Wonderland*. It is almost disappointing that, unlike the characters in Carroll's tale, the man remains the same size and the dog does not talk to him. It seems odd that the dog, 'man's best friend', does not undergo some kind of **anthropomorphic** transformation given the number of such changes in the collection as a whole. But Carter is mostly interested in the independence of spirit associated with cats, rather than the more manageable behaviour of dogs. This explains why the dog, at the end of this tale, remains a dog.

TRADITION AND SUBVERSION

As the man leaves the house, chance events reveal 'one last, single, perfect rose' (p. 46), which he takes to fulfil his daughter's wish. The connection between the girl and the rose as symbolic images of perfection and simple innocence is made succinctly by this action. The 'leonine apparition', part man, part lion, that seizes hold of him 'like an angry child' is the Beast of the fairy tale (p. 46). The mere image of Beauty's perfection is enough to calm the savage nature of the Beast. If readers are expecting an obvious feminist perspective in Carter's retelling of this tale, they will most likely be disappointed: so far, so conventional. The traditional characters are less distant from us in manners and dress than the traditional tale's Beauty and Beast, but in every other respect they clearly conform to the pattern of the tale as we know it of old.

Dutiful Beauty, 'possessed by a sense of obligation to an unusual degree' (p. 48), is obedient to her father and to the Beast throughout this story. When she neglects that duty, her good looks are spoiled. She is no longer the perfect woman. One has to consider exactly how **ironic** Carter is being in offering this version of the story to the reader – particularly when she warns the reader against judging her character: 'Do not think she had no will of her own' (p. 48). But it does seem that her options, such as they are, leave her little to choose between the idle 'enchantment' (p. 50) of the Beast's domain and the 'high living and compliments' (p. 52) of her father's new riches. Beauty's return to the Beast is the traditional race to save the dying lover by the guilty party. Beauty has neglected her duty and must atone for that fact. The rather pathetic humiliation of the Beast by his own loneliness is swiftly erased by her renewed love. There seems to be a rather mocking tone to Carter's depiction of the man recovering from a near-death experience.

STUDY FOCUS: MAN AND BEAST   A03

Although there is little structural difference between this retelling and the traditional fairy tale, Carter exaggerates the Beast's bestial qualities. He growls, he roars, he walks 'on all fours' (p. 50). He does not eat in front of Beauty, presumably to save her from the terrible sight. Anthropomorphisation and transformation – from man to beast and beast to man – are typical of fairy tales, and typical of this collection. Yet in this tale, Carter exaggerates the Beast's animal qualities, perhaps shocking a reader who has accepted the normality of beasts in the world of fairy tale. Throughout the story, Carter does not allow the reader to forget the conflict of the man within the beast – and the beast within the man.

CONTEXT   A03

Although the story of a beautiful girl loving or marrying a monster has many origins and variations, French author Gabrielle-Suzanne Barbot de Villeneuve is considered to be the original author of 'Beauty and the Beast'; her novella was published in 1740. In 1756 this was radically abridged by Jeanne-Marie le Prince de Beaumont; this shorter tale is the version we are most familiar with today.

INTERPRETATIONS

In many ways, this is the least satisfying story of the collection. It is engaging in the way it is told, and the familiarity of the **narrative** path is not without its own entertainments. However, the tale itself is not subverted by Carter at all. This is perhaps the most disturbing aspect of Carter's tale: in the new form the reader has to question the values embedded in such a story. 'Beauty and the Beast' offers the reader the romantic sentiment that the bestial nature of man can be tamed and humanised by the submissive sacrifice of woman.

This can be viewed as a kind of equality: the man loses an element of his masculinity, the woman loses her independence, yet each gains the other. However, it could be argued that Beauty does not gain the person she desired: she chooses to be with the Beast, but ends up only with the man she has to release from within the Beast. Perhaps there is a moral for our times that arises from this retelling: people need to recognise that they cannot always have what they want. Their life together is depicted as a 'walk in the garden' (p. 55), an **allusion** to the Garden of Eden and its associations of paradise regained and redemption. This image of happiness also suggests an acceptance of nature's imperfection: Mr and Mrs Lyon can enjoy the snowlike 'drift of fallen petals' (p. 55).

CHECK THE FILM A03

Walt Disney's *Snow White and the Seven Dwarfs* (1937), based on the fairy tale by the Brothers Grimm, is one of the first and most successful feature-length animated films. *Pinocchio* (1940), *Cinderella* (1950), *Sleeping Beauty* (1959), *The Little Mermaid* (1989) and *Beauty and the Beast* (1991) are all taken from the European fairy-tale tradition.

CHECK THE FILM A03

Shrek (2001) by DreamWorks Animation is based upon William Steig's fairy-tale picture book entitled *Shrek!* (1990). The film **parodies** Disney versions of fairy tales, inverting the values implied in the tale of 'Beauty and the Beast'.

GLOSSARY

43 **pallor** indicates an unnatural loss of colour; often applied to human features as a sign of ill health or death

44 **Palladian** Andrea Palladio (1518–80) was an Italian architect who imitated ancient Roman design. The Palladian style became popular in eighteenth-century England through the work of Inigo Jones (1573–1652)

45 **squirearchal** an adjective suggesting the self-importance of the minor landowning country gentry or squires

   impecunious having little or no money, derived from the Latin pecunia ('money')

47 **Queen Anne** a decorative style of furnishing and architecture from the early eighteenth century

49 **Apocalypse** the Christian biblical idea of the end of the world and the revelation of God's will to humanity – in apocalyptic terms the idea of the Beast is a **synonym** for the devil

REVISION FOCUS: TASK 2 A03

How far do you agree with the following statements?

● Carter's stories suggest that all human beings can change, or be changed.

● This story is not typical of the collection; it is a straightforward retelling of a fairy tale.

Try writing opening paragraphs for essays based on these discussion points. Set out your arguments clearly.

KEY QUOTATIONS: THE COURTSHIP OF MR LYON (A01)

Key quotation 1: Mr Lyon strikes a bargain with Miss Lamb's father: '"Take her the rose then, but bring her to dinner," he growled' (p. 47)

Possible interpretations:

- Portrays man as animal, beastly and unpredictable.
- A bargain is agreed, a feature typical of fairy tale narrative.

Key quotation 2: Miss Lamb agrees to stay with Mr Lyon to restore her father's fortune: 'Do not think she had no will of her own … [but] she would gladly have gone to the ends of the earth for her father, whom she loved dearly.' (p. 48)

Possible interpretations:

- Justifies her agreement to staying with the Beast.
- Carter is at pains to emphasise that Beauty has strength and independence.
- Links to the wider theme of patriarchal power and female submission.

Key quotation 3: When she realises Mr Lyon is dying, Miss Lamb returns to his house: 'It seemed December still possessed his garden' (p. 53)

Possible interpretations:

- A symbolic, physical representation of the Beast's pining for his love; links to Carter's frequent use of winter setting in these tales.
- Reflects the Beast's response to the lack of love, and of a loved one.
- Implies that, as his life fades without love, so does the life of his garden and of the earth itself, suggesting that love and life are inextricably linked.

CONTEXT (A04)

The possibility of transformation lies at the heart of the 'romance' genre, much of which follows the template established in Jane Austen's novels. In Austen's *Pride and Prejudice* (1813), for example, Elizabeth Bennet rejects Mr Darcy because of his pride. Only when she recognises his true qualities can their love blossom. In this sense 'Beauty and the Beast' – and Carter's 'The Courtship of Mr Lyon' – can be seen as falling within the romance genre.

THE TIGER'S BRIDE

SUMMARY

- A Russian nobleman travels with his daughter. They arrive in an unnamed Italian city.
- The father is a drunken, womanising spendthrift. He plays cards with The Beast – a mysterious and disguised figure.
- The Beast takes advantage of the nobleman's foolishness and soon he has lost everything. He then stakes his daughter's life in the hope of recovering his lost fortune. He loses and is crushed. The Beast scolds him for his lack of care.
- The girl is taken next morning by The Beast's valet.
- The Beast's valet tells the girl that The Beast will repay her father and reward her well for showing herself to him naked. She laughs and mocks his request with a false acceptance. This causes The Beast to shed a tear.
- The girl is presented the next morning with an earring in the shape of a teardrop, which she refuses to accept. When asked a second time to agree to The Beast's demands, she remains silent. Another tear falls from The Beast.
- Next morning, another teardrop earring is presented to her and again refused. She goes out riding with The Beast. He insists that she must see him without his disguising garments.
- The girl is profoundly moved by the sight of the Beast in animal form and exposes her naked body to him.
- Through a magic mirror, the girl sees that her father is now wealthy again: The Beast has kept his word. She decides not to leave the castle, sending the clockwork servant to take her place in her father's life.
- The girl strips again but chooses to wear the earrings to approach The Beast. The earrings turn back to water as The Beast licks her human flesh away to reveal the animal fur beneath.

ANALYSIS

COMPARISONS WITH 'THE COURTSHIP OF MR LYON'

The tone of this version of 'Beauty and the Beast' is in complete contrast to the previous tale, as if Carter is somehow acknowledging the unsatisfactory nature of her other attempt at reworking the myth into a new form (see **Part Two: The Courtship of Mr Lyon**). The narration is given this time to Beauty, and the reader immediately feels a sense that this is her story. She is not an idealised image of perfection. In this relationship, the daughter is attempting to cope with an inadequate father, but not from a sense of duty; this is a case of damage limitation. She has chosen to come to this region because she was told that there was no casino. Her attempt to protect the last of her inheritance from her father's hopeless gambling is thwarted by circumstance. Twice she makes the link between cards and evil. In the second instance, she identifies The Beast with the devil for the ease with which he deprives her father of everything.

The character of the feckless father provides the opportunity for the first moral difference between the tales. The warning of neglected paternal duty to protect the child is much more clearly expressed in this version: 'If you are so careless of your treasures, you should expect them to be taken from you' (p. 60). The father is not permitted to see The Beast's home in this version; Beauty is taken there as a prize, not as a hostage to her father's fortune.

SETTING

While the original 'Beauty and the Beast' perhaps underpins the tale in certain recognisable elements, this is not a simple updating. Nor does the **narrative** have much in common with its closest myth. In terms of setting, however, Carter remains true to the story. She has chosen to set this tale, in the best fairy-tale tradition, long ago, in a far-off place. The distance, in both time and space, helps the reader to accept the tale; the modern setting of the other version does not achieve this sense of distance in the same way.

BEAUTY

The Beast's requests to see the girl naked are expressed through an almost comically embarrassed valet, who gabbles the deal at top speed. Unlike the voyeurism in 'The Bloody Chamber', there is no sense of threat in this request, more a sense of the ridiculous. The girl is able to laugh the proposal off with a challenge of her own: pay no more than you would for 'any other woman in such circumstances' (p. 65). It is a riposte that exposes the cheap and degrading bargain on offer. Her argument is that, no matter what the price may be, the deal denies her identity, so why bother to look at her face? Her silence in the face of his repeated request is evidence of a much more resourceful and resilient character in this version of the story.

The mutual revelation that takes place between Beauty and The Beast is quite touching, despite its fantastic weirdness. The girl accepts The Beast as 'courteously curious as to the fleshly nature of women' (p. 72) and makes clear she will do him 'no harm' (p. 71).

In deciding not to return to the world of men, represented primarily by her father, the girl realises she has been changed by her experience. In her mirror she sees 'a pale hollow-eyed girl whom I scarcely recognized' and compares herself to the painted doll automaton 'whose face was no longer the spit of my own' (p. 73) The **narrator** describes the unseeing eyes of the automaton in an apparent reference to the **feminist** concept of the 'male gaze' – 'the market place, where the eyes that watch you take no account of your existence' (p. 74) – suggesting it is a manufactured and unnatural response in men, not a defining characteristic.

Art critic, painter and writer John Berger (b.1926) explores the idea of the male gaze in *Ways of Seeing* (1972). Men gaze at women, he says, in the assumption that they can do something to or for them; this gives them power. Women, however, view themselves being looked at and constantly carry their own image with them: 'Men look at women. Women watch themselves being looked at' (p. 47).

CHECK THE BOOK A03

John Webster's *The White Devil* (published in 1612) is a revenge **tragedy** that explores themes of murder, debauchery, corruption and revenge. It uses the device of an Italian setting to comment on English society, much in the way Carter's settings are a distancing device that allows the reader to make connections imaginatively. In Webster's case the device was a necessity to avoid censorship.

STUDY FOCUS: THE AUTOMATON   A02

The automaton, an imitation of Beauty, is an intriguing **symbol**. Beauty does not recognise herself at first, but later decides to send this imitation out into the world. The assumption that no one will notice the difference is a comment on how **patriarchal** society simultaneously idealises and reduces women. The young woman angrily compares her own life with her father to that of the doll: 'had I not been allotted only the same kind of imitative life amongst men?' (p. 70).

THE TEARDROP EARRINGS

The Beast's gift of teardrop earrings seems to be a coded plea for the girl to take note of his emotional distress. When she fixes them to her ears she finds them 'very heavy' (p. 73), but they are all she chooses to wear to meet The Beast again in his room. In one way this resembles the use of jewellery and nakedness in 'The Bloody Chamber'. However, in this tale the jewellery seems much more intimate and honest: a representation of male emotion, rather than the controlling lust of the Marquis. The earrings are the final transformation of the story, reverting to the tears from which they were formed. Perhaps Carter is suggesting that male ideas of women will not change until women have changed themselves and become as autonomous and independent as men, especially those who have dropped the mask of their masculinity. The ending of the story seems to be advising the reader that it might be a good idea for men and women to see each other as they really are and that mutual recognition of a shared animal nature is the basis of happiness in human relationships.

CHECK THE POEM **A03**

In *The World's Wife* (1999), a **satirical** collection which **revises** a number of myths and fairy tales, poet Carol Ann Duffy plays with gender roles and allows the female voice to be heard. In 'Mrs Beast' the Beast is not transformed into a man; instead he remains bestial, at the mercy of Mrs Beast: 'Bring me the Beast for the night' (line 91).

GLOSSARY

56	**grappa** a form of brandy made from grapes
57	**profligate** wasteful and self-indulgent
58	**civet** African mammal, sometimes compared to a cat, whose musk is used as the basis of perfume
59	**stock** a scarf worn around the neck, usually for riding
60	**capisco** Italian verb meaning 'understand'
63	**gracile** gracefully slender
65	**Desnuda** naked (Spanish)
66	**soubrette** in theatre, particularly opera, a female comedy character – a servant or friend of the leading female character – sexually provocative, talkative and irreverent
	settecento minuet a term normally used to describe eighteenth-century culture in Italian – literally meaning 'seven hundred' – here a reference to late baroque music style
	simulacra an image or representation, often unconvincing or vague
68	**Tantivy!** a hunting cry used to urge horses and their riders into a gallop
69	*trompe l'œil* an artistic optical illusion, used to trick the eye into believing an image is the object it represents
70	**Kublai Khan** thirteenth-century Mongol emperor, grandson of Genghis Khan

REVISION FOCUS: TASK 3 A03

How far do you agree with the following statements?

● In Carter's stories, women must become more like men if they are to become equals.

● Human weakness is at the heart of all these tales.

Try writing opening paragraphs for essays based on these discussion points. Set out your arguments clearly.

KEY QUOTATIONS: THE TIGER'S BRIDE **A01**

Key quotation 1: Beauty's father seems to enjoy losing his fortune at cards: 'he laughs, as with glee' (p. 56)

Possible interpretations:

- Suggests the absence of any paternal care or responsibility.
- A woman, specifically a daughter, is considered an object of financial value to be bargained with.

Key quotation 2: On the appearance of the automaton, the valet explains: 'We surround ourselves … with simulacra and find it no less convenient than do most gentlemen.' (p. 66)

Possible interpretations:

- Comments on male attitudes to women: they are painted dolls for men's convenience.
- Suggests that this independent, resourceful girl, in strong contrast, has no place in the world of men.

Key quotation 3: Beauty accepts she must witness The Beast naked: 'The lamb must learn to run with the tigers.' (p. 71)

Possible interpretations:

- Characterises men and women with animalistic stereotypes.
- Implies that women must change if they are to challenge male dominance.
- Foreshadows the tale's resolution.

CONTEXT **A03**

Danish author Hans Christian Andersen (1805–75), considered one of the world's greatest storytellers, began publishing his pamphlets of fairy tales in 1835. He wrote over 150 of these stories, including 'The Little Mermaid', 'The Wild Swans' and 'The Snow Queen'; they were translated into English in 1846.

PUSS-IN-BOOTS

SUMMARY

- Puss-in-Boots, a ginger tomcat, agrees to be servant to a young cavalry officer.
- The cat's master falls in love with old Signor Panteleone's young wife. He serenades her and succeeds in getting her attention. However, further contact is prevented by her chaperone.
- With the assistance of one of Puss-in-Boots's lovers, a female tabby cat, a scheme is plotted to divert the chaperone's attention with a sudden infestation of rats.
- Posing as expert rat-catchers, the young soldier and Puss-in-Boots gain admission to the house. The young wife sends the chaperone away.
- Puss keeps up a pretended noise of battle with imaginary rats to disguise the sound of the lovers' mutual pleasure.
- The young soldier becomes determined to find a way to be with his lover, and together the cats plot the murder of the husband, ensuring that they will benefit from the arrangements.
- The cats take control. The tabby cat sends the old man tumbling downstairs, and his neck is broken. The young man, posing as a doctor, is able to enjoy another happy moment with his lover.
- With her husband dead and the chaperone under her control, the young widow takes charge of financial matters to everyone's satisfaction.
- The story concludes with the tomcat conceitedly congratulating himself on his talents and failing to recognise that it was the tabby cat that had all the best ideas.

ANALYSIS

COMMEDIA DELL'ARTE

Carter clearly enjoys this tale. It is a bawdy romp drawing on the stock characters of *commedia dell'arte*, which transferred from the professional performance troupes of Italy to influence the theatrical traditions in Britain. Pantomime remains one of the most common early childhood memories of theatre for British theatregoers and non-theatregoers alike. In its current form pantomime has no equivalents in modern European theatre or elsewhere, despite the common heritage. Carter takes the familiar pantomime tale and resites it in Bergamo, the place of *commedia dell'arte*'s origins, returning it to its roots in popular entertainment and grossly exaggerated, often violent, physical comedy.

Anthropomorphism is not problematic in pantomime or fairy tale. Puss-in-Boots's enduring appeal as a rascally but inventive Everyman character (see page 92) is complemented by his narcissism. He represents the triumph of the 'little man'. Carter gives him some of the attributes of the *commedia dell'arte* servant character Arlecchino, or Harlequin, such as tremendous acrobatic agility. The young officer is the *inamorato* of the tale, the typical young male lover motivated by lust, love, music and passion but lacking in common sense.

The chief obstacles to youthful fulfilment in this tale are taken directly from the *commedia dell'arte* characters known as the *vecchi*, the old ones. Signor Panteleone is the equivalent of the Pantalone character. This typically rich, powerful, mean old man is usually played as impotent yet desperately pursuing younger women. His young wife appears to be modelled on the *commedia dell'arte* character of the *inamorata,* the young man's lover, usually called Isabella or Lucinda. However, her very active role in the resolution of the story makes her more like Columbine, the female counterpart to Harlequin: energetic, acrobatic and feisty. The role of Columbine, the agile and resourceful servant, is shared with the tabby cat that Puss-in-Boots so happily impregnates but fails to appreciate.

The chaperone, variously called 'dragon', 'hag' or 'man-hater' (p. 82) in the tale, is based on La Ruffiana, the gossiping old woman who keeps the *inamorati* apart. This is the role that would be performed by a man in drag on stage, the role of the pantomime 'dame'. There is a sense in which she is the substitute for the **patriarchal** figure in the story, acting as guardian of his property, so the idea that she is a man in woman's clothing is not as ridiculous as it might seem.

CHECK THE FILM **A03**

The *Carry On* films are a long-running series that began in 1958, directed by Gerald Thomas and produced by Peter Rogers. They are a combination of slapstick, **parody**, innuendo and double entendres, the comedy seen as typically British humour derived from **farce** and music hall. The humour stems as much from the same company of actors playing stock characters from film to film as it does from the script or situation in each film.

STUDY FOCUS: DISGUISE AND SELF-DECEPTION A02

Disguise and pretence are themes that Carter exuberantly explores in her use of the devices and characters of the *commedia dell'arte* tradition. The young man takes on the mask of Signor Furioso (Mr Frenzy) to enter both the house and his lover in a frenetic display of youthful energy. When he later returns as a bogus doctor, Carter is playing with the stock *commedia* character Il Dottore, who is useless as a medic, useless with women and speaks only pseudo-intellectual nonsense. Beneath his disguise, the young man is the very opposite of this member of the *vecchi*.

It is the only story in the collection in which the **narrative** voice is masculine, and its arrogance is punctured for the reader by the knowledge that it was the young female characters who took control of the situation and ensured a happy outcome. Puss-in-Boots remains very pleased with himself, unaware that in his new role as 'family man' he is still an impostor.

REVISION FOCUS: TASK 4 A02

How far do you agree with the following statement?

● 'Puss-in-Boots' is so different from the other tales, it seems out of place in the collection.

Try writing opening paragraphs for an essay based on this discussion point. Set out your arguments clearly.

GLOSSARY

76	**Figaro** central character in the comic opera by Rossini based on the traditional *commedia dell'arte* character Brighella, liar and schemer, from Bergamo
	obbligato usually a particularly difficult solo in a piece of music
77	**rococo** originally meaning 'old-fashioned', now applied to a definite and highly ornamental style of design and decoration popular in eighteenth-century France and Italy
	genuflection from the Latin *genuflectere*, meaning 'to bend the knee'; a sign of respect, particularly in Catholic rituals
	pontiff's the pontiff is a name for the pope
78	**billet-doux** a love letter
79	**Aldebaran** a star in the constellation of Taurus, one of the brightest stars in the sky
83	**discommoded** inconvenienced, given trouble or discomfort
	mountebank a confidence trickster, particularly a bogus medical doctor or 'quack'
	zany derived from the Italian *zanni*, 'buffoon', a familiar form of the name Giovanni, the nickname given to mad acrobatic clowns in the *commedia dell'arte* tradition
88	**saraband** a slow, graceful court dance of the seventeenth and eighteenth centuries

CHECK THE FILM A03

New versions of classic tales were shown in 2008 in the BBC series *Fairy Tales*. *Rapunzel* was set in the competitive world of tennis, *Cinderella* in the academic world of anthropology, *The Empress's New Clothes* in the celebrity world of award ceremonies, and *Billy Goat* in the music industry. The BBC's approach shared elements with Carter's – the head of drama for Northern Ireland, Patrick Spence, stated: 'these stories offer such fantastic scope for comedy drama'.

KEY QUOTATIONS: PUSS-IN-BOOTS A01

Key quotation 1: Puss is 'proud … of his fine, musical voice. All the windows in the square fly open when I break into impromptu song' (p. 76).

Possible interpretations:

- Suggests that others do not share Puss's opinion of his voice.
- Puss is selfish and self-obsessed.
- Male pride and arrogance are presented as self-deception.

Key quotation 2: Puss argues that 'love is desire sustained by unfulfilment' (p. 81).

Possible interpretations:

- Suggests a stereotypical male attitude to love.
- Attitude of male cynicism – though contrasted in the attitude of Puss's master.
- Links to the wider themes of love and sexuality.

KEY QUOTATIONS: PUSS-IN-BOOTS A01

Key quotation 3: On hearing Tabby's suggested plan 'I congratulate her ingenuity with a few affectionate cuffs round the head' (p. 86).

Possible interpretations:

- Suggests female ingenuity and male resentment of it.
- Stereotypical male response: an inability to show gratitude, or any emotion, in any way other than physical.

CRITICAL VIEWPOINT A03

It could be argued that 'Puss-in-Boots' is a tale of female empowerment, in which the young wife and the tabby cat achieve their own ends through ingenuity. Equally it could be argued that it is a comedy of male arrogance and the lengths to which lust can drive men.

THE ERL-KING

SUMMARY

- A young girl enters the forest and meets with the Erl-King, who transforms young girls into caged birds.
- Despite enjoying the dreamlike rapture of her time with the Erl-King, the girl resolves to kill him and release the trapped young women.

ANALYSIS

SOURCES

'The Erl-King' is an adaptation of a European tale that is likely to be less familiar to a modern audience, partly because it has not been recycled in the animated versions of 'classic' tales that dominate so-called 'family entertainment'. It draws heavily on folkloric traditions of the Green Man as the **personification** of nature or the energies of spring (see also **Part Three: Man, woman and nature**).

FORM

The basic shape of the tale is simple, but Carter's **narrative** is not easily reduced to a chronological account of events. Of all the stories in the collection, 'The Erl-King' is the most innovative and experimental in its narrative form.

THE OPENING

The opening sentence is concerned with the significance of light, in both material and **metaphorical** senses, and contains an **allusion** to the poetry of Emily Dickinson (1830–86), itself influenced by Christian scripture. Carter plays with the **paradox** 'perfect transparency must be impenetrable' (p. 96), immediately qualifying her introductory statements of 'lucidity' and 'clarity'.

The visual colour scheme – 'brass-coloured', 'sulphur-yellow', 'nicotine-stained', 'russet slime' – evokes the transition from autumn to winter, a hard and dirty season where everything is 'withered' and 'discoloured'. The idea of death is drawn out of the natural passage of the seasons: 'a haunting sense of the imminent cessation of being' (p. 96). Carter uses the annual, cyclical death of nature as a metaphor for mortality. But her expression hints at a more universal sense of total annihilation, where everything ceases to exist: 'All will fall still, all lapse' (p. 97).

CHECK THE BOOK A04

Although the Green Man is generally depicted as benevolent and kind, Kathleen Basford views the Green Man of medieval art as a demon in her work *The Green Man* (1978).

CHECK THE POEM A03

Compare the opening paragraph of 'The Erl-King' with Emily Dickinson's poem 'Light is sufficient to itself'.

STUDY FOCUS: NARRATIVE VOICE A02

The **narrative** voice of 'The Erl-King' is constantly shifting. This changing of perspective positions the readers in various ways and has an unsettling effect (see **Part Four: Narrative techniques**). The narrative cohesion is maintained by a sense of the tale continuing from moment to moment, but it is clearly not a chronological account of events. The sharp edges of space and time become blurred as Carter's 'wood swallows you up' (p. 96). The narrative voice is partially established by a distanced recount of 'that afternoon', described in the third person. It then moves through direct address in the second person – 'you are no longer in the open air' (p. 96) – to become a wholly involved first person narrative account from the perspective of the female **protagonist**. Carter also shifts between past, present and future tenses. The tale never settles into one narrative mode and the effect is both disorienting and entrancing.

GRADE BOOSTER A02

This densely written and challenging tale might not be the most accessible on which to base an exam response, yet reference to its narrative viewpoint, symbolism, language and ideas can add depth and breadth to your analysis of other tales in the collection.

SYMBOLISM

The threatening presence in the **metaphorical** wood becomes clear in a repeated phrase that acts as an almost poetic refrain: 'Erl-King will do you grievous harm' (p. 97). The dangerous creature or spirit Carter introduces as something that 'came alive from the desire of the woods' (p. 98) is a mocking and cruel embodiment of nature. His 'white, pointed teeth' (p. 99) immediately recall deadly predators, whether they be real wolves or imaginary vampires. The central **symbol** for this tale is the 'old fiddle' (p. 99) with its broken strings. The image suggests neglect and abuse alongside the possibility of harmony. Its presence next to the caged birds representing the trapped female spirit offers some uncertain hope of restoration and liberation from the patriarch's 'pretty cages' (p. 102).

The narration slips into dream-like rapture as the Erl-King enchants the narrator. She becomes a 'stream' and 'like a skinned rabbit' as she is stripped to her 'last nakedness' (p. 102). The joyous indulgence in nature is accompanied by a 'terrible fear' of entrapment (p. 103). The narrator revels in her enchantment and her imprisonment, though she recognises – and always has – the 'grievous harm' the Erl-King will do her. Carter returns to this paradox of fear and irresistible attraction a number of times: the Erl-King cages birds yet is loved and credited with 'innocence' (p. 103). When the narrator imagines herself killing the Erl-King, Carter employs an image used in 'The Bloody Chamber': long hair, a symbol of female beauty and masculine strength, wound around the neck in strangulation.

CHECK THE POEM A03

Carter **alludes** to Christina Rossetti's poem 'Goblin Market' (1862) when she writes 'Eat me, drink me; thirsty, cankered, goblin-ridden' (p. 102). In this poem one sister succumbs to the temptations of the 'goblin merchant men', while the other resists.

THE END

The tale ends with a vision of the future: the woman will liberate the trapped 'young girls' and enable the 'old fiddle' to play music once again (p. 104). But the hope of harmony is replaced by 'discordant' cries of a male voice. The last sentence of the story – 'Mother, mother, you have murdered me!' (p. 104) – twists the relationship of the narrator and the Erl-King into another dimension, suggesting the narrator is in some way mother to the Erl-King; the effect is startling and provocative.

CONTEXT **A04**

Michaelmas (p. 99), 29 September, is the Feast of St Michael in the Christian calendar. It falls just a few days after the autumn equinox, which marks the shortening of daylight hours, the beginning of autumn and the approach of winter.

GLOSSARY

96	**lancinating**	piercing or stabbing
97	**flossed**	a coined word, suggesting covered with fine silky fibres
98	**eldritch**	supernatural, weird
	blewit and **chanterelle**	types of edible mushroom
99	**osiers**	tough flexible twigs from a willow tree, used for wickerwork
101	**diatonic**	a musical scale of five whole tones and two half tones
	palliasse	a thin straw mattress
	dervishes	members of a Muslim religious order, known for their whirling dancing
102	**prothalamions**	a song celebrating a marriage
103	**numinous**	supernatural, holy
	lycanthropes	werewolves
	gelid	very cold

KEY QUOTATIONS: THE ERL-KING **A01**

Key quotation 1: The narrator walks through the woods at the start of the tale: 'There is no way through the wood any more … Once you are inside it, you must stay there until it lets you out again' (p. 96).

Possible interpretations:

- The wood is personified as a malevolent being.
- Connection with the Erl-King and his caged birds; suggests the wood and the Erl-King are one and the same.
- Links to the forest setting in other tales: a place of danger.

Key quotation 2: The narrator realises what the Erl-King intends: 'in his innocence he never knew he might be the death of me, although I knew from the first moment I saw him how Erl-King would do me grievous harm.' (p. 103)

Possible interpretations:

- An **ambiguous** viewpoint: the Erl-King is both malicious and innocent, or perhaps unknowingly malicious.
- Suggests innocence on the part of the narrator who cannot blame him for her death.

KEY QUOTATIONS: THE ERL-KING A01

Key quotation 3: The Erl-King captures and cages birds: 'and now I know the birds don't sing, they only cry because they can't find their way out of the wood … and now must live in cages.' (pp. 103–104)

Possible interpretations:

- Suggests the narrator has shaken off the Erl-King's enchantment and lost her naivety.
- Could suggest the shift in perception of the relationship between men and women, when the enchantment of love fades.

REVISION FOCUS: TASK 5 A02

How far do you agree with the following statement?

- The Erl-King represents the very essence of man: selfish, unthinking, innocent and destructive.

Try writing opening paragraphs for an essay based on this discussion point. Set out your arguments clearly.

GRADE BOOSTER A02

Comparing character, setting, language or viewpoint across the different tales in the collection shows breadth of knowledge and understanding, and an overview of the text as a whole. Consider ways in which the character of the Erl-King can be compared to other domineering patriarchs in Carter's stories: the Marquis in 'The Bloody Chamber', for example.

THE SNOW CHILD

SUMMARY

- An aristocrat riding with his wife wishes for a girl as beautiful as the objects he sees in nature.
- The child he has wished for appears before them.
- The Countess is jealous and attempts to kill her, but each attempt leaves the Countess worse off than before.
- She succeeds at the third attempt when the child pricks her finger on a rose and dies.
- The Count is upset and briefly has intercourse with the dead girl, who melts away.
- The Countess regains everything she has lost and the Count gives her the rose that killed the girl, which she drops.

ANALYSIS

CHARACTERS

'The Snow Child' is the shortest tale in the collection, yet its power to shock and disturb is not diminished by its relative brevity. The Countess is a striking figure, 'glittering' and 'shining' in black fur with a touch of scarlet (p. 105). She is dressed in the 'pelts of black foxes', an **anthropomorphic** image of sly and cunning sexuality. The Count, however, has inexplicable desires for another, an imaginary girl he wishes into existence. Carter suggests that the Count, yet another aristocrat, is a cold-blooded killer in his desire for a girl 'as red as blood' (p. 105). The tale then allows him to have the girl he wishes for: he has fathered the girl of his dreams. This may be a comment on how **patriarchy** shapes women in the image of men's desires and, as can be seen, not much good comes of this.

SYMBOLS

The **symbolic** significance of the Count's desires is communicated in the **similes** of his three wishes: snow, blood and a raven. His desire is a mixture of coldness, bloodthirstiness and death. The raven is an icon of **Gothic** literature, epitomised in Edgar Allan Poe's **narrative** poem 'The Raven', but the mythic association of this black, carrion-eating, croak-voiced bird with death and omens of death is much older and more widespread in cultures across the world.

JEALOUSY AND DEATH

The envious Countess makes two attempts to rid herself of the girl. First she plans to abandon the girl, then to drown her. Both attempts are thwarted by the Count – and both have magical consequences, leaving the Countess naked and the girl 'furred and booted' (p. 105). The **symbols** of clothing and jewellery represent the transference of affection from an older to a younger woman that is commonplace in society. The Countess is left with only the Count's pity. The third symbolic device she employs against the girl is more devious: the picking of the rose. It is a typical deception as practised by the stepmother and evil old crone in 'Snow White', a seemingly harmless gesture or act of kindness concealing murderous intent. The symbol of the rose combines the perfection of natural beauty and the thorn as a **metaphor** for the inevitable pains of loving. In allowing the picking of the rose, the Count fails to protect his child from the jealousy of his wife, and the girl dies bleeding and screaming.

CONTEXT A03

The **revision** of fairy tales and myths is common in women's poetry. A poem may contain a single image from a myth or tale, or a complete collection may be given over to rewritings, such as Carol Ann Duffy's *The World's Wife* (1999), Liz Lochhead's *The Grimm Sisters* (1981) and Anne Sexton's *Transformations* (1971).

CONTEXT A03

Edgar Allan Poe's 'The Raven' (1845) was published in the newspaper the *New York Evening Mirror* to popular acclaim.

The scene of graphic necrophilia that follows is perhaps the most extreme image in the whole collection. The Countess is reduced, briefly, to the role of spectator. Carter seems to suggest here that women know men would rather indulge themselves with dead fantasies than accept women as they really are, a depressing and morbid view of human relationships.

STUDY FOCUS: INTERPRETATIONS A03

As a version of 'Snow White', 'The Snow Child' is an enigmatic tale that may be interpreted in a number of ways. It can be seen as an exploration of sexual jealousy and competition between women for the attention of men. Alternatively, and perhaps in addition, it is an **allegory** of the tension between parents and children, more particularly the triangle of relationships between mother and daughter, father and daughter, and mother and father.

THE THORN

The conclusion of the tale is somewhat **ambiguous**. Has the Countess been hurt by the rose thorn herself? Or does she recognise that the rose 'bites' (p. 106) and drop it before it can hurt her as it hurt the man's fantasy child? If it is the latter, is she rejecting love itself in trying to avoid the pain of love? If it is the former, would that suggest in hurting another woman she has only hurt herself and left the real villain, the Count, unscathed and unpunished?

GLOSSARY

105	**immaculate**	pure, without stain or blemish, perfect – the **paradox** of virgin birth in Christian doctrine is solved with the notion of immaculate conception
106	**virile member**	the phallus or erect penis

KEY QUOTATIONS: THE SNOW CHILD A01

Key quotation 1: The Count wishes for a child: 'she was the child of his desire and the Countess hated her' (p. 105).

Possible interpretations:

- Suggests the child is a fantasy realised.
- Creates ambiguity: does desire refer to her creation at the Count's wish? Or does it suggest his sexual desire? The Countess's reaction suggests the latter.

Key quotation 2: The Snow Child picks a rose, pricks her finger and dies: 'The Count picked up the rose, bowed and handed it to his wife' (p. 106).

Possible interpretations:

- Suggests an empty gesture, attempting forgiveness and reconciliation.
- Could also suggest the Count intends the Countess to die as the child did.

REVISION FOCUS: TASK 6 A01

How far do you agree with the following statement?

- This is the most shocking of the tales in the collection.

Try writing opening paragraphs for an essay based on this discussion point. Set out your arguments clearly.

CONTEXT A04

Carter wrote in an afterword to her short story collection *Fireworks* (1974): 'I'd always been fond of Poe, and Hoffman – Gothic tales, cruel tales, tales of wonder, tales of terror, fabulous narratives that deal directly with the imagery of the unconscious – mirrors; the externalised self; forsaken castles; haunted forests; forbidden sexual objects.'

THE LADY OF THE HOUSE OF LOVE

SUMMARY

- A beautiful vampire, doomed to eternal life, lurks in a Carpathian chateau. She occasionally feasts on a traveller or shepherd boy.
- The vampire's Tarot cards foretell death for visitors until the arrival of a young officer.
- In his innocence, the young officer changes the order of her deck of Tarot cards, replacing Death with the Lovers. She expects to devour him but her ritual does not follow the usual pattern, and she finds herself becoming human once more.
- He puts her to bed, but when he awakes, full of hope for the future, he discovers his new love has died as an old woman.
- He is roughly dispatched by the housekeeper and returns to his regiment, in time to depart for the war in France.

ANALYSIS

SLEEPING BEAUTY AND VAMPIRES

'The Lady of the House of Love' is set in the Carpathian mountain region in central Eastern Europe. The main action of the tale takes place just before the outbreak of the First World War. Among other references, this vampire tale turns the story of the passive female Sleeping Beauty on its head. The princess is not sleeping; she is preying on unwary men – and she is not waiting to be rescued. She is neither alive nor dead; she is undead. There are multiple **allusions** to Bram Stoker's *Dracula* (1897) and its many cinematic adaptations.

In the original fairy tale, the princess is saved from an evil death by being put to sleep. She then does not age a day until she is rescued by a handsome prince whose love revives her to live happily ever after. In Carter's version the Countess craves some kind of release from her ritualised and repetitive immortality; her rescue comes in the form of death. The love of the handsome prince restores her true age and humanity. He escapes death at her hands only to enter the bloodbath of the First World War, where the average life expectancy among junior officers was measured not in years but in months.

A VICTIM OF IMMORTALITY

The abandoned village is a place of ghosts, shadows and distant sobbing, and has 'a sense of unease' (p. 107). But Carter balances the vindictiveness of her criminal monsters with hints that they cannot help themselves. They are helplessly sleepwalking through eternity, with little variation in diet, and the chief emotion of the vampire is 'sadness'.

Carter points out how the vampire merges two opposite images into one monstrous form: she is both 'death and the maiden' (p. 107), a murderer and a beautiful, helpless victim of her murderous nature. In Renaissance art, young women are often depicted as vulnerable victims menaced by a bony skeleton representing death. The images are **allegories** of the mortality of the human form, the impermanence of beauty and the inevitability of death. The skeleton always appears as a masculine and predatory figure. In a sense, the female vampire has paid the price for taking on the role of the male, preserving her beauty at the cost of becoming the thing that threatened her. The song of the caged lark pleases her because it mirrors her own imprisonment in her unnaturally preserved beauty. Her perfect beauty is a 'deformity' (p. 108) because it is so perfectly inhuman.

THE VAMPIRE

The vampire queen is a malevolent sexual presence, whose 'army of shadows' (p. 109) interfere with nature, turn good things into bad, sweet into sour and generally cause young women, in particular, 'diseases of the imagination' (p. 109).

The vampire's self-fulfilling and inescapable prophecy is seen in the Tarot cards: a cycle of 'wisdom, death, dissolution' (p. 109). The obscene consumption of human flesh is only depicted in the housekeeper's careful manicure of her mistress's fingernails afterwards, 'to get rid of the fragments of skin and bone' (p. 111). The voice of the man-eating giant from 'Jack and the Beanstalk' interrupts the **narrative** to boom out his cannibalistic desires. The juxtaposition of the prim rituals of the vampire and the relatively safe monster of childhood tales is a startling narrative link to the arrival of the hero.

THE YOUNG MAN

The young man is a soldier, a cheerfully rational adventurer. Throughout the tale, it is made clear that he is of a generation of young men doomed to a horrible death in unimaginable circumstances. Yet he is unable to imagine himself capable of failure or defeat: 'This lack of imagination gives his heroism to the hero' (p. 120). The **irony**, of course, is that Carter has already signalled her soldier's doom: 'He will learn to shudder in the trenches' (p. 120), while also recognising the 'special glamour' (p. 112) of those prevented from growing old by war. In this sense, the allure of youth and beauty is shared by the vampire and the young man. She becomes old before eventually dying, whereas he will never grow old.

As in other tales in the collection, powerful aromas intoxicate the senses. The young man's response to their 'rich, faintly corrupt sweetness' as he moves through the thorn bushes surrounding the chateau is 'Too many roses' (p. 113) suggesting his masculine indifference to perfume. Carter does not overplay the allusion to Prince Charming hacking his way through the undergrowth to reach his bride-to-be. The man is surprised by the 'ruinous' state of the interior (p. 115), which is entirely in keeping with the 'Gothic eternity' (p. 112) of vampire legends: 'cobwebs, worm-eaten beams … endless corridors … winding staircases … eyes of family portraits briefly flickered as they passed' (p. 115). Carter has included most of the **clichés** of terrible, spooky interiors from the **Gothic** genre. In addition, the vampire can be seen as a striking reinvention of Charles Dickens's famous character from *Great Expectations*, Miss Havisham, who, jilted on her wedding day, shuts out the light and rots in the decay of her wedding feast. This places the young man in the role of Pip from *Great Expectations*: an innocent child, who will be manipulated by Miss Havisham.

CONTEXT **A04**

The 'diseases of the imagination' (p. 109) which the vampire induces are the extremes of behaviour that might now be termed manic depression. Carter is alluding to the work of the Renaissance scholar and depressive Robert Burton, who wrote *The Anatomy of Melancholy* (first published in 1621). Among the diseases Burton considers are St Vitus's dance – 'the lascivious dance' – and 'lycanthropia … or wolf-madness', as well as 'frenzy' and 'possession of devils'.

CHECK THE BOOK **A03**

In Chapter 8 of *Great Expectations* (1860–1) Pip describes his first meeting with Miss Havisham: 'I saw that the bride within the bridal dress had withered … and had no brightness left but the brightness of her sunken eyes. I saw that … the figure … had shrunk to skin and bone. … Now, waxwork and skeleton seemed to have dark eyes that moved and looked at me.'

DEATH

At the vampire's death, she seems to have become an irrational impossibility, 'an invention of darkness' (p. 124), banished by the morning light. The soldier's reaction to her 'pathetic' death is one of vague curiosity to keep something of her alive in the impulse to 'resurrect her rose' (p. 124). The rose, an intimate memory of her, is an omen of his imminent death. Although the 'maiden' (p. 107) in the vampire has been defeated, 'death' (p. 107) regains its 'corrupt, brilliant, baleful splendour' in the 'monstrous flower' the soldier has revived (p. 125). Carter is pointing us towards the fact that, no matter how bizarre or unpalatable our fantasies of death may be, the real world of men can be horrible beyond the scope of imagination.

STUDY FOCUS: THE YOUNG MAN AS MOTHER   A03

Although the vampire tries to maintain her ritualistic consumption of prey, she is unable to resist the young man. It can be argued that the rational, unimaginative male ends up destroying the irrational, fantastic female. He comforts her when she cuts herself and seems to play the role of parent to her as the helpless child. Carter compares him to a mother as he deals with her wound and tries to 'kiss it better' (p. 123).

GLOSSARY

107	**revenants**	ghosts from the past – from the French *revenir*, 'to return'
	somnambulist	sleepwalker
	Tarot	derived from fourteenth-century playing cards, a stylised set of **symbolic** images used in fortune-telling
	death and the maiden	title of an oil painting by sixteenth-century artist Hans Baldung; also a poem by German writer Matthias Claudius set to music by Franz Schubert in the nineteenth century; more recently a play by Ariel Dorfman (1990)
109	**tenebrous**	dark and gloomy
	catafalque	a raised platform on which the body of a dead person lies
111	**escritoire**	writing desk
116	**bedizened**	dressed up or overdressed in fine clothes
118	**carillons**	sounds resembling a peal of bells
119	**Vous serez ma proie**	You will be my prey (French)
121	**Suivez-moi**	Follow me (French)
	Je vous attendais	I was waiting for you (French)
122	**lugubrious**	mournful

CONTEXT   A03

Bram Stoker allows the legends of werewolf and vampire to be almost indistinguishable in his novel *Dracula* (1897). His vampire assumes many different animal shapes through the story, and it is particularly thanks to cinematic adaptations that Dracula is now identified with the vampire bat rather than the wolf.

KEY QUOTATIONS: THE LADY OF THE HOUSE OF LOVE   A01

Key quotation 1: The Lady of the House of Love is an archetypal vampire in almost every way: 'Everything about this beautiful and ghastly lady is as it should be, queen of night, queen of terror – except her horrible reluctance for the role.' (p. 110)

Possible interpretations:

- The vampire is a monster who is not reconciled to her nature.
- The vampire is a woman condemned to perpetual beauty and sexual predation.
- Carter subverts central elements of the Gothic, creating a reluctant monster.

KEY QUOTATIONS: THE LADY OF THE HOUSE OF LOVE A01

Key quotation 2: When she was a girl, the vampire was happy to feed on baby rabbits, voles and field mice, but 'now she is a woman, she must have men.' (p. 110)

Possible interpretations:

- **Ambiguous** suggestion of her sexual and cannibalistic impulses.
- Emphasises Carter's dual portrayal of the character as vampire and as woman.

Key quotation 3: The vampire considers her attraction to the young soldier: 'And could love free me from the shadows? Can a bird sing only the song it knows?' (p. 119)

Possible interpretations:

- Suggests the possibilities of liberation which love and sexuality can bring.
- Links to the wider themes of metamorphosis, and the possibilities of change.

REVISION FOCUS: TASK 7 A02

How far do you agree with the following statements?

- This tale draws more fully on the Gothic tradition than any other in the collection.
- Carter's characters cannot help themselves: they are victims of circumstance or victims of their own nature.

Try writing opening paragraphs for essays based on these discussion points. Set out your arguments clearly.

CONTEXT A04

The Tarot card 'La Papesse' (p. 109), the Female Pope, is a **symbol** of the superior intellectual powers **feminists** attribute to women. La Papesse is linked to the legend of Pope Joan, who is said to have disguised herself as a man and been elected to the papacy, but been finally exposed by giving birth in public. This tale is cited as an example of how women have been written out of history by men.

EXTENDED COMMENTARY

THE LADY OF THE HOUSE OF LOVE, PP. 113–16

From 'At the mauvish beginnings of evening' to 'all the freshness of morning'.

The young hero arrives at the abandoned and ruined village as the day is ending. Carter has just indicated a turning point in the tale by the use of the giant's threatening **couplet** from 'Jack and the Beanstalk'. The young man approaching is both Jack, the slayer of giants, and the handsome prince rescuing the princess. He is the lady's fortune as told in the cards: 'love and death' (p. 112).

Carter has the hero arrive at the end of his quest 'hot, hungry, thirsty, weary, dusty' (p. 113). He has struggled to come 'a great way' to this place, and he is momentarily disappointed by the 'uninhabited' village with its roofs 'caved in', 'fallen tiles' and 'shutters hanging disconsolately'. The hero's 'faint unease' is not an awareness of the 'foul secrets' of the place, as he is not 'sufficiently imaginative' to see beyond the 'poignant brightness of the hollyhocks' and 'the beauty of the flaming sunset' (p. 113).

The hero is drawn towards the mansion by the housekeeper's mimed invitation through the 'obscene … excess' of the 'jungle' of red roses (p. 114). Here his actions mimic those of the handsome prince in 'Sleeping Beauty', who has to hack his way into the castle through thickets of thorn. The **imagery** is inverted, as the roses in this tale are not a barrier; they intoxicate with their 'heavy scent' (p. 113). They are also, of course, the **symbol** of romantic love, inviting and welcoming the hero.

Carter is once again taking the **protagonist** hero from the exterior of an 'immense, rambling' (p. 114) ruin into the intimate heart of a private chamber. The man is reminded of 'ghost stories' but dismisses his memories as 'fancies'. His refusal to participate in imaginary terrors protects him from danger: he is 'no child' (p. 114). His defining male characteristic is his rejection of childhood and of imagination. In his **patriarchal** view of the world, such irrational things have no place and therefore must be dismissed. His 'virginity' acts as a 'pentacle', a magic charm to ward off the evil he is approaching so unawares. Carter is jokingly linking the young man with Sleeping Beauty's Prince Charming by inverting the charm of sexuality. Whereas Prince Charming draws Sleeping Beauty to him through his physical appearance, the soldier is unknowingly protected from the beautiful vampire by his innocence. He is brought through 'melodramatically creaking hinges' to a 'lightless, cavernous interior'. Lewis Carroll's *Alice's Adventures in Wonderland* is recalled by the use of the grammatically incorrect phrase 'Curiouser and curiouser' (p. 114), and again the hero dismisses his 'childish lack of enthusiasm' (p. 115) for the place. Called to his doom, the hero displays understated Englishness by tidying himself to meet the 'more elevated member of the household'. Carter underscores this point by mentioning his 'tweed jacket' (p. 115), an item of clothing **synonymous** with the English aristocracy.

As he approaches the inner sanctum, the 'ruinous … interior' is briefly described: 'worm-eaten … crumbling' (p. 115). The choice of adjectives connects with the general atmosphere of death and decay.

CONTEXT   **A04**

In the fairy tale 'Jack and the Beanstalk' the hero climbs a magic beanstalk and finds a giant's castle. Jack hides himself in the castle, but the giant can smell him. The tension builds as the giant chants, 'Fee fi fo fum, I smell the blood of an Englishman. Be he alive, or be he dead, I'll grind his bones to make my bread.' The most widely known retelling of this traditional English folk tale is from Joseph Jacobs' *English Fairy Tales* (1890).

CONTEXT **A04**

The expression 'the lady of the house' has been in use since the nineteenth century to refer to the housewife. It has become an archaic **euphemism** for a woman who remains without an independent career or income after marriage. Carter is emphasising the limitations of marriage for women.

Once again the interior of the **Gothic** location is represented as a labyrinth of 'endless corridors', 'winding staircases' and 'galleries' of 'family portraits'. Carter playfully reiterates the hero's tendency to underestimate danger in the understatement that the vampire family portraits are 'of a quite memorable beastliness'.

The hero's approach is halted at the final door, its significance signalled by the deliberately **melodramatic** use of the 'harpsichord' (p. 115). This harks back to the previous description of the vampire 'strumming the bars' of her pet lark's cage as she 'likes to hear it announce how it cannot escape.' (p. 108). In this, the young man's impending doom and the vampire's eternal doom of imprisonment are linked. The 'liquid cascade' of the vampire's pet songbird disarms the hero completely as he waits to enter 'Juliet's tomb' (p. 116). Carter's reference to Shakespeare's *Romeo and Juliet* (c.1595) reminds us that the vampire is neither alive nor dead, in the same way that Juliet in her drugged state is both alive and dead to different characters at the end of the play. 'Juliet's tomb' is also the place where the 'star-crossed lovers' die, as Romeo in his grief is unable to recognise that Juliet is only sleeping. The **irony** that the virginal Prince Charming enjoys the 'freshness of morning' (p. 116) on the threshold of a tomb encapsulates his naive masculinity.

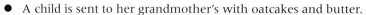

THE WEREWOLF

SUMMARY

- A child is sent to her grandmother's with oatcakes and butter.
- She encounters a huge wolf. Unafraid, she draws her knife and cuts off its right forepaw. The wolf limps away and the girl wraps up the paw, placing it in her basket.
- As snow falls and covers any tracks, the child comes to her grandmother's and finds her unwell.
- As the child takes a cloth from her basket, the wolf's paw falls out – but it has transformed into a human hand. The child recognises it as her grandmother's.
- The child cries out and the neighbours come. They beat the old woman and stone her to death.
- The girl moves into her grandmother's house and prospers.

ANALYSIS

STUDY FOCUS: WOLVES AND MOTHERS   A04

Carter takes the fairy tale 'Little Red Riding Hood' for an outing in a different form in this story of inter-generational female rivalry. Whereas in other tales the wolf or animal represents predatory male sexuality or **patriarchal** tyranny, here the wolf represents the preceding generation of mothers. This is another perspective on society's expectations of women – to marry, have children and never be independent.

A HARD LIFE

Carter prepares the ground for the tale by emphasising the link between the environment and the inhabitants of the 'northern country' (p. 126). This invites the reader to identify, through **pathetic fallacy**, the reflection of the people's 'cold hearts' in the 'cold weather'. The **narrator** seems rather condescending towards the people, implying that their beliefs are naive or merely ignorant superstition: 'the Devil holds picnics in the graveyards and invites the witches'; garlic keeps vampires away; the mysterious power of 'second sight' is granted by difficult and particular circumstances of birth; and old women are stoned to death for being witches (p. 126). The reader is invited to view such cruel behaviour as a characteristic of people with simplistic beliefs.

Carter then turns this condescending perspective on its head by telling a tale of a shape-shifting witch – one who can transform herself into a wolf – that ends with her execution by stoning. Carter does not overplay the resonances of this form of execution as a specifically masculine revenge on women (prescribed as punishment for adultery in ancient Christian texts). Carter's 'Winter and cold weather' (p. 127) **alludes** to Shakespeare's mockery of rustic simplicity in *As You Like It* (c.1599–1600), where exiled noblemen sing reassuring verses about the freedom of the forest, their **conceit** being that there is 'no enemy' in the forest but 'winter and rough weather' (Act II Scene 5). Carter has been hinting that the enemies of these simple 'upland woodsmen' (p. 126) are non-existent, but this linking allusion signals there is more to the forest's dangers than just weather.

THE CHILD

After the preamble, the 'Little Red Riding Hood' tale begins. The girl is equipped with her 'father's hunting knife' (p. 127) for protection and she is skilled in its use. The absence of the father is not explained, and the phallic **symbolism** of the knife as the representation of a masculine strength is not emphasised. The weapon becomes 'her knife' as she turns to face her attacker. The encounter with the wolf and the second encounter with the injured grandmother show the 'child' (p. 127) to be strong and able to defend herself. The conflict is resolved by the girl summoning her neighbours to her aid. In giving the neighbours the task of stoning the witch, Carter allows the child to retain some of our sympathy.

HAPPILY EVER AFTER

The conclusion of the tale, after the grandmother-witch-wolf has been stoned to death, is a swiftly delivered 'happily ever after': she takes over her grandmother's house and 'she prospered' (p. 128). Carter's ending suggests that, whatever the mistakes of previous generations, it may be possible for this generation of women to benefit from their ancestors' wealth of experience without, **metaphorically** speaking, inheriting their dangerous shape-shifting tendencies – in other words, without having to pretend to be what they are not.

> **CONTEXT** A04
>
> Witchcraft trials continued long after the reign of James I of England; the last person to be executed for witchcraft in England was Alice Molland in 1684. European persecution of women for the alleged crimes and heresy of witchcraft did not come to an end until the eighteenth century.

KEY QUOTATIONS: THE WEREWOLF   A01

Key quotation 1: The child goes to visit her grandmother: 'she knew the forest too well to fear it' (p. 127).

Possible interpretations:

- Suggests the girl's strength and resourcefulness.
- A new perspective on the symbol of the forest: knowledge can guide you through it.

Key quotation 2: The girl recognises her grandmother's severed hand: 'There was a wedding ring on the third finger and a wart on the index finger' (p. 127).

Possible interpretations:

- The grandmother is effectively condemned to death at this recognition.
- The tradition of marriage and the superstition of witchcraft are given equal significance and are implicitly linked.
- The superstitions which Carter earlier mocked are verified: a wart can be the sign of a shape-shifter.

REVISION FOCUS: TASK 8   A02

How far do you agree with the following statement?

- Many of the characters in these tales are symbols: they represent aspects of human nature or society.

Try writing opening paragraphs for an essay based on this discussion point. Set out your arguments clearly.

GLOSSARY

126   **Walpurgisnacht**   Walpurgis Night, the night of 30 April, the eve of May Day, is named after the English nun Walpurga, a missionary to Germany in the eighth century

       St John's Eve   23 June, the eve of the feast day of St John the Baptist; coincides with the Midsummer solstice

       supernumerary   exceeding the standard number

       familiar   a spirit in the shape of an animal that is the close companion of a witch

> **CONTEXT** A04
>
> According to German folklore Walpurgisnacht (p. 126) is the night when witches gather in places such as the Brocken, the highest point of the Harz Mountains in the north, and celebrate the arrival of spring with satanic revels and lustful dancing.

THE COMPANY OF WOLVES

SUMMARY

- The wolves in the winter forest are hungry.
- A young girl sets off through the forest to her granny's house.
- On her journey a stranger appears and walks along with her, challenging her to a race to granny's house. It is agreed that he can kiss her if he wins.
- The stranger arrives at granny's house and pretends to be the girl to trick the old woman into inviting him inside. Stripping naked, he turns into a wolf and eats her. He then disguises himself with granny's nightcap and waits for the girl to arrive.
- The young girl arrives and is trapped by the man. The house is surrounded by howling wolves.
- She strips off her clothes and burns them in the fire. She kisses the stranger, takes off his shirt and burns it, thus making the man completely into a wolf.
- Christmas Day arrives and the blizzard outside dies down. The fearless girl sleeps in granny's bed with the wolf.

ANALYSIS

CONTEXT   A04

Jacob and Wilhelm Grimm published *Kinder- und Hausmärchen* (*Children's and Household Tales*), containing eighty-six folk tales, in 1812. Later editions expanded to include 200 stories plus ten children's legends. The Brothers Grimm are usually thought of as the source of most well-known fairy tales.

STUDY FOCUS: STORIES WITHIN A STORY   A02

Here is an outline of the three stories told within this story:

- A man traps a wolf in a pit, cuts its throat and cuts off its paws, only to find it transformed into the corpse of a man.
- A witch transforms the guests at a wedding into wolves.
- A man relieves himself outside at night and disappears. His wife remarries and has children, only for her first husband to return. Enraged by her behaviour, the first husband turns into a wolf and is killed after savaging one of her children. The wolf turns back into the man again when he is dead. An urgent warning is given about the importance of running away from naked men in the forest.

WEREWOLVES

Carter delays the development of plot and the introduction of main characters as she describes the nature of wolves and the dangers of encountering these 'forest assassins' (p. 129). The instruction on how to take precautions and defend children from the wolves is followed immediately by an ominous note of warning that hints at other, more fantastical dangers: 'the wolf may be more than he seems' (p. 130). The two miniature tales of encounters with werewolves act as a preface to the main story. The only hint of protection against a werewolf is the belief of 'old wives' (p. 132) that clothing can keep the wolf at bay. Burning a wolf's clothes prevents him regaining his form as a man.

THE GIRL

Once the tale itself begins, the narrative unfolds swiftly. As she sets off into the forest, the young girl is cloaked with the protection of 'the invisible pentacle of her own virginity' (p. 133). The **allusions** to 'Little Red Riding Hood' draw upon the significance of menstrual blood as the physical evidence of passing from girl to woman. Carter describes her as 'an unbroken egg' to emphasise her vulnerability, but adds that 'she is afraid of nothing' (p. 133). Her mother allows her to make the journey that her father, if he were around, would prevent. Carter seems to be suggesting that men prefer girls not to change into women, preferring to keep them in a dependent position and so maintain **patriarchal** authority.

GRANNY AND THE STRANGER

The scene between the young girl and the stranger is swiftly, and somewhat dismissively, summarised by Carter as 'Commonplaces of a rustic seduction', and the girl is happy to lose her bet with the 'handsome gentleman' (p. 135). Her God-fearing granny is also speedily dispatched by the werewolf. The nakedness of the young man and the impressive size of his genitals, is menacing and deadly: 'The last thing' (p. 136) seen by the 'pious old woman' (p. 135). In many versions of the original tale, granny is rescued from the belly of the wolf. However, Carter allows no such comforting possibility here. Granny is not coming back in this story. Anything that is of no use to the wolf, he burns or hides away out of sight.

WOLVES AND MEN

The language refrains of the original tale focusing on the size of the bodily features of the wolf, are interspersed with the girl's realisation of the danger she faces. Even at this moment, she can feel pity for the wolves outside in the cold. She has no use for fear as she strips to reveal herself to the man. Her kiss, though freely given, is an act of deception. This self-confident young woman, who knows she is 'nobody's meat' (p. 138), seizes control of the situation and burns the werewolf's clothing. As he can no longer take the shape of a man, he is no threat to her. Carter is making the point that masculinity can be more dangerous and deadly to women than any carnivore. The insistence on the idea of 'meat' reflects the **feminist** perspective that the media presents women as mere objects of flesh for the consumption of men. The declaration of defiance is a model of Carter's view that women should refuse to accept the passive role of victim.

CONTEXT A03

Charles Perrault's 'Le Petit Chaperon Rouge' ('Little Red Riding Hood') is the original source of this fairy tale (1697). In it the child is eaten, and a moral on the virtues of obedience accompanies the story. A new version, 'Rotkäppchen' ('Little Red Cap'), appeared in the Brothers Grimm collection in 1812.

CHECK THE BOOK A03

Women and Media (1980), edited by Helen Baehr, was one of the first texts of feminist media analysis to explore the stereotyping of women in the mass media and the related question of women as media executives.

THE WINTER SOLSTICE

The ending of the story emphasises the peacefulness of reconciliation, with the man-beast tamed. Carter's assertion that Christmas Day is 'the werewolves' birthday' (p. 139) is a deliberately confrontational one. While the depiction of Christian believers in the story is not tremendously sympathetic – the 'mad old man' (p. 130) and the 'Aged and frail' granny trying to keep the wolf from the door by 'living well' (p. 135) – it is unlikely that Carter is suggesting Jesus was a werewolf. It is more likely that she is drawing our attention to the winter solstice when the balance between day and night shifts, 'the hinge of the year when things do not fit together as well as they should' (p. 131). The passing of the shortest day in winter (usually 21 or 22 December) is an event that was marked with pagan celebrations before Christian festivals were placed in December. Carter is drawing on a mystic tradition of magic and the belief in solstices as particular, special moments when transformation is possible. It is an image of the redemption of man through realising the virtues of his animal nature, a theme Carter returns to throughout these tales.

CONTEXT · A04

Paganism is best understood as a diverse group of religious faiths that share a respect for the natural world. Modern-day pagans might identify themselves as Wiccans, Druids, shamans, sacred ecologists, Odinists or heathens.

STUDY FOCUS: SYMBOLIC LANGUAGE · A02

Look out for, and try to comment on, patterns of symbols and language within and across the tales. For example, in 'The Company of Wolves', compare the description of the smell of human 'meat' (p. 129) attracting the wolves' attention; the girl laughing in the knowledge that she is 'nobody's meat'; and the description of her red shawl as the 'colour of sacrifices' (p. 138).

GRADE BOOSTER · A03

It is vital that you express your viewpoint in responding to and interpreting Carter's tales – but it is equally important that you offer and explore a range of viewpoints and interpretations. What different ways, for example, are there of interpreting Carter's intentions in writing 'The Company of Wolves' – or any of the tales in the collection?

GLOSSARY

129	**incarnate** in the flesh, in human form, or naked or blatant
	wraiths a fifteenth-century term for ghosts or spectres
131	**irremediable** something that cannot be cured or remedied
133	**cuneiform** wedge-shaped, particularly applied to early Persian writing
135	**prophylactic** a precaution that prevents or guards against disease
138	**prothalamion** a celebratory song or poem sung before a wedding, a term invented by the poet Edmund Spenser (c.1552–99) with his 1596 marriage poem 'Prothalamion', based on the Greek word *epithalamium* – a song celebrating a marriage
	threnody a sad poem or song, often recited or sung for the dead
138	**Walpurgisnacht** Walpurgis Night, the night of 30 April, the eve of May Day, when according to German folklore witches meet and revel with the devil; named after the English nun Walpurga, a missionary to Germany in the eighth century

---

KEY QUOTATIONS: THE COMPANY OF WOLVES · A01

Key quotation 1: The wolves in the forest 'cluster invisibly round your smell of meat as you go through the wood unwisely late.' (p. 129).

Possible interpretations:

- Humans are reduced to mere 'meat'.
- Direct address of 'you' places the reader in danger.
- Wolves presented as almost supernatural monsters, silent and invisible.

KEY QUOTATIONS: THE COMPANY OF WOLVES A01

Key quotation 2: The girl enters the woods on her way to visit her grandmother: 'The forest closed upon her like a pair of jaws' (p. 133).

Possible interpretations:

● The forest is presented again as a place of fear.

● The image of wolf and forest merge into one; each encapsulates and incorporates the other.

Key quotation 3: The girl's red shawl is laden with symbolism: 'her scarlet shawl, the colour of poppies, the colour of sacrifices, the colour of her menses' (p. 138).

Possible interpretations:

● Poppies suggest death.

● Sacrifice suggests the sacrifice of women to the appetites of men.

● Menses suggests the transition from girl to woman.

REVISION FOCUS: TASK 9 A03

How far do you agree with the following statement?

● Each of Carter's tales is intentionally open to a number of different interpretations.

Try writing opening paragraphs for an essay based on this discussion point. Set out your arguments clearly.

CHECK THE BOOK A03

Routledge's *Complete Fairy Tales* (2002) includes every one of the 210 tales collected by the Brothers Grimm, including 'Little Red Cap'.

CHECK THE FILM A03

Neil Jordan's 1984 film, *The Company of Wolves*, is a conflation of several of the stories, including 'The Company of Wolves' and 'Wolf-Alice'.

WOLF-ALICE

SUMMARY

- A girl raised by wolves is brought back to human society.
- The nuns charged with her care find her intolerable and hand her over to the Duke, who, as it happens, is a werewolf.
- She acts as his servant, using the little training given by the nuns, but remains ignorant of his nature.
- She is bewildered by her first menstrual bleeding and begins to discover her identity as her body changes and matures.
- She finds a white dress behind the mirror and puts it on.
- The Duke is out hunting as a wolf. He is wounded by the angry widower of one of his victims.
- The girl tends to the wolf's wounds and he regains his shape as the Duke, and recovers his own identity.

ANALYSIS

THE WILD CHILD

This tale combines werewolf mythology with legends of feral children raised by wolves. The idea of human children being raised by animals has many precedents. The most obvious is the tale of Romulus and Remus, founders of Rome, being suckled by wolves. There are documented cases of feral children acting very much in the way Wolf-Alice behaves, seeing the world in an undeveloped and, in some senses, inhuman way. Helen Simpson in her introduction to the 2006 Vintage edition of *The Bloody Chamber* (p. xviii) points to the origins of this tale in medieval literature, suggesting it is an early version of 'Little Red Riding Hood'.

CHECK THE BOOK **A03**

Lucien Malson's *Wolf Children and the Problem of Human Nature* (1972) includes early accounts of Jean-Marc Gaspard Itard's attempts to teach the feral child 'Victor of Aveyron' to speak. Itard, a nineteenth-century physician, believed that the capacity for empathy and language distinguished humans from animals. Despite failing to teach Victor to speak, Itard believed Victor's ability to empathise was evidence of the child's increased humanity after being brought back to civilisation.

NOT ONE OF US

The **narrator** of the story is clearly implicated in the rejection of the child brought in from the forest, but masks personal responsibility with the pronoun 'we'. The tale begins with the fact that the child's nature and behaviour are alien to the narrator. The information that she cannot speak 'like we do' (p. 140) invites the reader to view the child from the narrator's perspective, as something not like 'us'. The point is stressed again, later, that the child has 'little in common with the rest of us' (p. 142). She has neither language nor perception of time, suggesting that the narrator considers these the most important assets of human identity.

The story itself gives away no identifiable place or time. The tale is set in a dukedom somewhere in Europe at some point after the invention of gunpowder weapons that fire bullets, though the narrator's reference to 'Man Friday' (p. 147), a character in Daniel Defoe's novel *Robinson Crusoe* (1719), suggests the eighteenth century.

THE DUKE

Abandoned by the nuns for resisting their teachings, the girl is put into the service of the Duke. The most significant thing we are told about him is that 'nothing can hurt him since he ceased to cast an image in the mirror' (p. 142). This combines the werewolf and vampire myths and returns to Bram Stoker's novel *Dracula* (1897). Stoker similarly combined Eastern European folklore of werewolves and vampires to create his monstrous villain, adding the inability to cast a reflection in a mirror as his contribution: this revealing characteristic is not found in vampires of earlier tales. The Duke regards himself to be 'both less and more than a man' (p. 146), even though he cannot see himself.

> **CHECK THE BOOK** **A03**
>
> Daniel Defoe (1660–1731) published *Robinson Crusoe* under the title *The Life and Strange Surprizing Adventures of Robinson Crusoe, of York, Mariner: Who lived Eight and Twenty Years, all alone in an un-inhabited Island on the Coast of America … Having been cast on Shore by Shipwreck … Written by Himself.* Friday is the name Crusoe gives to the native he befriends from another island.

> ### STUDY FOCUS: GROWING UP **A02**
>
> In 'Wolf-Alice' as in a number of other tales, Carter explores the significance of the physical process of becoming a woman. The child learns a sense of time through her physical connection to the cycles of the moon and her menstrual period. But it is the discovery of her reflection in the mirror that is more significant in her discovery of her personal identity. She begins to see that the image in the mirror is 'herself within it' (p. 147). She is learning the processes of imagination, the ability to understand the form and content of images – a human characteristic that sets us apart from animals – and she becomes less wolf-like from this point in the story. She adopts a white dress she finds behind the mirror, another 'sign of her difference' from the wolves (p. 147), and walks out of the castle on two legs. Wolf-Alice is 'far more sentient' than the Duke, and this gives her the ability to survive the revenge attack upon 'the lord of cobweb castle' (p. 148).

THE MIRROR

The mirror almost becomes a character in the story, recalling the uses of magic mirrors in 'The Tiger's Bride', in the original fairy tale of 'Snow White' and in Lewis Carroll's *Through the Looking-Glass and What Alice Found There* (1871). This last example is perhaps particularly significant bearing in mind the name of the main character in Carter's story. The mirror is 'rational' (p. 148) and impartial, recording the image of the girl, and then the image of the duke, 'as vivid as real life itself' (p. 149). The duke is brought into being by the touch of the girl's tongue – perhaps implying wolf-like care, but also suggesting the means of human speech, the language which has restored Wolf-Alice's humanity. In yet another version of a happy ending, both the wolf man and the wolf child have recovered their true selves: the woman has allowed the man to recover and see his own true nature in the same way that she has come to know herself: through her own image.

STUDY FOCUS: THE 'RATIONAL GLASS' A04

Carter was a firm believer in **materialism** – a theory which argues that everything can be explained in physical terms of matter and energy. The question of who controls the representation of women and men, a key theme in **feminist** debate in the 1970s, is still worth asking in the twenty-first century. It is a principle of the materialist outlook that in order to appear to be something over any sustained length of time, it is necessary to be it. So appearances, images, however deceptive they might be, are important in knowing who we are and what we are becoming. That is why the 'rational glass' (p. 148) is so important to Carter; it is art, it is literature and it is life: warts and all.

GLOSSARY

140 **counterpoint** a melody added as an accompaniment to another melody

145 **circumambulatory** to walk all the way round – also has a connotation of 'beating around the bush' in speech, or time-wasting

146 **diadem** a crown

147 **débutante** a young girl making her debut in society, an aristocratic tradition of introducing children as candidates for marriage, a ritual of coming of age

litany a form of chanted prayer, led by a priest, who recites a series of petitions to which the congregation respond in unison; typically an appeal for divine intervention in human affairs

148 **Mycenaean** denoting the civilisation of an ancient Greek city

GRADE BOOSTER A02

The story of 'Wolf-Alice' is not directly derived from a traditional fairy tale. Consider the significance of Carter's use of symbolism and her intentions, though, in the light of other, connected tales: 'The Werewolf' and 'The Company of Wolves'. How are wolves and humans presented in this trio of tales? How do any connections you can make between these tales throw light on the story of 'Wolf-Alice'?

KEY QUOTATIONS: WOLF-ALICE A01

Key quotation 1: It is only Wolf-Alice's appearance that is human: 'it is as if the fur she thought she wore had melted into her skin and become part of it.' (p. 141)

Possible interpretations:

- Wolf-Alice, like the werewolf Duke, has a dual nature: part human, part wolf.
- Appearance and self-image are strongly connected: we are as we see ourselves and vice versa.

Key quotation 2: The duke's 'eyes see only appetite' (p. 142).

Possible interpretations:

- The wolf as a symbol of appetite, of voracious consumption.
- 'Appetite' implies sexual greed: the consumption of flesh both for nourishment and sexual gratification.
- Echoes Carter's other wolves – and some of Carter's male characters.

KEY QUOTATIONS: WOLF-ALICE   A01

Key quotation 3: The nuns hide Wolf-Alice away from the world: 'we secluded her in animal privacy … because it showed us what we might have been' (p. 144).

Possible interpretations:

- Humans fear and deny their animal nature.
- Links to the symbolic significance of transformation from beast to human, or human to beast.

REVISION FOCUS: TASK 10   A02

How far do you agree with the following statement?

- The end of 'Wolf-Alice' – and the collection as a whole – suggests there are possibilities of harmonious and balanced relationships between men and women.

Try writing opening paragraphs for an essay based on this discussion point. Set out your arguments clearly.

CHECK THE FILM   A03

François Truffaut's film *L'Enfant sauvage* (1970) retells the story of Victor, the wild boy of Aveyron, and a doctor's attempts to educate him.

CHARACTERS

It is partly the nature of the short story as a **narrative** form that dictates characters be defined by the use of carefully selected detail. Carter is not creating her characters from scratch in this collection; many are stock characters from fairy-tale convention dressed in new clothes. Some are amalgamations of recognisable character types drawn from other literary genres. The Erl-King is the most singular character in the tales as a whole; he is a kind of pagan wood spirit, elusively representing a complex combination of ideas about nature (see the **Part Two: The Erl-King** and **Part Three: Man, woman and nature** for more on 'The Erl-King'). Carter allows some of the characters to perform the role of **narrator**, though none of them tell their stories in exactly the same way. Transformation and metamorphosis are the key functions of Carter's characters: some are shape-shifters; others are disguised or masked in one way or another. The revelation of the true identity of Carter's characters is often accomplished through a thoroughly other-worldly moment of magic.

The women in *The Bloody Chamber* are in general given domestic roles, whether they be aristocrats, middle class or peasants. The men are mostly figures of authority whose power or wealth has been inherited in one way or another. These Notes will consider together those who take the role of narrator and **protagonist**; the villainous patriarchs and the predatory male characters; the male characters who are less threatening; the positive and negative models of motherhood; the few female characters who may be seen as victims of their circumstances; the female characters that represent the vivacity of life; and, finally, the human animal.

THE NARRATOR PROTAGONIST

- The new bride, 'The Bloody Chamber'
- The girl, 'The Tiger's Bride'
- Puss-in-Boots, 'Puss-in-Boots'

A **protagonist** is usually taken to be the principal character causing most of the events in a story to be enacted. Carter frequently returns to the question of who has the initiative at any moment in her stories. She wants to show who has the power to make things happen.

The bride of 'The Bloody Chamber' recalls how her innocence was stripped away from her through a flashback of linked memories (on the train, thinking of her mother alone at home, the delivery of the wedding dress, the courtship, going to the opera on the night before her wedding). Subsequently, the tale follows a traditional chronological recounting of events. She is a creature of sensations, delighting in the 'impeccable linen of the pillow' (p. 1); her satin nightdress, 'supple as a garment of heavy water' (p. 2); and the Marquis's kiss 'with tongue and teeth in it' (p. 2). Though very aware of her immediate surroundings, she only glimpses the truth of the Marquis – and herself – in 'gilded mirrors' (p.6): she reports the moment of consummation of her marriage through the reflections in the mirrors, as if she only exists in the Marquis's eyes.

When left alone, her idle existence as a rich man's wife is oppressive. The creative act of making music is her escape. After she has discovered the truth of the secret room, she copes with the imminent threat to her life through the 'therapeutic task' (p. 30) of playing the piano. She remains an odd combination of fearlessness and resignation – 'I knew I must meet my lord alone' (p. 33) – dependent on her mother, her 'avenging angel' (p. 39), for her salvation.

The girl in 'The Tiger's Bride' is presented as a tougher personality, a survivor, but is equally powerless in many respects. She resents her inability to escape her father's neglect. She describes his 'special madness' (p. 56), his 'debauchery' (p. 59), as the 'sickness' (p. 59) of gambling. Her 'heartless mirth' in response to The Beast's request to see her 'Desnuda' (p. 65) is the response of a person hardened by experience. Although she initially feels she is part of a 'humiliating bargain' (p. 68), she changes her view when The Beast changes his demand. Carter **alludes** to the well-known axiom that refers to an unlikely meeting between the powerful and the powerless: 'The lion shall lie down with the lamb.' Typically, Carter's woman understands this by turning it around: 'The lamb must learn to run with the tigers' (p. 71). The **anthropomorphic** transformation she undergoes at the end of the tale is a remarkable compromise. She rejects the values of her father's civilisation but confirms the possibility of a 'peaceable kingdom' (p. 74) by becoming the tiger's bride and rejoicing in the revelation of her 'beautiful fur' (p. 75).

Puss-in-Boots is an amusing anthropomorphic character who boasts he is 'a cat of the world, cosmopolitan, sophisticated' (p. 76). He relishes his role as a raconteur and his language is overloaded with **rhetorical** flourishes, particularly when embellishing his part in the story. His habit of referring to himself in the third person – 'Puss takes his promenade' (p. 77) – also demonstrates his egocentricity.

He is also a **caricature** of masculine opportunism. He refers to Shakespeare's *Hamlet* (1601) when he says cats 'smile and smile'. Carter neatly connects politicians – 'all cats have a politician's air' (p. 77) – and 'villains' (p. 78) through this **allusion** to Hamlet's bitter observation that 'one may smile and smile and be a villain' (Act I Scene 5).

It is, perhaps, misleading to call Puss-in-Boots a **protagonist**, as the real protagonist, the 'sleek, spry tabby' (p. 82), is hidden in his story. Puss-in-Boots claims all the credit, but the success of his ventures has, in fact, entirely depended on the tabby cat's resourcefulness – and she finds time to provide him with three 'fine, new-minted ginger kittens' (p. 95). This is perhaps an example of 'history' that should be rewritten as '*her* story'.

CONTEXT A04

The saying 'The lion shall lie down with the lamb' is adapted from the Old Testament: 'The wolf also shall dwell with the lamb, and the leopard shall lie down with the kid' (Isaiah 11:6). The Quaker William Penn wrote in 1693: 'Nor is it said the lamb shall lie down with the lion, but the lion shall lie down with the lamb.' The Quaker Edward Hicks (1780–1849) painted *The Peaceable Kingdom* inspired by these verses.

KEY QUOTATIONS: THE NARRATOR PROTAGONIST A01

Key quotation 1: As the girl travels to The Beast's palazzo, 'my own skin was my sole capital in the world and today I'd make my first investment' ('The Tiger's Bride', p. 62).

Possible interpretations:

- Suggests her independence now her father has lost her.
- Implies the lack of economic options available to lone women.
- Links to the transformation at the end of the tale: the skin she will lose to reveal her animal nature.

Key quotation 2: On hearing The Beast's request to see her naked: 'I let out a raucous guffaw; no young lady laughs like that! my old nurse used to remonstrate. But I did. And do.' (The Tiger's Bride', p. 65)

Possible interpretations:

- Suggests the girl's strength in the face of male power.
- Characterises the girl's independence and unwillingness to conform to stereotype.
- Links to the wider theme of patriarchal power and female submission.

THE PREDATORY PATRIARCH AND THE ABSENT FATHER

CONTEXT A04

Melodrama was a popular nineteenth-century theatrical genre known for its moralistic plots that reflected yet sensationalised the reality of class conflict in Britain. Typically predatory aristocrats menaced beautiful young women who were then rescued by the handsome hero.

- The Marquis, 'The Bloody Chamber'
- The Count, 'The Snow Child'
- The father, 'The Tiger's Bride'
- The father, 'The Courtship of Mr Lyon'

The Marquis in 'The Bloody Chamber' and the Count in 'The Snow Child' are manifestations of extreme cruelty. Their power and authority stands in stark contrast to the aristocratic father's weakness in 'The Tiger's Bride' and the businessman father in 'The Courtship of Mr Lyon'. The comparison seems to suggest the authority of aristocracy makes a patriarch more powerful and therefore dangerous. Whether powerful or weak, however, they are all patriarchs – male heads of a family or household. Carter presents no positive model of the father in these tales.

STUDY FOCUS: THE MARQUIS A02

The most dangerous patriarch of all, the Marquis, combines the inherited wealth and position of the aristocrat with the power of wealth. He represents selfish indulgence – his title alone is an obvious reference to the Marquis de Sade (who gave his name to an entire range of activities considered to be beyond the norms of sexual behaviour). He is a dangerous and menacing predator. The narrator compares him to a lily and almost immediately describes that flower as 'cobra-headed' (p. 3). The cold-blooded, reptilian nature of the Marquis is suggested alongside more obvious references to his 'leonine' (p. 2) head with its 'dark mane' (p. 3). He has the ability to move with the stealth of a hunter, creeping coldly around 'as if his footfall turned the carpet into snow' (p. 3). He is a serial killer and torturer of women.

One of Carter's most provocative acts in these stories is to make the Marquis's female prey respond to his attentions with arousal. But this character is incapable of considering the possibility of female fulfilment. For the Marquis, sex is an act performed on another body, not something shared with another person. He rejects his prey as soon as there is evidence of mature independent sexuality. One could even argue he is the patriarch as child abuser, the deepest and darkest betrayal of the father's role. This idea is hinted at when the **narrator** links the aroma of the Marquis's cigars, 'a warm fug of Havana', with 'little girl' memories of her father 'before he kissed me and left me' (p. 7).

CHECK THE BOOK A03

Re-Visiting Angela Carter: Texts, Contexts, Intertexts (2006), edited by Rebecca Munford, includes Gina Wisker's view that 'Incest terrifies and disgusts the conventional, and those who seek to control, because it recognises sameness' ('Behind Locked Doors: Angela Carter, Horror and the Influence of Edgar Allan Poe').

The Count of 'The Snow Child' is a repellent figure, indulging his desires far beyond any notion of acceptable behaviour. Carter's sardonic comment on his sexual prowess – 'he was soon finished' (p. 106) – shows the short-lived nature of his virility and undermines the power that his sexuality might have.

The Duke in 'Wolf-Alice' is yet another aristocrat. He is completely unaware of himself as a monster. It is only through the care and support of Wolf-Alice that he can see himself as others see him. Here Carter is using the device of a wolf-man, with no real character, to show how identities can be transformed through care and compromise.

Carter's patriarchs generally offer two models of the father: tyrant or traitor. Mr Lyon, the Beast in 'The Courtship of Mr Lyon', is a manipulator. His courtship of Beauty is conducted through the father, as would be expected in the traditional **patriarchal** manner. He persuades Beauty's father to hand over his daughter through economic blackmail and ensures Beauty returns to him through emotional blackmail. His decision to starve to death in her absence is reminiscent of self-pitying, jilted lovers who threaten suicide. He recovers his appetite swiftly enough on her return.

The impoverished nobleman of 'The Tiger's Bride' and the ruined businessman of 'The Courtship of Mr Lyon' are examples of the absent father, the father who fails to provide for and then abandons his child: a common enough villain in folklore and myth alike. Both characters put business affairs and riches ahead of their real 'treasures' ('The Tiger's Bride', p. 60), their daughters.

The Erl-King, though not an aristrocrat in any human sense, is perhaps Carter's most disturbingly predatory patriarch. His influence, which is both natural and supernatural, seems limitless and irrefutable – until the narrator strangles him.

REVISION FOCUS: TASK 11   A03

How far do you agree with the following statement?

● In Angela Carter's world, all men are monsters.

Try writing opening paragraphs for an essay based on this discussion point. Set out your arguments clearly.

KEY QUOTATIONS: THE PREDATORY PATRIARCH   A01

Key quotation 1: The Marquis finds the narrator looking at his collection of erotic art: 'Have the nasty pictures scared Baby? Baby mustn't play with grownups' toys until she's learned how to handle them, must she?' ('The Bloody Chamber', p. 13).

Possible interpretations:

● Emphasises the Marquis's controlling, patronising attitude to his young, vulnerable wife.

● Introduces an increased and tangible danger to the narrator.

● The first explicit depiction of the Marquis as villain, a character type typical of fairy tales.

Key quotation 2: The narrator is enchanted by the Erl-King: 'when he shakes out those two clear notes from his bird call, I come, like any other trusting thing that perches on the crook of his wrist.' ('The Erl-King', pp. 100–101)

Possible interpretations:

● The Erl-King is presented as a controlling patriarch, preying on innocent girls.

● Could also suggest the power of nature to which we all are drawn and over which we have no control.

CONTEXT A04

Brewer's Dictionary of Phrase and Fable (seventeenth edition, 2007) notes that in German legend the erl-king is 'a malevolent goblin who haunts forests and lures people, especially children, to destruction. … Erlking means "king of the alders" but has popularly been understood to mean "elf king"'.

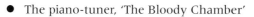

THE INNOCENT MALE

- The piano-tuner, 'The Bloody Chamber'
- The soldier, 'The Lady of the House of Love'

A few of Carter's male characters are relatively innocent in comparison with the more obviously predatory examples. The piano-tuner of 'The Bloody Chamber' is blind. He is helpless and non-threatening; he listens; he is supportive and gentle. He is also unable to see the evidence of his lover's past transgressions: the indelible stain which she carries on her forehead. This can be seen as a very forgiving and unusual trait in a man.

The soldier in 'The Lady of the House of Love' typifies the bumbling, if well-intentioned, idiot who messes up the world for a woman. His defining characteristic is 'lack of imagination' (p. 120). Given that the imagination is so important to Carter, and such a fundamental human quality, it makes this 'blond beauty' (p. 114) appear almost inhumanly dull.

THE MATRIARCH

- The mother, 'The Bloody Chamber'
- The Countess, 'The Snow Child'
- Wolf-Alice, 'Wolf-Alice'
- The werewolf, 'The Werewolf'

CONTEXT **A04**

In Greek mythology Nemesis was the goddess of retribution or vengeance, believed to be the daughter of Nox, the night. An unforgiving deity who punished mortals, particularly those who set themselves against the gods, she avenged their crimes and administered justice.

These female characters are Carter's devices for exploring the role of motherhood and the relationship of women to other women. The bride's mother in 'The Bloody Chamber' has all the traits of a masculine hero from the world of adventure stories: she shoots wild animals and fights off pirates. Carter also makes her a capable nurse, something more commonly thought of as a passive female role, but here given equal status with more conventionally heroic deeds. She is also equipped with *'maternal telepathy'* (p. 41) – Carter avoids using the patronising and **clichéd** phrase 'feminine intuition' – so she is the very model of **feminist** virtue.

She is an empowered mother, taking on the conventionally male roles of the capable parent and rescuer of distressed females. She is romantic, having 'gladly, scandalously, defiantly beggared herself for love' (p. 2). As a widow, she is 'magnificently eccentric' (p. 2) in black silk. Carter is presenting an all-action female who is not obliged to abandon

her femininity to compete with men. At the beginning, Carter seems to suggest that this is all part of her wild youth, an 'adventurous girlhood' (p. 1) which she has grown out of by becoming a mother. But her reappearance at the end of the tale, crashing through the waves on horseback with her 'black skirts tucked up around her waist' (p. 38), is even more romantic and glamorous. The wild and wind-blown image of the mother, 'black lisle legs exposed to the thigh' astride a 'rearing horse' (p. 40), also identifies her with the power of the natural elements. She is the Marquis's nemesis, the embodiment of 'furious justice' (p. 40).

The Countess of 'The Snow Child' is a more complex examination of the mother role. She is closer to the fairy-tale figure of the wicked stepmother, in the sense that the child is not her daughter but is 'conceived' in the Count's imagination. Through the Countess's actions, Carter examines the jealousies involved in competing for male attention with another woman. The **symbols** of her sexual appeal, the furs and riding boots, are transferred to the child despite the Countess's efforts to shake off her rival. The rose, as a symbol of romance, is a dangerous weapon in her hands. Having ensured the death of the Count's child, she is once more in control of the situation, highlighted in the way she restrains her 'stamping mare' (p. 106). As the Countess reasserts of her position and identity, she makes a sensual gesture of possessiveness: 'With her long hand, she stroked her furs' (p. 106).

The **eponymous** character in the story of 'Wolf-Alice' is an exploration of the idea of natural instinct in relation to stereotypical instinct, for example the 'maternal instinct'. Stripped of the inhibitions of civilisation, Wolf-Alice finds her own way of growing into a role which seems to be part daughter, part lover and part mother, with no clear distinction. Carter describes Wolf-Alice's 'tender gravity' (p. 148) as she heals the wounds of the Duke at the end of the story, enabling him to be seen as himself again.

STUDY FOCUS: THE WOLF GRANDMOTHER (A04)

The wolf's transformation into the grandmother in 'The Werewolf' is a particularly disturbing image of the difficult relationship between different generations of women. The child discovers that the wolf's severed paw has become 'a hand toughened with work and freckled with old age' (p. 127). This shows her learning that she cannot trust or respect women of previous generations who have taken on the role created for them by men. Carter's description of the matriarch as 'crone', 'old woman' and 'witch' (p. 126) is a mirror image of the tyrannical patriarch. When the child acts against the grandmother, her circumstances are transformed. Her 'hard life', part of the cold pattern of 'Harsh, brief, poor lives' (p. 126) in a difficult and hostile climate, becomes less difficult. The tale ends with the simple announcement that 'she prospered' (p. 128). Carter seems to be suggesting that each generation of women has to free itself not only from the tyranny of **patriarchal** society, but also from women whose identity and nature have been transformed by men into something monstrous.

REVISION FOCUS: TASK 12 (A04)

How far do you agree with the following statement?

● In Carter's stories, the role which society expects of women is much more complex than the role it expects of men.

Try writing opening paragraphs for an essay based on this discussion point. Set out your arguments clearly.

KEY QUOTATION: THE MATRIARCH (A01)

Key quotation: The girl's mother kills the Marquis: 'without a moment's hesitation, she raised my father's gun, took aim and put a single, irreproachable bullet through my husband's head.' ('The Bloody Chamber', p. 41)

Possible interpretations:

● The narrator's mother takes on the traditionally male role of avenging hero.

● The word 'irreproachable' suggests that no blame can be attached to this death; the Marquis has received what he deserved.

● Links to the wider theme of men and women.

GRADE BOOSTER (A02)

The role of women in the tales – and Carter's presentation of that role – is absolutely central to their analysis and interpretation. Compare, for example: the bride and her mother in 'The Bloody Chamber'; the Countess in 'The Snow Child' and the grandmother in 'The Werewolf'; 'Wolf-Alice' and the narrator in 'The Tiger's Bride'. What does each suggest about the nature, role and relationships of women?

CONTEXT A03

Simone de Beauvoir in her essay 'Must We Burn Sade?' (originally published in 1951–2 in *Les Temps Modernes* as 'Faut-il brûler Sade?') writes: 'Never in his stories does sensual pleasure appear as self-forgetfulness, swooning, or abandon. … The male aggression of the Sadean hero is never softened by the usual transformation of the body into flesh. He never … loses himself for an instant in his animal nature'.

THE VICTIM

- The bride, 'The Bloody Chamber'
- Beauty, 'The Courtship of Mr Lyon'
- The child, 'The Snow Child'
- The Countess, 'The Lady of the House of Love'

Angela Carter was particularly interested in the portrayal of women as victims of male aggression, and in particular how this limited the feminist perspective of the time. Her argument was that women need not accept that role, and she uses these stories to explore how that may be achieved.

Aside from her role as **narrator**, the bride in 'The Bloody Chamber' is passive. Although she considers escape, she makes no real attempt to evade the Marquis's plans for her. This is one aspect of Carter's examination of the nature of sadomasochistic relationships. It is related to her controversial views on the writings of the Marquis de Sade (see **Part Five: Critical debates**). The character of a submissive woman enables Carter to explore the attractions of dominance in human relationships. She also looks at the extent to which the young wife might be seen as a willing victim. Despite her claim that she is 'innocent but not naïve' (p. 13), the wife does not know what she is dealing with.

Beauty in 'The Courtship of Mr Lyon' is a worrier, an obedient daughter who becomes a 'spoiled child' (p. 52). In the end, however, she is redeemed as a prodigal daughter. She transfers her love for her father to the Beast so she can 'come home' (p. 54). She is clearly manipulated, first by her father and then by Mr Lyon: though she demonstrates little independent will, she surrenders it to him. Her most defining characteristic is her 'desolating emptiness' (p. 51).

The Count's 'child of his desire' (p. 105) in 'The Snow Child' is a male fantasy who vanishes almost as soon as she is called into existence. She is the ideal woman of male fantasy, unrealisable and impossible to compete with. Yet she is vulnerable to the **symbolic** touch of love, and she falls victim to 'the thorn' (p. 106) which represents the painful aspects of human emotion.

CHECK THE BOOK A03

In Oscar Wilde's **Gothic melodrama** *The Picture of Dorian Gray* (first published in *Lippincott's Monthly Magazine* in 1890), Dorian Gray sells his soul for eternal youth and beauty. Year after year his unchanging features retain the appearance of innocence and beauty, while his portrait ages as a result of his behaviour.

STUDY FOCUS: THE VAMPIRE A04

The vampire Countess in 'The Lady of the House of Love' is imprisoned by her permanent youthful beauty. She cannot age. Her release from this empty 'imitation of life' (p. 110) and her 'balked tenderness' (p. 122) is an accident of fate. She experiences the 'pain' (p. 123) of being human – for Carter, to be human is to suffer feelings for others – and then she dies. But the tale begins by presenting her as a predator. Her intended victim, the 'handsome bicyclist' (p. 121), unwittingly seals her doom. Carter often explores how seeming opposites can be transformed into one another, and here shows how hunter and hunted are interchangeable roles. The idea of the victim is enlarged at the end of this story to include the millions who perished in the First World War. The imaginary terrors of Gothic horror are dwarfed in comparison with the real and unimaginable horrors of the trenches in France.

KEY QUOTATIONS: THE VICTIM   A01

Key quotation 1: Miss Lamb feels she has been offered as a sacrifice to Mr Lyon: 'Miss Lamb, spotless, sacrificial.' (p. 48)

Possible interpretations:

- Implies danger and builds tension, suggesting that Carter will subvert the traditional happy ending.
- A typical fairy tale presentation of women: vulnerable, virtuous, in danger at the hands of ruthless men.
- Links to the wider theme of transformation: in the hands of Mr Lyon, Beauty becomes a lamb.

Key quotation 2: The Countess cannot control her vampire nature: 'the timeless Gothic eternity of the vampires … whose cards will always fall in the same pattern.' ('The Lady of the House of Love', p. 112)

Possible interpretations:

- Presents the vampire as someone to be pitied, a victim of her vampiric nature.
- Links to, and subverts, the Gothic tradition.

THE INDEPENDENT WOMAN

- The bride, 'The Bloody Chamber'
- The girl, 'The Tiger's Bride'
- The child, 'The Werewolf'
- The child, 'The Company of Wolves'

Most of Carter's characters are defined by their relationships to others: daughter, wife, mother, lover, husband, father. But Carter also uses these stories to explore the **feminist** notion of a female identity existing independently of, and not limited by, male identity.

The **narrators** of 'The Bloody Chamber' and 'The Tiger's Bride' alternate between strength and passivity. However, Carter gives the reader repeated images of female assertiveness. Her two versions of the character of Little Red Riding Hood (the rather anonymous child in 'The Werewolf' and the clever virgin in 'The Company of Wolves') are both far less passive than the girl in the original tale. The 'mountaineer's child', born and raised in harsh conditions, is a tough character who 'knew the forest too well to fear it' ('The Werewolf', p. 127). She is prepared and able to act in her own self-defence when threatened. When Carter says 'the child was strong' (p. 128), she is deliberately turning around the power relationship, and the gendered stereotyping, of the adult and the child in the original fairy tale. The weak female is replaced by a more positive and capable female. The defiance and ingenuity of the girl in 'The Company of Wolves', turning the tables on her attacker by burning his clothing in the fire, are defined by her laughter. When Carter's 'wise child' laughs at the werewolf 'full in the face' (p. 138), she is seen to be strong enough to cope with any situation. This 'strong-minded child' (p. 132) enjoys her moment of power.

CONTEXT   A04

Not all the young female characters in traditional fairy tales are sweet and helpless victims. In one traditional version of 'Little Red Riding Hood', the girl and her grandmother use their ingenuity to lure the wolf to his death. In the Brothers Grimm version of 'Snow White', the young woman appears to condone (although not initiate) her wicked stepmother's punishment of being made to dance to death in a pair of red-hot iron shoes!

KEY QUOTATION: THE INDEPENDENT WOMAN   A01

Key quotation: The wolf announces he will eat the girl: 'The girl burst out laughing; she knew she was nobody's meat.' ('The Company of Wolves', p. 138)

Possible interpretations:

- The girl is capable and fearless.
- Wider links to the presentation of strong women throughout the tales.

THE HUMAN ANIMAL

- The Beast, 'The Tiger's Bride'
- Wolf-Alice, 'Wolf-Alice'
- Granny, 'The Company of Wolves'

This character type is a definitive feature of many of the stories, and a crucial element in the whole collection. In the tiger, 'La Bestia' ('The Tiger's Bride', p. 57), Carter has created her definition of the male, and of female desire for the male. He is an aristocrat, but of a different kind. He is 'impeccable' (p. 57), 'potent' (p. 58) and 'chaste' (p. 58), a 'dreadful' (p. 60) warning to careless fathers. He cries jewelled teardrops when he wrongs the girl with his clumsy and embarrassing demands; he is no bully like the Marquis or the Count, taking advantage of his power. He has a 'sculptured calm' (p. 67) in his male disguise, which hides the 'annihilating vehemence' (p. 71) of the animal. Carter's Beauty offers herself as sacrifice to this Beast, as in the original story, but understands 'his appetite need not be my extinction' (p. 74). She rejects her father's world and becomes an animal in a union of sensual pleasure with The Beast. In this story the tiger is a **symbol** of realised mutual passion that affords men and women equal respect, and regards sexual desire as beautiful and natural.

While Carter creates a collection of beasts that are supposed to disgust, they also offer their apparent victims the hope of transformation. In becoming most true to the animal within the human, both men and women can become 'fully human' ('The Lady of the House of Love', p. 124).

CHECK THE BOOK · A03

Robert Louis Stevenson's novella, *The Strange Case of Dr Jekyll and Mr Hyde* (1886) tells the story of an Edinburgh doctor, Dr Jekyll, who has discovered a potion which, when drunk, allows him to free himself of all conscience and be transformed into the evil Mr Hyde.

KEY QUOTATIONS: THE HUMAN ANIMAL · A01

Key quotation 1: On seeing the wounded duke, Wolf-Alice 'leapt upon his bed to lick, without hesitation, without disgust … the blood and dirt from his cheeks and forehead.' ('Wolf-Alice', p. 138)

Possible interpretations:

- Wolf-Alice takes on a maternal, caring role to save the duke.
- At the same time, her empathy for the duke suggests her humanity.
- The lines between human and beast are blurred in the positive resolution of the tale.

Key quotation 2: When the girl realises 'granny' is in fact a wolf, she recognises that appearances are not always the surest way to recognise danger: 'she knew the worst wolves are hairy on the inside' ('The Company of Wolves', p. 137)

Possible interpretations:

- The girl is aware of the nature of men.
- Grotesque image suggesting all men have an inner 'wolf'.
- Transformation is used to present man's dual nature.

REVISION FOCUS: TASK 13 · A02

How far do you agree with the following statements?

- Every character in the collection is either a predator or a victim.
- Carter's stories explore how love can transform or destroy us.

Try writing opening paragraphs for essays based on these discussion points. Set out your arguments clearly.

THEMES

MARRIAGE

Throughout the collection, marriage is identified with the past, with corruption and with deception. The first story in the collection opens with the new bride eagerly looking forward to and travelling excitedly towards her future life married to the Marquis. However, 'The Bloody Chamber' goes on to portray marriage as a moral and literal equivalent of death. Similarly, in 'The Courtship of Mr Lyon', the marriage contract is financially motivated: a woman, owned and controlled by the father, passes into the ownership of another man. This is a historically accurate representation of marriage, referring back to the time when the law stated that all property belonging to a woman became her husband's on marriage. This is no longer the case but Carter is suggesting that men behave as if they still have the right to control women, and her stories challenge that.

CHECK THE BOOK **A03**

Betty Friedan's *The Feminine Mystique* (1963) attacked the notion that women could only find fulfilment through being a mother and a housewife.

STUDY FOCUS: MARRIAGE AND MONEY **A04**

The passing of the female from the care of the father to the care of the husband, **symbolically** enacted in the rituals of the wedding ceremony, is mocked in 'The Tiger's Bride'. The 'parlour' (p. 57) where the father gambles away his daughter to 'La Bestia' (p. 57) is a substitute casino that emphasises the role that chance plays in human relationships. Yet she, as 'a woman of honour' (p. 68), is bound by the contract her father has made with the Beast, which is sealed by the turn of 'A queen, a king, an ace' (p. 59). Carter is pointing out the economic circumstances or financial arrangements that govern people's actions, as strongly as, if not more so than, their personalities or their beliefs.

In 'The Courtship of Mr Lyon' the bankrupted father brings 'Miss Lamb' (p. 48) to lie with 'Mr Lyon' (p. 55) and so resolve a dispute about the rose he stole from Mr Lyon's garden. Her cooperation with the arrangements made between the men guarantees 'on some magically reciprocal scale, the price of her father's good fortune' (p. 48). The benefits of economic alliances formed through marriage arrangements are demonstrated in her 'new-found prosperity' (p. 51). Yet she is not committed to a marriage at this point in the story. Beauty and her father enjoy 'life … as she had never known it' on 'credit', so their status is temporary and subject to terms and conditions. Her absence from the Beast's home causes his domestic affairs to fall into neglect and 'disillusion' (p. 53). Flower arranging is an activity stereotypically associated with the housewife, and generally taken for granted by their husbands. The dying flowers symbolise not only the Beast's romantic pining for his love but also hint at the future Miss Lamb will have as Mrs Lyon: domestic servant.

'Wolf-Alice' and 'The Company of Wolves' portray different versions of partnership between the sexes which have little to do with any recognisable ceremony or convention of marriage. Although Wolf-Alice is dressed as a 'white bride', her 'pitiful' (p. 148) 'ministrations' (p. 149) to the wounds of the Duke at the end of the story bear no resemblance to any kind of formal ceremony. Marriage is a major aspect of human civilisation, but Wolf-Alice exists outside all such norms. That is why she can lead the Duke into a realisation of his identity beyond the traditional values of **patriarchy**. Carter is suggesting that any realignment of male and female relationships can only be 'brought into being by her [Wolf-Alice]' (p. 149), even though 'she lives without a future' (p. 141). This implies that the ideal of marriage as a binding contract, or life sentence, is unrealistic.

'The Company of Wolves' shows through its table-turning conclusion that women can take charge of their own destiny and have relationships with men on their own terms. Carter's 'savage marriage ceremony' (p. 139) is followed by a collection of images that conveys the idea of a peaceful and prosperous future. It suggests the 'happily ever after' promised in every fairy tale yet rarely glimpsed in reality. The 'blizzard died down' after the violence of the tale to leave the forest 'All silent, all still' on 'Christmas Day' (p. 139). Carter's words echo the well-known Christian carol 'Silent Night', concluding her tale with a hopeful and powerful **metaphor** of reconciliation.

REVISION FOCUS: TASK 14 **A02**

How far do you agree with the following statement?

● The traditional fairy tale rewards its heroes with a happy marriage. Carter, however, presents marriage as a dark and frightening prospect.

Try writing opening paragraphs for an essay based on this discussion point. Set out your arguments clearly.

SEXUALITY

The collection offers an impression of sexuality as a frightening and exciting aspect of adult behaviour. Carter certainly does not shrink from portraying the extremes of desire at its most perverse. In 'The Bloody Chamber' the risks involved in being submissive in a relationship are made very clear. Carter does flirt with ideas of sadomasochism here, i.e. deriving sexual pleasure from inflicting pain on oneself or others, but in the end rejects masochistic submission as empty and unfulfilling.

SEXUALITY AND 'THE BLOODY CHAMBER'

In 'The Bloody Chamber' Carter emphasises the appeal – and the risk – in marrying an older, more experienced man. The attention and prestige the young wife acquires through her association with a powerful man are flattering to her. She knows 'nothing of the world' (p. 4) and is wholly unprepared to deal with the conflicting responses she feels when her husband delays the moment of consummation of their marriage. They give rise to both 'a kind of fear' and 'repugnance' (p. 11). It is her sexual response – a 'strange, impersonal arousal' (p. 11) – which she fears. The Marquis suggests that the anticipation of the event is far more pleasurable than the event itself, and that is certainly true for her.

Her disturbing realisation that she, like the Marquis, is capable of almost anything is a moment of self-awareness: 'I sensed in myself a potentiality for corruption that took my breath away' (p. 6). But it is also a realisation of how far from corrupt she is, having led an 'innocent and confined life' (p. 6). As she is stripped in the 'formal disrobing of the bride' (p. 11), her responses are **ambiguous**. The 'trembling' (p. 10) and blushing could be nervousness or sexual arousal, until she confesses: 'I was aghast to feel myself stirring' (p. 11). But this physical sensation is complicated by the fact that she has 'seen [her] flesh in his eyes' (p. 11). The Marquis's pleasures are visual; he enjoys looking at her. Her surprise is that she seems to enjoy being looked at by him in this way. This was a controversial sentiment for a **feminist** writer to give to a female character in the 1970s, particularly as it comes close to confirming a male chauvinist attitude around at the time that women enjoyed being dominated and humiliated.

The **narrator** is entirely passive at this stage, taking no active part in the consummation of their marriage: 'my husband beds me' (p. 12). After losing her virginity, she recalls the moment with hints of the violence involved. The Marquis seems so exhausted, he might have been 'fighting' with her; his composure was shattered 'like a porcelain vase flung against a wall'; she heard him 'shriek and blaspheme' (p. 14); and there was blood. Her 'spent body' (p. 14) has been used up; her virginity consumed by the Marquis as 'connoisseur' (p. 13) and 'gourmand' (p. 11). Her unfulfilled desire, which seems to survive the Marquis's attentions, is thwarted by his decision to abandon her on their honeymoon for business. Her frustration is expressed when she has 'to be content' (p. 15) with only having dinner with him.

STUDY FOCUS: CONTRADICTIONS AND CONFLICTS A02

Carter represents human sexuality as something dangerous and animalistic. This is shown in the violent images in 'The Bloody Chamber'; the voyeurism and exhibitionism in 'The Tiger's Bride'; the comical contrast of the rutting cats and the energetic coupling of the lovers in 'Puss-in-Boots'; the imprisonment of the women in 'The Erl-King'; the intimate moments of transformation in 'The Tiger's Bride', 'The Company of Wolves' and 'Wolf-Alice'. However, the various endings of the tales offer different insights into the ways in which the contradictions and conflicts of male and female relationships can be resolved. Try making a list of how the relationships are resolved at the end of each tale. How do they differ?

CONTEXT A03

Erica Jong's novel *Fear of Flying* (1973), published six years before *The Bloody Chamber*, was controversial in its frank discussion of female sexuality.

STUDY FOCUS: THE FEMALE VIEW A03

The view of sexuality within the stories is exclusively a female view, presented as a challenge to some attitudes of the 1970s. Male sexuality is represented mostly as aggressive and selfish. The men in the stories do not face any life-threatening rite of passage or dilemma: their sexual destiny seems assured. The Marquis is a serial killer who has followed in the footsteps of his ancestors to enter 'the kingdom of the unimaginable' ('The Bloody Chamber', p. 36). Mr Lyon, lying down with Miss Lamb at the end of 'The Courtship of Mr Lyon', can depend on her self-sacrifice for his survival. The advances of The Beast in 'The Tiger's Bride' are only rejected at first because they are so timid. Puss-in-Boots is an insensitive boaster: 'what lady in all the world could say "no" to … a fine marmalade cat?' ('Puss-in-Boots', p. 76).

Even when men face difficulties, female ingenuity steps in to help: when Puss-in-Boots's master cannot get to the lady he desires, the female tabby cat makes it happen. The soldier in 'The Lady of the House of Love' will not take 'criminal advantage' (p. 122) of the vampire he believes to be in need of medical treatment for 'nervous hysteria' (p. 124). The certainty of all these men, their self-assurance, is their most deadly attribute.

FEAR AND RISK

Some of the women in the tales express a fear of sex. This may have its roots in the fact that for women sexual activity brings with it the possibility of pregnancy and the inevitability of the pain of birth. In the past, childbirth also brought with it a considerable risk of death for the mother. Sexuality is seen as a kind of doorway through which a woman passes towards possible fulfilment, perhaps motherhood, or even death. The sensation of fear, particularly fear that is proved or known to be unfounded, is thrilling. It is this thrill that underpins the reader's experience in the **Gothic** and horror genres; humans find fear a pleasurable sensation, up to a point.

CHECK THE BOOK A03

In his introduction to *Supernatural Horror in Literature* (published in 1973), Howard Phillips Lovecraft writes: 'The oldest and strongest emotion of mankind is fear, and the oldest and strongest kind of fear is fear of the unknown. These facts few psychologists will dispute, and their admitted truth must establish for all time the genuineness and dignity of the weirdly horrible tales as a literary form.'

The bride does not mention any personal fear of the Marquis until she is approaching the forbidden chamber itself. She only admits a 'dreadful anguish' (p. 28) when she realises she is to join this macabre display of dead wives. When she mistakes the sound of Jean-Yves for her husband returning she finds that 'fear gave me strength' (p. 30). Yet the return of her husband does cause genuine fear and she only has sufficient resourcefulness to delay the moment of execution long enough for her mother to rescue her.

This thrill of risk-taking accompanies all the experiences of the young women in these tales as they find themselves confronted by strange men who exert power over them. Even Beauty in 'The Tiger's Bride', though openly annoyed, is a little disappointed to discover The Beast has not asked for more than a quick look at her naked: 'That he should want so little was the reason why I could not give it' (p. 68).

METAMORPHOSIS

Metamorphosis can be used in fiction to represent the presence of two 'natures' in one person. As in the **Gothic** double of Robert Louis Stevenson's 'The Strange Case of Dr Jekyll and Mr Hyde' (1886), Carter explores how man can also be beast: 'hairy on the inside' ('The Company of Wolves', p. 137).

Transformation revealing some idea of truth is a common theme of folk and fairy tales. In the original 'Beauty and the Beast' the creature is rescued by the goodness of a true woman who restores him to his handsome self. Carter's two retellings of the tale offer something quite different. Mr Lyon loses his attractive and powerful animal qualities and ends up looking 'unkempt' ('The Courtship of Mr Lyon', p. 54). In 'The Tiger's Bride' it is not The Beast, but Beauty who is transformed. Having dispatched her replica to the real world of her father, she is free to shed 'all the skins of a life in the world' (p. 75) and become a beast herself. Carter inverts the traditional transformation from beast to human and its **symbolism**. To be beast-like is to be virtuous; to become 'manly' is to be vicious.

'The Snow Child' offers a different view on metamorphosis: a wish can become reality, but can just as easily be wished away. The transitory nature of male desire is emphasised by the melting away of the child: 'Soon there was nothing left of her but a feather … a bloodstain … and the rose' (p. 106).

'The Lady of the House of Love' turns the traditional tale of 'Sleeping Beauty' upside down. In the original tale, the princess pricks her finger on a poisoned object and is about to die. Saved by the limited magical powers of good fairies, the princess does not die but lies sleeping for a hundred years. She is magically restored by the kiss of a handsome prince who has fought his way through the undergrowth to rescue her. The moral conveyed celebrates the virtue of patience, and suggests that enduring suffering is worthy of reward. In 'The Lady of the House of Love', a beautiful aristocratic vampire is transformed into a 'far older, less beautiful' woman (p. 124). The vampire cannot sleep (sometimes a **euphemism** for death) and is only able to find some peace after cutting her finger. The handsome prince kisses her – but not in any romantic or sexual sense – and is too dim to understand the changes going on around him. Carter makes the Countess become 'less beautiful' (p. 124) after her lover tries to 'kiss it better' (p. 123). Although the Countess and her soldier are separated, unlike Prince Charming and Sleeping Beauty, it becomes clear the Countess will find some kind of union with her lover, and many others, in death.

CONTEXT A03

Ovid's *Metamorphoses* was written approximately two thousand years ago. The poem tells of the creation and history of the world and contains tales of transformation in which a mortal or a god is changed into a plant or animal. Tales of transformation are common in ancient myths.

STUDY FOCUS: TAMING THE WOLF A03

The transformations of the wolf – a powerful **symbol** of the ferocity of nature, the dangers of the unknown and all-consuming desire – are seen in the different versions of 'Little Red Riding Hood'. In 'The Company of Wolves', however, the metamorphosis is prevented by the 'wise child' (p. 138). She tames the threat of the werewolf and domesticates his dangerous nature. Unable to return to the form of a man, he is now merely a 'tender wolf' (p. 139). Carter here draws on another strand of folk tale which sees women having the wit to outsmart the devil himself.

BEAUTY AND WEALTH

A recurring theme in the stories is that beauty can, but should not, be bought or owned by the wealthy. In 'The Bloody Chamber' the bride is bought with jewels and clothes. In 'The Tiger's Bride' and 'The Courtship of Mr Lyon', Beauty is bought through dishonest dealing, both financial and at the card table. In each case wealth corrupts beauty: the 'tell-tale stain' on the narrator's forehead takes 'the shape and brilliance of the heart on a playing card' ('The Bloody Chamber', p. 36); Beauty in 'The Courtship of Mr Lyon' becomes vain: 'she smiled at herself in mirrors a little too often' (p. 52); Beauty in 'The Tiger's Bride' learns to accept her father's cynical view 'that, if you have enough money, anything is possible' (p. 69). Their appearance and their emotional state show that being groomed for their master's pleasure damages them. Unlike the lovers in standard fairy-tale happy endings who become rich, marry and live happily ever after, Carter's characters show the escape from the material world as freedom from corruption. 'The Bloody Chamber' narrator's redistribution of her dead husband's wealth is a **revision** of the fairy-tale 'she became rich and lived happily ever after' and indicates socialist principles.

The Beast in 'The Tiger's Bride' wears a mask of a painted 'beautiful face' but it is 'too perfect' to be 'entirely human' (p. 58). Carter is playing with the reader's expectations and understanding of the character at this point in the story. She is deliberately hiding the real identity of The Beast, but subtle suggestions are made that the wealth, which enables and requires the disguise, distances humans from each other and from themselves. Carter is influenced here by the **Marxist** analysis of capitalism and its effects on people.

CONTEXT A04

Marx and Engels explored the concept of alienation in their early works such as *The German Ideology* (written in 1845–6) and *Economic and Philosophical Manuscripts of 1844*: 'it is clear that the more the worker spends himself, the more powerful becomes the alien world of objects which he creates over and against himself, the poorer he himself – his inner world – becomes, the less belongs to him as his own' (*The Germany Ideology*, 1997 edition, p. 63).

STUDY FOCUS: KARL MARX   A04

Karl Marx (1818–83) described how people become obsessed with the things they make, buy, sell and use, and are unable to see themselves in any meaningful way as part of the world. Marx referred to this as alienation, where people become strangers to themselves. This is clearly represented in the Marquis and his private collections of art and literature: he flaunts his enjoyment of the finest things in life without the necessity of working for a living. His degrading attitudes and actions **symbolise** the degenerate nature of the idle rich. Hoarded personal wealth becomes a destructive power. Carter clearly wants us to realise the opposite: that great wealth shared has the power to do good. But part of the problem for Carter is that she presents the world of luxury with such sensuous delight in language – in her rich depiction of grandiose buildings, lustrous furnishings, fine clothing and rare works of art. As a result the question of ownership and access to great wealth is lost amidst the display of luxury itself (for more on this see **Language and style**).

MAN, WOMAN AND NATURE

The use of the masculine noun 'man' to mean humanity as a whole was a common **cliché** being challenged at the time Carter was writing *The Bloody Chamber*. Carter, however, makes a clear distinction between 'man' and 'woman'. Man is shown to be disconnected from nature in these tales, while woman is potentially a creature of nature. For Carter, womankind has the power to heal the rift between man and nature.

STUDY FOCUS: THE ERL-KING   A03

'The Erl-King' shows the spirit of nature as a man, but an isolated and feminised man: 'He is an excellent housewife' (p. 99). In the middle of the wild forest, the Erl-King tends to domestic chores, looking after all living and growing things in his garden. Carter describes him as a primitive hunter-gatherer, with emphasis on his gathering of 'unnatural treasures'. What Carter means by this is not immediately clear, as we are first told of all the natural things collected by the Erl-King: pigeons' eggs, dandelions, goat's milk, goat's cheese and rabbit stew. It is only at the end of that paragraph that Carter describes the Erl-King's 'cruel' habit of keeping 'singing birds' (p. 99) in cages.

We are then told that his 'green eye' (p. 103) reduces women to the size of birds, and his 'regard' (p. 104) innocently imprisons them. The Erl-King's 'green eye' is an **intertextual** reference to Shakespeare's play *Othello* (c.1602–4), and Iago's **ironic** warning to Othello that jealousy is 'the green-eyed monster which doth mock / The meat it feeds on' (Act III Scene 3). This and the imprisoning 'regard' seem to suggest that men are 'naturally' possessive and jealous. Carter also suggests that women do not have to be limited by this element of man's 'human nature'.

AN EVIL TRICK?

The concept that man hides his true nature behind a mask is presented in 'The Bloody Chamber' and 'The Tiger's Bride', where the Marquis and The Beast are at their most dangerous when the mask is removed. In other tales, the power of nature is disfigured or disguised in man, for example the Beast in 'The Courtship of Mr Lyon' or the werewolf in the last three stories. It is the figure of the werewolf which most clearly presents the relationship between man and nature as an evil trick played upon woman: 'Carnivore incarnate, only immaculate flesh appeases him' ('The Company of Wolves', p. 138). This statement applies equally to the Marquis in 'The Bloody Chamber'. In repeatedly returning to the transformation of this triangular relationship between man, woman and nature, Carter challenges the notion that there is such a thing as an unchanging human nature or a 'natural order' in human society.

Through the **eponymous** character in 'Wolf-Alice', Carter clearly expresses the problems of a human who has been overtaken by their inner animal. Part of being human is being able to communicate in sophisticated visual and verbal language. A child raised in a wild state of nature cannot crack the codes of human society. Wolf-Alice cannot imagine any other moment of time than 'the present tense' (p. 141). For her there is no past and future. While there is 'sensual immediacy' (p. 141) to her existence, there is no future. The point here is that we humans can adapt our environment to our needs, and have been more successful at doing this than animals, because of our ability to imagine, and to remember and share the **narratives** of our lives. Carter is pointing out in her stories that by adapting the natural environment we have created a social environment that does not allow all our human needs to be fulfilled. She argues that this is particularly true for women because the social environment that has evolved is often a **patriarchal** one.

CONTEXT   A04

Representations of the spirit of the wood or the spirit of spring are associated with paganism. The Green Man is a **symbol** of fertility often found in old European churches. His head is usually wreathed in leaves and branches. In Christian terms the Green Man is viewed as a symbol of Easter.

CHECK THE BOOK   A03

A photograph of a Green Man carving in Rosslyn Chapel can be seen, along with a description of the Green Man in British folklore, in Marc Alexander's *Companion to the Folklore, Myths and Customs of Britain* (2002).

CHECK THE BOOK   A03

Kate Millett's *Sexual Politics* (1970) was a controversial attack on patriarchal values that advanced the **feminist** agenda in American and Europe. Later feminists such as Camille Paglia have criticised Millett, causing much controversy among academic feminists.

COLD NATURE

With few exceptions, nature in the stories is a cold and unwelcoming place that begins where human civilisation ends. Nature in Carter's stories can be interpreted in a number of ways: it can refer to the physical world itself, or to the physical world as a **symbol**, or to a character's instinctive nature that breaks the social codes of civilised behaviour.

CHECK THE BOOK **A03**

Simon Schama's *Landscape and Memory* (1995) contains a chapter on forests in the Western imagination.

The climate is as much a feature of the natural world as the landscape in these stories, and most are set in the coldest parts of the world in the coldest season. 'The Courtship of Mr Lyon' unfolds in a 'winter's landscape' (p. 43) that is slow to leave Mr Lyon's home – although the image of 'a drift of fallen petals' (p. 55) suggests the arrival of spring and a more hopeful ending. The aristocrats fleeing the Russian winter in 'The Tiger's Bride' find no comfort in the 'treacherous South' (p. 58) where parlours can be 'cold as hell' (p. 59). 'The Erl-King' takes place in an autumnal world with 'Introspective weather' (p. 96). 'The Snow Child' is set in midwinter, as are 'The Company of Wolves' and 'The Werewolf'. The depressive effect of the cold weather in each story in succession is relieved by contrasting settings for other stories. 'Puss-in-Boots' anticipates the arrival of the first 'vernal hint of spring' (p. 94) as the cats and lovers mate so enthusiastically. The main action in 'The Lady of the House of Love' takes place in 'hot, ripe summer' (p. 111) and the events of 'Wolf-Alice' span a period that is not tied to one season.

CHECK THE POEM **A04**

The poet Anne Sexton (1928–74) retells seventeen Brothers Grimm tales in her verse collection *Transformations* (1971). Her writing questions many of the conventional ideas of femininity found in the tales.

The way human behaviour is shaped by a harsh and bleak environment is a theme Carter uses frequently. It forms part of the introduction to the main story in both 'The Werewolf' and 'The Company of Wolves'. The combination of 'cold weather' and 'cold hearts' (p. 126) in the 'The Werewolf' is related to the fear of hungry wolves, 'grey as famine' ('The Company of Wolves', p. 130), made more dangerous in wintertime when food is scarce.

The distance from civilisation, or how far society is from being truly civilised, is **symbolised** by the emptiness of the landscape that surrounds the fortresses of the patriarchs. The 'amphibious' (p. 9) isolation of the Marquis's castle in 'The Bloody Chamber' is echoed in the 'bereft landscape' (p. 70) surrounding The Beast's palace in 'The Tiger's Bride', 'a burned-out planet' (p. 63) dominated by the 'sad browns and sepias of winter' (p. 70).

STUDY FOCUS: THE SEA AND THE FOREST   **A04**

The sea in 'The Bloody Chamber' is linked to the matriarch and by extension to ideas of the earth mother. The narrator describes the 'amniotic salinity of the ocean' (p. 8) as she arrives at her destination. This compares the sea to the amniotic fluid that surrounds a baby in the womb during pregnancy. The watery connection between mother and child is followed through the 'melting' landscape (p. 8), and formed in the tears that flow over 'gold bath taps' (p. 21) while they talk on the telephone. Perhaps the clearest expression of this connection between mother, sea and child comes when the narrator's 'avenging angel' (p. 39) emerges from the sea, shoots the Marquis and so saves her life. She is not only her daughter's saviour, she is the **personification** of the protective maternal instinct.

The forest is a **paradoxical** symbol in the stories. The fairy-tale forest is physically unwelcoming and alluring at the same time. This is most obvious in 'The Erl-King', where the narrator enjoys the 'delicious loneliness' (p. 97) at the same time as she is aware of the fact that 'there is no clue to guide you through in perfect safety' (p. 96). The forest is a place where civilisation and its restricting boundaries do not apply, a place where humans can discover their true nature, or be saved, or sacrificed.

PART FOUR: STRUCTURE, FORM AND LANGUAGE

STRUCTURE

As a collection of stories, the structure of *The Bloody Chamber* is not entirely cohesive. There is no obvious thread or theme that flows from story to story, except, perhaps, that they are all inspired by fairy tales. 'The Bloody Chamber', 'The Courtship of Mr Lyon' and 'The Tiger's Bride' form a trio of tales about women marrying monstrous men. 'Puss-in-Boots' provides an entertaining comic interlude, its exuberance giving way to the slower pace of 'The Erl-King', a dark and disorienting exploration of the fairy-tale forest. 'The Snow Child' moves along briskly, its simple structure following the fairy-tale formula of patterns of three. 'The Lady of the House of Love' is an elaborate **Gothic** romance. The last three stories, 'The Werewolf', 'The Company of Wolves' and 'Wolf-Alice', are concerned with how to deal with the big, bad wolf. All the stories, even 'Puss-in-Boots', deal with death and with monsters of the imagination. But the 'bloody chamber' (p. 35) of the opening story provides the title that unites the collection. Considering them as tales from 'the kingdom of the unimaginable' ('The Bloody Chamber', p. 36) or as stories of 'the fated sisterhood' (p. 27), Carter has set up a display of horrors to arouse the emotions and celebrate curiosity.

NARRATIVE TECHNIQUES

'THE ERL-KING'

Carter employs a different **narrative** style for each story and often changes style within a story. The most complex and subtle experiments with narrative form come in 'The Erl-King' whose folk-tale origins are likely to be the least familiar of all the sources from which Carter has drawn her inspiration.

Carter uses first person narrative forms in 'The Bloody Chamber', 'The Tiger's Bride', 'Puss-in-Boots' and 'The Erl-King'. Only in 'The Erl-King' is the identity of the **narrator** at first concealed. The narrator's role in the story is unclear, shifting in and out of the action in an unsettling and dreamlike manner. Although clearly female, the narrator never becomes a defined character as the other identifiable – but unnamed – narrators do. Puss-in-Boots has a charismatic personality but is known by a descriptive label rather than a given name and lacks individuality, even for a cat.

'The Erl-King' begins its narrative in the third person in the past tense; moves to direct address in the second person, present tense; and shifts to the third person, future tense, over the first three paragraphs. This uncertainty of tense and person in the narrative voice continues throughout the story. The effect is disorienting. Time and space are not fixed. The story proceeds only because Carter retains enough descriptive detail to form a recognisable chronological recount and create an expectation of narrative: something is bound to happen. The forest is as much a passing of time as it is a place, and autumn is felt rather than observed as 'the approach of winter': 'cold … grips hold of your belly and squeezes it tight' (p. 96). Carter suggests a place that is not yet dead but is dying: 'All will fall still, all lapse' (p. 97). The vague sense of narrative confusion is deliberately and carefully controlled by Carter and it creates an eerie sensation of being lost in her forest. The reader relies on the narrator to guide us back to the path, but has the uneasy suspicion that Carter is not in a hurry to find the quickest way home.

CHECK THE BOOK A03

In her essay 'Notes from the Front Line' Carter writes: 'I believe that all myths are products of the human mind and reflect only aspects of material human practice. I'm in the demythologising business' (in *On Gender and Writing*, edited by Michelene Wandor, 1983, p. 71).

CRITICAL VIEWPOINT A02

Metamorphosis is a significant feature of the collection of tales. Perhaps reflecting this, the narrative changes its form throughout Carter's tales. Carter employs metamorphosis for different effects within the stories, changing the forms of the tales as she does so.

CHECK THE POEM A03

Johann Wolfgang von Goethe (1749–1832) wrote a poem called 'Der Erlkönig' ('The Erlking', 1782) in which a supernatural being tries to entice a young boy to go with him. Unsuccessful, the Erl-King kills him while he is held in his father's arms: 'my father, he seizes me fast, / Full sorely the Erl-King has hurt me at last' (27–8). This poem was later set to music by Franz Schubert (1797–1828).

'WOLF-ALICE'

'Wolf-Alice' has some touches that suggest the narrator is possibly involved in the action of the story, but these implicate the reader in the rejection of the wild child rather than create an identifiable narrator. The opening sentence invites a sense of collusion: Carter uses the first person plural pronoun to draw attention to the child as an alien being who does not speak 'like we do' (p. 140). Later in the story, the **narrator** admits: 'we secluded her in animal privacy out of fear of her imperfection because it showed us what we might have been' (p. 144).

THE OMNISCIENT NARRATOR

CHECK THE BOOK **AO3**

In his essay 'The Storyteller' German philosopher Walter Benjamin (1892–1940) points out that the early folk tale would have contained something useful for the listener, perhaps a moral or some practical advice. This essay can be found in Benjamin's collection *Illuminations* (the 1999 translation by Harry Zohn is a good edition, with an introduction by Hannah Arendt).

The **narrative** voice in the other tales is the third person **omniscient narrator**. It is safe to assume that this is the voice of Carter herself. She is not a participant in the events of the stories. However, she frequently makes an **aside** to the reader in the knowing way that raconteurs often do to change the pace of an anecdote.

Occasionally characters will speak through the narrator, their dialogue not marked with conventional speech punctuation. This often happens with the language refrains of fairy tales, such as 'What big eyes you have' ('The Company of Wolves', p. 137) and other familiar fairy-tale elements. This device implies that the words are the inner thoughts of the character, something that happens naturally when stories are verbally exchanged and read aloud. They are **allusions** that assume a shared understanding of the storytelling conventions of fairy tales. For example, in 'The Lady of the House of Love', the narrative follows an image of the Countess being cleaned up after devouring her prey with the introduction of the hero through the refrain from 'Jack and the Beanstalk': 'Fee fie fo fum / I smell the blood of an Englishman' (p. 111). The refrain is completed to bring him into the story fully with his arrival at the village, under threat of being devoured: 'Be he alive or be he dead / I'll grind his bones to make my bread' (p. 112).

FORM

THE GOTHIC TRADITION

MEDIEVAL GOTHIC

The term **Gothic** originally described a style of art and architecture which was widespread in medieval Europe. It is associated with crude, grotesque and exaggerated features and is, to an extent, a fusion of early Christian and pagan **symbolism**. The style came to be seen as a primitive attempt to incorporate the power of wild nature within the structures of civilisation, and was viewed in the sixteenth, seventeenth and eighteenth centuries as the sign of a superstitious and brutal age. (The medieval influence on Carter is discussed in more detail in **Part Five: Literary background**.)

EARLY GOTHIC

It is possible to trace a cultural connection between medieval mystery plays, one of the means by which Christian ideas were communicated to an illiterate society, and later works of drama that employ **allegorical** or supernatural devices. Shakespeare's plays *Macbeth* (1606) and *Hamlet* (1601) are early examples of plays with **Gothic** features, such as ghostly apparitions and a preoccupation with insanity. Feigned madness, the passions of revenge and elaborate crimes of murder are found in John Webster's revenge **tragedy** *The White Devil* (1612), which is seen as foreshadowing the Gothic literature of the eighteenth century.

EIGHTEENTH- AND NINETEENTH-CENTURY GOTHIC

Horace Walpole's *The Castle of Otranto* (1764), Ann Radcliffe's *The Mysteries of Udolpho* (1794) and Matthew G. Lewis's *The Monk* (1796) are considered to be the 'classic' Gothic tales that established the conventions of the genre in English literature. Each takes in an unfamiliar location, set in a distant past. The characters tend to be rather two-dimensional, their main characteristic being frequent exposure to extreme stress and terror at the hands of various supernatural phenomena.

Jane Austen's *Northanger Abbey* (begun in 1798 and published posthumously in 1818) shifted the focus of the genre. Austen was more concerned with the psychology of her characters than the hysterical victims of the supernatural. Mary Shelley's *Frankenstein, or The Modern Prometheus*, which appeared in 1818, relies so little on the traditional elements of Gothic fiction that it almost appears to be outside the genre altogether. However, it is an enquiry into the nature of resurrection, and all the essential questions of life and death are posed by Frankenstein's creature. Supernatural power, fearful locations and terrible madness make up the investigation of what it is to be human. Emily Brontë's *Wuthering Heights* (originally published under the gender-disguising name Ellis Bell in 1847), with its intricate **narrative** structure and desolate setting, also features a mysterious and violent man who destroys a strong woman, amid ghosts, passions and revenge.

LATER GOTHIC

CHECK THE BOOK **A03**

In *Two Women of London: The Strange Case of Ms Jekyll and Mrs Hyde* (1989) Emma Tennant takes Robert Louis Stevenson's classic exploration of the divided self and gives it a **feminist** slant.

The later Victorian Gothic novels explore the darker aspects of the human psyche in the familiar setting of the modern world. This is a conscious attempt to question social progress by bringing the terrors of the past into conflict with the assumed certainties of the present. Robert Louis Stevenson's *The Strange Case of Dr Jekyll and Mr Hyde* (1886) and Oscar Wilde's *The Picture of Dorian Gray* (1890) use the idea of multiple personality to explore the dual nature of humanity as man-beast, god-devil, angel-demon. In *The Bloody Chamber*, Carter reworks this typical theme of the Gothic genre, not only in the magical transformations of the collection, but also in the way these transformations explore the dual nature of humanity as both human and animal. As in H. G. Wells's *The Island of Doctor Moreau* (1896), science and religion are called into question as the authors dwell on the potential horrors and glories within the individual.

Bram Stoker's *Dracula* (1897) imports European folklore in a highly theatrical, eroticised and **melodramatic** combination of Gothic elements as civilisation is threatened by an ancient menace. In this way these novels reflect the powerful revolutionary changes taking place in the nineteenth century that inspired and still influence our understanding of personal identity and social responsibility.

In the twentieth century the influence of **modernism** and the all too real horrors of human history saw the genre decline in popularity. Its influence has fragmented into genres such as science fiction and horror, though it has maintained a presence in the popular imagination. Aspects of the Gothic were used by writers such as Daphne du Maurier (1907–89) and Mervyn Peake (1911–68); and other writers, such as Anne Rice (b.1941) and the master of modern horror, Stephen King (b.1947), incorporate elements of the Gothic genre in their work as they continue to explore the dark horrors of the human imagination.

CHECK THE BOOK **A04**

If you wish to find out more about the lives and work of many of the authors mentioned in these Notes, *The Oxford Companion to English Literature*, edited by Margaret Drabble (revised sixth edition, 2006), is a good place to begin.

STUDY FOCUS: CARTER AND THE GOTHIC TRADITION A02

Carter positively revels in extreme sensations, perceptions and locations. The gruesome display of dead wives in 'The Bloody Chamber', the disorientation of the senses in 'The Erl-King', and the descriptions of wilderness and the palazzo in 'The Tiger's Bride' all demonstrate how Carter exaggerates the Gothic content of fairy tales. Only 'The Bloody Chamber' and 'Puss-in-Boots' do not explicitly focus on the supernatural. 'Puss-in-Boots' seems less obviously Gothic in its lecherous comedy, but Carter certainly delights in the bawdy and murderous adultery of her anarchic heroes. The **narrator** in 'The Bloody Chamber' experiences the thrills and near-fatal consequences of going beyond social and moral boundaries.

In *The Bloody Chamber* Carter is both sensational and entertaining while promoting unconventional ideas that challenged the accepted beliefs of her time. The collection proposes some radical alternatives to the traditional fairy tale or Gothic 'consequences' of personal action.

ORIGINS

THE FAIRY-TALE TRADITION

Carter generally takes one particular fairy or folk tale as the basis of each story in this collection. However, recognisable elements of other tales reappear at various moments. Carter almost makes a seamless connection between all the stories, as if they could all be traced back to one great original story that has been long forgotten.

STUDY FOCUS: PERRAULT A03 A04

The traditions of the fairy tales that form the basis of Carter's tales can be traced back through the centuries across Europe and beyond to the oral tradition. In the sixteenth century writers began to make records of these tales. As print technology advanced so particular versions of the tales became known. Giovanni Francesco Straparola's *The Facetious Nights* (published in two parts as *Le Piacevoli Notti* in 1550 and 1553, and also referred to as *The Pleasant Nights*) introduced various folk tales to European literature, and certainly influenced later versions of the tales. Carter's chief source is the seventeenth-century French writer Charles Perrault (1628–1703), whose tales provide the source material 'Bluebeard', 'Puss-in-Boots', 'Sleeping Beauty' and 'Little Red Riding Hood'. Though Perrault is the most well-known source, his versions are pre-dated by other writers. The earliest known written version of 'Puss-in-Boots', for example, comes from the sixteenth century.

THE BROTHERS GRIMM

Later versions of most of Perrault's stories were recorded by the German academics known as the Brothers Grimm in the nineteenth century. The Disney animation features of these tales (recently **satirised** in the *Shrek* series of animated films) are yet another form of the tales to be considered. Some obscure sources are cited for particular stories. 'The Snow Child' is linked by Helen Simpson (in her introduction to the 2006 Vintage edition of *The Bloody Chamber*, p. xvi) to an unpublished variant of 'Snow White' collected by the Brothers Grimm. However, it bears direct resemblance to the story 'Snegorotchka' included in the French illustrator Edmund Dulac's *Fairy Book* (1916), where it is introduced as a Russian fairy tale. Yet Carter's telling of the tale is very far from the sentiments expressed in 'Snegorotchka'. This is just one example of how difficult it can be to define the origin of tales which were told for centuries before they were ever written down.

WIDER INFLUENCES

Carter freely interweaves references and direct quotations from other well-known children's tales: Lewis Carroll's *Alice's Adventures in Wonderland* (1865) and *Through the Looking-Glass and What Alice Found There* (1871) are both drawn upon directly and indirectly in several of her tales; the giant from 'Jack and the Beanstalk' or the Grimms' 'The Brave Little Tailor' makes his presence felt in 'The Lady of the House of Love'. But it is quite striking that, while Carter freely draws upon the magical element of shape-shifting creatures, the only fairy or magical being in the collection taken directly from fairy tale is the wood spirit in 'The Erl-King'. This tale is derived from Germanic and Scandinavian traditions concerning evil elf creatures that lead children to their destruction in the forest.

While the heritage of Carter's tales can be traced to a certain extent, the stories are neither backward looking nor nostalgic. Neither can the collection be adequately summarised as an attempt to reclaim those old stories for a modern era. The stories that Carter chooses to tell are her stories; stories of a twentieth-century woman writing 'to please herself'. In the 1970s that intention was revolutionary, no matter how idealistic or limited in its achievements it may seem from the vantage point of the twenty-first century.

CHECK THE BOOK A03

In his 1957 collection of essays, *Mythologies*, Roland Barthes looks at the powerful nature of ancient stories and the way in which they have come to affect our values and beliefs.

CONTEXT A03

In 'Snegorotchka' a childless couple make a snow child that magically transforms into a little girl. They take her home and all live happily until the spring comes and she melts away. It is a sad tale of love and loss, relating death to the passing of the seasons and also showing how, though parents can make children, they cannot always keep them forever.

CHECK THE BOOK A03

Edmund Dulac (1882–1953) was one of the most influential illustrators of children's books during the early twentieth century. His *Fairy Book* (1916) contains stories from around the world and has been reprinted several times, as the illustrations are considered to be highly influential in the art of children's literature.

LANGUAGE

Jack Zipes's *Breaking the Magic Spell: Radical Theories of Folk and Fairy Tales*, first published in 1979, states: 'Once there was a time when folk tales were part of communal property and told … by gifted storytellers who gave vent to the frustration of the common people and embodied their needs and wishes in the folk narratives. … Today the folk tale as an oral art form has lost its aura … and has given way to the literary fairy tale and other mass-mediated forms of storytelling' (2002, p. 6).

Helen Simpson in her introduction to the 2006 Vintage edition of *The Bloody Chamber* defines Carter as 'an abstract thinker with an intensely visual imagination' (p. x). This is the chief characteristic of Carter's language in the collection. Whether she is exploring the sexual politics of erotic literature in 'The Bloody Chamber', male pomposity in 'Puss-in-Boots', or **Gothic melodrama** in 'The Lady of the House of Love', Carter seeks to entertain.

VOCABULARY

Carter's visual imagination is complemented by other compelling features of her language use. Her vocabulary is richly diverse and often startling. It ranges from the complex and detailed language of classic literature to monosyllabic expletives that still shock in print. Words such as 'prothalamion' ('The Company of Wolves', p. 138) and 'chthonic' ('The Bloody Chamber', p. 35) evoke the mythology of earlier civilisations and display Carter's acquaintance with literature of academic interest.

STUDY FOCUS: THE FIVE SENSES   A02

Carter portrays location and setting through densely textured detail and a combination of visual awareness with the other senses. In 'The Bloody Chamber' the 'misty blue' (p. 8) turrets of the Marquis's castle are presented with 'seabirds mewing' and the 'green and purple, evanescent departures of the ocean' (p. 8). Her use of double negatives – 'No room, no corridor that did not rustle with the sound of the sea' (p. 9) – emphasises the way the landscape seems to melt into the interior while hinting that no part of the castle offers any kind of peace. This complements the description of the 'refracted light from the waves' on the walls to create the 'luminous, murmurous castle' (p. 9) as a place that inspires a sense of awe in the narrator: it is, literally, an awful place.

ALL IN THE DETAIL

Carter leaves spaces in the **narratives** for meaning to be supplied by the reader. Sometimes this is done simply through omitting details or not stating the obvious fact. In 'The Tiger's Bride' Carter shapes an entire paragraph of incomplete sentences to describe the impact of the first glimpse of The Beast in his animal form. The paragraph – from 'A great, feline, tawny shape' to 'eyes, like twin suns' (p. 71) – functions as an incomplete list of The Beast's imposing features and subtly conveys a sense of wonder. The narrator is incapable of coherent thought under the spell of the animal.

In other places Carter's prose is made up of complex sentences with multiple clauses. From the first sentence of 'The Lady of the House of Love', the story tumbles out through a torrent of words describing the tangible 'presences' of the 'revenants' who haunt the village in 'shadows', 'sound' and 'a sense of unease' (p. 107). The 'beautiful queen of the vampires' is introduced in one sweeping sentence that describes her 'antique bridal gown'; her 'dark, high house'; the 'baleful posthumous existence' of her 'atrocious ancestors' (p. 107); her sad and somewhat obsessive reading of Tarot cards; her desire to escape; and her fatal youth. It seems as if the narrator simply cannot stop herself from embellishing the tale even as it is being told. This tale (like many others) also makes use of the shortened sentence, to create moments of tension or heighten the impact of a detail. Sentences such as 'I will be very gentle' (p. 119) and 'Now it is dark' (p. 120), stand out in ominous contrast to the majority of the text.

POETIC LANGUAGE

Elsewhere in her tales, Carter's prose takes on a more poetic voice. In 'The Erl-King' a passage describing the Erl-King's eyes is punctuated by a line of text that stands alone: 'Eyes green as apples. Green as dead sea fruit' (p. 103). Carter uses this technique of placing isolated **similes** to punctuate the rhythm of the narrative in other tales. In 'The Bloody Chamber' she morbidly links the disconnected telephone line with the murders the Marquis has already committed: 'Dead as his wives' (p. 29). In 'The Company of Wolves' Carter makes an **alliterative** line create the emphasis needed to turn rational fear to irrational superstition: 'Fear and flee the wolf; for, worst of all, the wolf may be more than he seems' (p. 130). The line stands alone in the text as a turning point in the narrative.

METAPHOR

The unexpected use of names or descriptive terms to create a surprising effect is at the heart of Carter's style. Though she employs many **metaphoric** images, there are a few common metaphors that unite a number of these stories. Perhaps the most striking are the **Gothic** elements of the stories that are associated with journeys from the exterior to the interior, penetration of secret spaces, rites of passage, transformations and quests. The metaphor of the forest, suggesting the unknown or the threat of the wilderness beyond human civilisation, is central to the imaginative landscape of the fairy tale and recurs in Carter's tales again and again.

This idea of a wilderness or inhospitable landscape does not always appear as a woodland. In 'The Bloody Chamber' the new bride's journey terminates at 'an unknown, never-to-be visited station' (p. 6). The Beast in 'The Courtship of Mr Lyon' is first encountered in the garden of a mansion isolated in a 'snow-filled' (p. 44) world. In 'The Tiger's Bride' Beauty travels across a 'wide, flat dish of snow' (p. 62) to The Beast's 'megalomaniac citadel' amid a 'dead' world (p. 63). In 'The Erl-King' it is almost as if the Erl-King and his domain are interchangeable: 'the wood swallows you up' (p. 96) and the Erl-King is 'the tender butcher' waiting to 'skin the rabbit' (p. 100). In 'The Lady of the House of Love' the vampire's castle emerges out of the 'jungle' of 'enormous thickets' (p. 114) of rose bushes. In 'The Werewolf' the forest resumes its identity as a place of 'Cold; tempest; wild beasts' (p. 126), while in 'The Company of Wolves' the forest is a place of 'teeming perils' (p. 130) filled with 'assassins' (p. 129): 'ghosts, hobgoblins, ogres ... witches' and 'the wolf' (p. 130).

CONTEXT A03

Arthur Rackham (1867–1939) was a successful children's book illustrator, whose works include *Fairy Tales of the Brothers Grimm* (1900). The fantasy worlds he created were often sinister, full of gnarled trees and goblins and monsters.

STUDY FOCUS: THE CASTLE AND THE ANIMAL A02

The ruined castle, the iconic image of the Gothic genre, is featured in one way or another in all of the stories. It can appear as a grand **symbol** of power and wealth, or a domestic shelter from the challenges of the world, or a protection from the psychological pressures of moving from childhood to adulthood.

The other dominant metaphor is that of 'the animal' in opposition to 'the human'. Carter does not have one particular view of the relationship of animal and human in these stories; sometimes it is positive, sometimes it is negative. This is one reason why identifying thematic links in the collection is not a simple matter. For example, should each of the transformations of man or woman into beast be understood to signify the same view of human society and human nature?

MOTHER GOOSE

In approaching these stories and considering their meaning, the central metaphors of 'the journey', 'the home', 'the wilderness' and 'the beast' provide a basis for Carter's rearrangement of the traditional tales. In each case, Carter employs a powerful interaction of ideas to deal with sex, class and gender and present them as matters of life and death. Folk tales were not originally created for, or told exclusively to, children. Fairy tales have a moral and **didactic** purpose. They function as warnings and instruction, based on the experience of people with little power in the world, on how best to recognise and survive predictable dangers. Carter felt that fairy tales had become isolated from the reality in which they were created and the reality which they addressed (see **Origins**). Carter as a modern-day version of Mother Goose, aims to revive their relevance by making the fairy tale a metaphor for her analysis of social class and gender.

CONTEXT A03

The first written evidence of the name Mother Goose as a teller of tales for children is in Jean Loret's *La Muse historique* (1650), a weekly gazette.

IMAGERY

STUDY FOCUS: BLOOD

A02

Blood is a key image that is obviously related to the **Gothic** element of the tales. It is related at different points to menstruation, sexual maturity, the loss of virginity, wounds, pain, death and sexual pleasure. In 'The Bloody Chamber' the stain or the mark of shame is transferred to the woman when she disobeys her husband and discovers the chamber's gory contents. In 'The Snow-Child' blood is present at the birth of the child and at its death as a consequence of the Count's shocking sexual assault. In 'The Lady of the House of Love' blood is the vampire's means of survival and the means of her release.

CONTEXT **A04**

Shakespeare's Macbeth broods on the nature of crime and punishment after Banquo's ghost attends the feast: 'It will have blood, they say: blood will have blood' (*Macbeth*, Act III Scene 5). As a literary symbol, blood has many different meanings but historically it has represented life, truth, family and purity. Its connotations of death, sacrifice and martyrdom are present in many different belief systems.

FLOWERS

Several central images are reworked throughout most of the stories in the collection. Flowers, for example, are a key image. Lilies in 'The Bloody Chamber' signify death and mourning through their association with funerals. The rose is a **symbol** of love and beauty – also agony and danger – in 'The Courtship of Mr Lyon', 'The Snow Child' and 'The Lady of the House of Love', to very different effects. The white rose brings the Beast and Beauty together in 'The Courtship of Mr Lyon' and symbolises a link of some kind of purity between the two: 'one white, perfect rose' (p. 47) is robbed from the Beast's garden by the father for his daughter; she returns white roses when away from the Beast and knows 'perfect freedom' (p. 51); her flowers are later discovered to be 'all dead' (p. 54). For the Countess in 'The Snow Child', the rose is a weapon. For the heroic cyclist in 'The Lady of the House of Love', the rose is a powerful omen of impending catastrophe on an unimaginable scale.

CONTEXT **A04**

The rose is a potent symbol in the literature and oral tradition of many cultures. The red rose is associated with blood and passion, and often identified with the female. The many layered petals of the rose, likened by artists to female genitalia, symbolise the complexity of the universe. In modern times the beauty, sweetness and defensive thorns of the rose symbolise the paradoxical nature of love as beautiful and intoxicating yet painful.

THE SONGBIRD

The caged songbird is a potent symbol of the loss of individual freedom, particularly for women. It is used in 'The Lady of the House of Love' and functions as a major plot device, in so far as there is any plot, in 'The Erl-King'.

MISTER WOLF

The wolf – 'Mister Wolf' – is a key symbol from the **imagery** of fairy tales and folklore. The wolf posed very real danger to human beings in early civilisations, and so represents the threat of unknown and uncontrollable nature. The wolf also represents greed, deceit and insatiable appetites. There are fewer references to the wolf's positive attributes of bravery and strength, though the female wolf is often portrayed as a generous and protective mother. On a simple level, wolf tales suggest that children should be wary of strangers. In a Freudian, **psychoanalytical** interpretation, the wolf in fairy tales represents the dangers of suppressed or repressed sexual desire. As the embodiment of danger, the wolf is an ever present predator.

Carter's various presentations of 'the wolf' (representing the different dangers she perceives in modern society) lead to contradictions that are not easily resolved. In 'The Werewolf' the threat is female but defeated. In 'Wolf-Alice' the wolf is humanised and the danger resolved. In 'The Company of Wolves' the threat is male and the wolf is dehumanised to resolve the threat it poses. The Beast in 'The Courtship of Mr Lyon' and 'The Tiger's Bride'

CONTEXT **A04**

The psychoanalyst Sigmund Freud (1856–1939) is considered to be one of the most influential thinkers of the modern era for his investigations into the workings of the unconscious mind and his studies on repression and sexual drives. Freud considered myths to be an expression of repressed thoughts.

is a variation on the idea of the werewolf. In presenting a variety of metamorphoses between woman, beast and man, Carter is exploring what it is to be human and questioning whether it is possible to understand the reality of human nature.

LITERATURE, ART AND BEYOND

Helen Simpson notes in the introduction to the 2006 Vintage edition that annotating *The Bloody Chamber* in detail would be a lengthy task (p. xiv). Sometimes Carter's references to works of literature and art are open and direct; often the allusions are entwined in several overlapping references that play with meaning. Other explicit references are totally fictitious, as if Carter is daring the reader to challenge her knowledge of literature and culture while at the same time mocking her own tendency to be esoteric.

When Carter gives the Romanian aristocrat in 'The Bloody Chamber' the name Carmilla, she is making reference to the **Gothic** novella 'Carmilla' published in 1872 by Joseph Sheridan Le Fanu (1814–73). The novella features a predatory lesbian vampire some twenty-five years before Bram Stoker's *Dracula* appeared. In a similar vein, Carter refers to 'Vlad the Impaler who picnicked on corpses in the forests of Transylvania' (p. 109) as the ancestor and source of the vampire beauty in 'The Lady of the House of Love'. Here she is recalling a legend that distorts history for the benefit of good storytelling, as this account of Vlad Tepes is based on propaganda and the alleged connection between Tepes and Stoker's villain Count Dracula is disputable.

Carter does not confine her allusions to the so-called higher forms of culture, literature and art. Children's literature, horror movies, luxury commodities, recognisable brand names and icons of fashion are all used to support her storytelling.

CHECK THE FILM A03

Blood and Roses (1960), directed by Roger Vadim, is an adaptation of Le Fanu's 'Carmilla'. Another version of this tale is the Hammer film *The Vampire Lovers* (1970), directed by Roy Ward Baker.

CHECK THE BOOK A03

In *The Uses of Enchantment: The Meaning and Importance of Fairy Tales* (1976), Bruno Bettelheim examines the instructive function of fairy tales from a **psychoanalytical** perspective. 'If we want to function well, we have to integrate the discordant tendencies that are inherent in our being. Isolating these tendencies and projecting them into separate figures … is one way fairy tales help us visualize and thus better grasp what goes on within us.'

PART FIVE: CONTEXTS AND CRITICAL DEBATES

HISTORICAL BACKGROUND

POST WAR

The post-war period in which Angela Carter grew up was dominated by the Cold War. The USSR emerged from the Second World War as a major international power and Eastern Europe disappeared behind what Winston Churchill in 1946 called the 'Iron Curtain'. Britain was no longer able to sustain its empire and America became the dominant capitalist power in the West, with increasing influence on British culture.

Post-war Britain was dominated by the 'make do and mend' approach. Rationing for some items did not stop until the mid 1950s and Britain was, as it had been during the war, heavily dependent on American aid. The welfare state was introduced in 1945, bringing free health care and education for all. This was followed in 1948 by the establishment of a National Health Service with medical treatment available to all.

1950s AND 1960s

In the 1950s austerity gave way to renewed prosperity and hope for a future where scientific and technological advances would solve many of humanity's problems. The introduction of the oral contraceptive pill in 1960 was to have a profound impact on relations between men and women. The so-called 'baby boom' generation, born in the aftermath of the war, came to adulthood in the 1960s and defined that decade as one of protest against the mistakes of previous generations. The assassination of the American president John F. Kennedy on 22 November 1963 is often viewed as a turning point in the Cold War, while the American war in Vietnam became the focus of unprecedented levels of international protest. Old values and traditional views were challenged as the televisual age shrank the world to fit into a smaller screen.

1970s AND 1980s

The 1970s brought political scandals in America; economic upheaval; increasing unemployment and industrial strikes in Britain; and challenges to 'male chauvinism' by the **feminist** movement.

Margaret Thatcher's policy of monetarism and privatisation in the 1980s was opposed by the trade union movement, and legislation was introduced to limit the unions' power. Britain went to war against the Argentinian occupation of the Falkland Islands in 1982, and after the war the Tories were returned to power with a huge majority.

The political confrontations that characterised the mid 1980s, in particular the miners' strike of 1984, redefined British society. Thatcher's view that 'There is no such thing as society. There are individual men and women and there are families', given in an interview with *Woman's Own* magazine (31 October 1987), summed up the change in outlook.

CONTEXT A04

William Beveridge (1879–1963) was a liberal economist commissioned by the British government to report on the ways Britain could be rebuilt after the Second World War. He recommended that the government should take steps to overcome the five 'Giant Evils' facing society – 'Want, Disease, Ignorance, Squalor and Idleness' – and in 1945 the Labour government announced the introduction of the welfare state as suggested in his 1942 Beveridge Report.

The end of the Cold War era was in sight when Mikhail Gorbachev, leader of the USSR, rejected Stalinist dictatorship and announced the policies of glasnost and perestroika in 1985. Within six years the USSR had ceased to exist and the Cold War was officially over. With the demolition of the Berlin Wall starting in 1989, the 'Iron Curtain' in Eastern Europe was no more. But in China in the same year, student protests for reform were crushed in Tiananmen Square.

1990S AND BEYOND

In 1990 South Africa ended years of apartheid rule and released Nelson Mandela after twenty-seven years in prison. In the 1990s satellite communications made the internet available to the public, creating the possibility of instant global communication. America took its main European ally, Britain, into the first war in the Gulf in 1991.

STUDY FOCUS: TWENTIETH-CENTURY WOMEN A04

Carter was very much aware of herself as a late twentieth-century woman. As she once stated: 'The sense of limitless freedom that I, as a woman, sometimes feel *is* that of a new kind of being. Because I simply could not have existed, as I am, in any other preceding time or place. I am the pure product of an advanced, industrialised, post-imperialist country in decline' ('Notes from the Front Line', in *On Gender and Writing*, edited by Michelene Wandor, 1983, p. 73).

CHECK THE FILM A03

The television drama series *Boys from the Blackstuff* was first broadcast in 1982. Written by Liverpool playwright Alan Bleasdale (b.1946), the series is regarded as a definitive dramatic response to the Thatcher era. Both comic and tragic, it is a sweeping depiction of individuals whose lives are being changed by governmental policies of privatisation and monetarism.

LITERARY BACKGROUND

MEDIEVAL INFLUENCES

Angela Carter's wide interests in literature and philosophy are represented in the depth and range of **intertextual** reference in her stories. She is a self-consciously literary writer. Her interests in medieval literature influence *The Bloody Chamber* in two important and definitive ways.

Medieval writers were conscious that they were writing for an audience that would hear their tales rather than read them. The element of the human voice in the **narrative** is something Carter strives to achieve. She is always present as the storyteller, even when the narrative voice is given to a character within the story. In the Middle Ages, illiteracy was the norm. Visual **imagery** was, therefore, second only to the spoken word in its power to communicate. Carter is a highly visual writer, and her use of **symbol**, **metaphor** and **allegory** harks back to that time.

Allegory – where the story has a deeper, hidden meaning – is a significant narrative device in medieval literature and works in a variety of ways to speak to the reader. Medieval texts were written to be read aloud to non-readers, and allegory is another way of showing to the reader the meanings within the story. Carter uses her characters in a similar way to that in which Everyman is used in medieval morality plays. Just as Everyman is both a character in the drama, and a device representing not only mankind but every individual in the audience, so Carter's readers – female readers in particular – are drawn to sympathise and identify with her characters, their personal dilemmas and their moral journeys.

POSTMODERN AND MANNERIST INFLUENCES

The influence of **postmodernism** is also present in Carter's writing (see also **Contemporary approaches**), most specifically the idea of 'systems of significance' – signs and symbols which, when experienced in conjunction with other signs and symbols, create meaning. The most familiar 'system of significance' is, perhaps, language: the spoken and written word. For example the word 'chair' can be seen as a symbol representing a thing that you sit on.

Carter distanced herself from postmodernism. She considered it introverted, an academic exercise that involved merely writing 'books about books' without any connection to the world beyond literature. She compared this approach to the sixteenth-century **Mannerist** movement in art. Not meant as a compliment, this comparison shows that she thought postmodernism to be the opposite of a progressive development in theory.

But there are also connections between Carter's work and the style of Mannerism, particularly it the way that it rejects symmetry and harmony. Mannerist painters typically depicted emotional intensity through the use of distorted perspectives, intricate composition and vivid imagery. They also used **ambiguity** in a way that is also present in Carter's work. Carter was careful in her construction of her stories and concerned that her readers found her meaning, but was also quite relaxed about being read in different ways, and at different levels of meaning, by different readers: her stories acknowledge and allow that possibility.

CRITICAL DEBATES

READING CRITICALLY

This section provides a range of critical viewpoints and perspectives on *The Bloody Chamber* and gives a broad overview of key debates, interpretations and theories proposed since the collection was published. It is important to bear in mind the variety of interpretations and responses this text has produced, many of them shaped by the critics' own backgrounds and historical contexts.

ORIGINAL RECEPTION

Ellen Cronan Rose in 'Through the Looking Glass: When Women Tell Fairy Tales' (1983, pp. 207–27) was one of the first critics to give a serious critical response to *The Bloody Chamber*. She approved of the reversal of stereotypical gender roles as 'a critique of the idea of adult womanhood sanctioned by patriarchy and a suggested alternative to it'. This approval was not shared by Patricia Duncker in 'Re-Imagining the Fairy Tales: Angela Carter's Bloody Chambers' (1984, pp. 3–14), and she pulled no punches in her attack on Carter: 'But the infernal trap inherent in the fairy tale, which fits the form to its purpose, to be the carrier of ideology, proves too complex and pervasive to avoid.' In other words, Duncker believed Carter had attempted an impossible and ultimately pointless task, in that the form of the fairy tale cannot be used without the new version being contaminated by the ideas and values of the original tale.

LATER CRITICISM

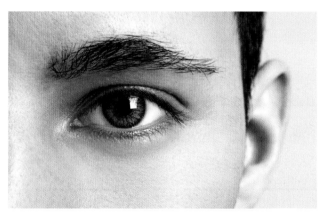

On Angela Carter's death in 1992, many obituaries were written in praise of her writing. However, Merja Makinen, in 'Angela Carter's *The Bloody Chamber* and the Decolonization of Feminine Sexuality' (1992, pp. 2–15), argued against the obituarists who praised her as a 'benign magician', creating a mystic aura around her craft as a writer. This approach, Makinen suggested, misrepresented the true power of Carter's writing: 'Carter's work has consistently dealt with representations of the physical abuse of women …, of women alienated from themselves within the male gaze, and conversely of women who grab their sexuality and fight back, of women troubled by and even empowered by their own violence' (p. 3).

In 1998 Aidan Day in *Angela Carter: The Rational Glass* prefaced his views with the **oxymoronic** statement 'Carter's fiction is a bit extreme' (p. 1), and he is clearly ill at ease with aspects of sexuality represented by Carter in *The Bloody Chamber*, particularly 'female sexuality' (p. 151). Day believes this to be 'difficult ground … for a male critic'. He later disqualifies himself from commenting on Carter's representation of female desire on the grounds that 'As a man, I am not competent to judge the psychological veracity or otherwise of this image of positive female response to male pornographic attention' (p. 160). It could be argued, however, that Day fails to see the irony in his attitude. It is men's refusal to understand women that Carter seeks to overthrow in her stories.

Other critics have commented on Carter's tendency to return to and retell certain tales. Jacqueline Pearson in her foreword to *Re-Visiting Angela Carter: Texts, Contexts, Intertexts* (2006), suggests that: 'for Carter allusion helps to provide a language for ambiguity' and that 'one way of achieving this is to tell and retell certain central narratives' (p. ix).

Jago Morrison in *Contemporary Fiction* (2003) summarises *The Bloody Chamber* as 'an archaeological investigation of gender representation, coupled with a set of creative attempts at subversion', and so dismisses it as purely **feminist** fiction (p. 168). Morrison seems to regard Carter's stories as academic exercises in creative writing that have failed.

Sarah Gamble in *Angela Carter: A Literary Life* (2005) comments on how the fairy-tale form 'places the figure of the story-teller centre stage' (p. 156) and how Carter created a new public identity as a storyteller following the publication of *The Bloody Chamber*. Gamble recognises that Carter won this identity on her own terms, as 'pleasing her audience by providing them with a comfortably reassuring read did not feature on her list of priorities' (p. 156). Gamble gives what she believes is evidence of the enduring value of Carter's work: 'Most of Carter's writing remains in print: it is read by general readers and studied at universities, and has lost none of its capacity to shock, startle and delight' (p. 205).

CONTEMPORARY APPROACHES

FEMINISM

Despite the individual power of these tales, another theme can be traced through them as a collection – the development of the female role. This development is striking in its simplicity: Carter's female 'victims' become gradually empowered by embracing desire and passion as a human animal. To exaggerate this aspect of the collection would diminish the impact of each tale in itself, but it does reveal *The Bloody Chamber* as very much a product of its time and of the concerns of the feminist movement in the late 1970s. The issue of the empowerment of women and, particularly, the challenge to conventional depictions of heterosexual relationships in literature, art and the media were part of the controversial agenda of feminists of the period. Feminists today might argue that it is easy, with hindsight, to underestimate how male-dominated British society was at the time. They might also argue that it is just as easy to over-estimate the progress towards equal opportunity that has made a feminist point of view almost passé for many young people now.

Feminist criticism has many different strands, each of which views Carter in a very different way according to its political and sexual orientation. Patricia Duncker in 'Re-Imagining the Fairy Tales: Angela Carter's Bloody Chambers' (1984, pp. 3–14) voices a particularly hostile perspective: 'Carter envisages women's sensuality simply as a response to male arousal.'

Certainly Carter won little praise from feminist critics for *The Sadeian Woman* (1979), and the reaction to her attitude towards the Marquis de Sade and sexuality in that work was applied to *The Bloody Chamber*. In *The Sadeian Woman*, Carter suggested that pornography could be used to question and overturn 'the contempt for women that distorts our culture'. Carter also thought that the writings of the Marquis de Sade suggested the possibility of 'moral pornography' because she found his **ideology** of individual freedom 'an ideology not inimical to women'. This was not a popular view among feminists and remains controversial. Andrea Dworkin in *Pornography: Men Possessing Women* (1981) denounces Carter as a 'pseudo-feminist' (p. 84); Susanne Kappeler in *The Pornography of Representation* (1986) accuses Carter of attempting a kind of literary rehabilitation of de Sade, 'the multiple rapist and murderer' (p. 133). Duncker simply dismisses Carter's belief that de Sade 'put pornography in the service of women' as 'utter nonsense' (in 'Re-Imagining the Fairy Tales: Angela Carter's Bloody Chambers', p. 8).

Nanette Altevers in 'Gender Matters in *The Sadeian Woman*' (1994, pp. 18–23) argues in Carter's defence that fairy tales perpetuate 'contempt for women' and that Carter's stories explore 'the current relations between the sexes' and challenge the convention that sexual freedom is the preserve of men only.

Sarah Gamble argues in *The Fiction of Angela Carter: A Reader's Guide to Essential Criticism* (2001) that for the later critics, such as Lucie Armitt, 'the issue of sexual politics is removed from the central position it has hitherto occupied in analyses of this text' (p. 132). Influenced by **postmodernism**, she notes that commentaries are more interested in the shifting and interrelated forms of the **narratives**. Armitt suggests in 'The Fragile Frames of *The Bloody Chamber*' that 'one of the major problems facing the reader of these ten stories is that they seem always to be dissolving into each other' (1997, p. 97).

MARXISM

Marxism is the philosophy for social change established by Karl Marx (1818–83) and Friedrich Engels (1820–95) in the nineteenth century.

In approaching *The Bloody Chamber* from the perspective of Marxist literary criticism, the text becomes a prism which refracts the society in which its writer lived: a time when every

element of society – class, politics, social status, morality – was open to question (see **Part Five: Historical background**). Carter questions society's values from a **feminist** and socialist perspective. Issues of gender dominate the tales. She questions the restricted choices and limited economic independence of the female characters, all of whom are expected to play out the roles defined for them by the male characters. She focuses on female empowerment and self-reliance; and the need to resist and escape tradition through personal choice. Above all, she recognises that changes in a **patriarchal** society will come from women, not from men, who are unwilling to give up their positions of power. But these issues of gender are not easily disentangled from issues of class for Carter, and class struggle is a key tenet of Marxism. As a **materialist**, Carter grounds her fantasy in carefully selected realistic detail; as a storyteller, Carter explores how fantasy frees the imagination from the constraint of **realism**.

For Carter, the most important aspect of the tales is her characters making changes happen in their lives; they are not passive victims of circumstance. In this respect they can be viewed as icons of the 'call to action' of the 1970s feminist and socialist movements.

CHECK THE BOOK **A03**

In *The Penelopiad* (2005) Margaret Atwood revisits Homer's *The Odyssey* from the viewpoint of Penelope, the long-suffering wife of Odysseus.

CHECK THE BOOK **A04**

The Marxist academic Terry Eagleton asserts in *Marxism and Literary Criticism* (1976) that his aim is 'to explain the literary work more fully … giving sensitive attention to its forms, styles and meanings … as a product of a particular history'.

PART SIX: GRADE BOOSTER

ASSESSMENT FOCUS

WHAT ARE YOU BEING ASKED TO FOCUS ON?

The questions or tasks you are set will be based around the four **Assessment Objectives**, **AO1** to **AO4**.

You may get more marks for certain **AOs** than others depending on which unit you are working on. Check with your teacher if you are unsure.

WHAT DO THESE AOs ACTUALLY MEAN?

ASSESSMENT OBJECTIVES	MEANING?
AO1 Articulate creative, informed and relevant responses to literary texts, using appropriate terminology and concepts, and coherent, accurate written expression.	You write about texts in accurate, clear and precise ways so that what you have to say is clear to the marker. You use literary terms (e.g. **metaphor**) or refer to concepts (e.g. **Gothic**) in relevant places.
AO2 Demonstrate detailed critical understanding in analysing the ways in which structure, form and language shape meanings in literary texts.	You show that you understand the specific techniques and methods used by the writer(s) to create the text (e.g. **symbolism**, **imagery**, etc). You can explain clearly how these methods affect the meaning.
AO3 Explore connections and comparisons between different literary texts, informed by interpretations of other readers.	You are able to see relevant links between different texts. You are able to comment on how others (such as critics) view the text.
AO4 Demonstrate understanding of the significance and influence of the contexts in which literary texts are written and received.	You can explain how social, historical, political or personal backgrounds to the texts affected the writer and how the texts were read when they were first published and at different times since.

WHAT DOES THIS MEAN FOR YOUR REVISION?

Depending on the course you are following, you could be asked to:

- Respond to a general question about the text as a whole. For example:

Explore Carter's presentation of men in *The Bloody Chamber*.

- Write about an aspect of *The Bloody Chamber* which is also a feature of other text(s) you are studying. These questions may take the form of a challenging statement or quotation which you are invited to discuss. For example:

'Gothic literature is concerned with the breaking of normal moral and social codes.' Discuss.

- Focus on the particular similarities, links, contrasts and differences between this text and others. For example:

Compare and contrast how writers present power in *The Bloody Chamber* and the other text(s) you have studied.

EXAMINER'S TIP

Make sure you know how many marks are available for each **AO** in the task you are set. This can help you divide up your time or decide how much attention to give each aspect.

TARGETING A HIGH GRADE

It is very important to understand the progression from a lower grade to a high grade. In all cases, it is not enough simply to mention some key points and references – instead, you should explore them in depth, drawing out what is interesting and relevant to the question or issue.

TYPICAL C GRADE FEATURES

FEATURES	EXAMPLES
A01 You use critical vocabulary accurately, and your arguments make sense, are relevant and focus on the task. You show detailed knowledge of the text.	*The narrator of 'The Bloody Chamber' is young and naive, having seen little of the world. Her perspective is not unreliable, but she does not recognise the danger of her situation as clearly as the reader.*
A02 You can say how some specific aspects of form, structure and language shape meanings.	*Carter presents the forest as a place of danger, a symbol of the wild desires that lie within human nature.*
A03 You consider in detail the connections between texts and also how interpretations of texts differ, with some relevant supporting references.	*Carter's monsters are not supernatural, like Stoker's Dracula, or the result of scientific ambition like Frankenstein's monster. Carter's monsters are simply men.*
A04 You can write about a range of contextual factors and make some specific and detailed links between these and the task or text.	*These stories reflect a period of great change for women, from the sexual liberation of the 1960s to the battle for sexual equality in the workplace, at home and in society in general.*

TYPICAL FEATURES OF AN A OR A* RESPONSE

FEATURES	EXAMPLES
A01 You use appropriate critical vocabulary and a technically fluent style. Your arguments are well structured, coherent and always relevant, with a very sharp focus on task.	*The image of the girl 'between the paws of the tender wolf' becomes a metaphor for the balance and harmony that female acceptance of human nature, and the animal nature within, can bring. This is not a degradation of human nature but a broadening of our understanding of the term.*
A02 You explore and analyse key aspects of form, structure and language and evaluate perceptively how they shape meanings.	*Carter's use of traditional fairy-tale settings provides a familiar background against which unfamiliar perspectives stand out. The castle becomes a symbol of power, the forest a symbol of the unknown, within which Carter's women face archetypes of danger and oppression.*
A03 You show a detailed and perceptive understanding of issues raised through connections between texts and can consider different interpretations with a sharp evaluation of their strengths and weaknesses. You have a range of excellent supportive references.	*It is easy to dismiss Carter's male characters as the typical monsters of Gothic fiction, perverted by their sexual depravity, distorted in their animal nature. Yet, just as Frankenstein's creature achieves our sympathy more readily than his creator, so we come to empathise with the Duke trapped in his werewolf nature, and the Tiger hidden behind his mask.*
A04 You show deep, detailed and relevant understanding of how contextual factors link to the text or task.	*Carter does not simply present women escaping the oppression of men. Hers is not the struggle for equality which was a focus of society throughout the decade in which these stories were written. Carter takes on the feminist ideas of the oppression of gender to present women escaping the image and self-image impressed on them and inherited by them.*

HOW TO WRITE HIGH-QUALITY RESPONSES

The quality of your writing – how you express your ideas – is vital for getting a higher grade, and **AO1** and **AO2** are specifically about how you respond.

FIVE KEY AREAS

The quality of your responses can be broken down into **five** key areas.

1. THE STRUCTURE OF YOUR ANSWER/ESSAY

- First, get **straight to the point in your opening paragraph**. Use a sharp, direct first sentence that deals with a key aspect and then follow up with evidence or detailed reference.
- **Put forward an argument or point of view** (you won't **always** be able to challenge or take issue with the essay question, but generally, where you can, you are more likely to write in an interesting way).
- **Signpost your ideas** with connectives and references which help the essay flow.
- **Don't repeat points already made**, not even in the conclusion, unless you have something new to add.

TARGETING A HIGH GRADE   A01

Here's an example of an opening paragraph that gets straight to the point, addressing the question: **Explore Carter's presentation of women in *The Bloody Chamber*.**

Carter's presentation of women focuses on their sexuality and their ability to change. Some of Carter's female characters must take control of their lives from the men who seek to control them, while others must change themselves, even their species in one case.

Immediate focus on task and key words and example from the text

2. USE OF TITLES, NAMES, ETC.

This is a simple, but important, tip to stay on the right side of the examiners.

- Make sure that you spell correctly the titles of the texts, chapters, authors and so on. Present them correctly too, with single or double quotation marks and capitals as appropriate. For example, 'The Tiger's Bride'.
- Use the **full title**, unless there is a good reason not to (e.g. it's very long).
- Use the term 'text' or 'collection' rather than 'book'. Using the word 'text', shows the examiner that you are thinking about *The Bloody Chamber* as a work of literature, created by the author.
- It's also important that you remember to distinguish between 'The Bloody Chamber' the short story, and *The Bloody Chamber* the collection as a whole. You can do this by consistently referring to either the story of 'The Bloody Chamber' or the collection.

EXAMINER'S TIP ✓

Answer the question set, not the question you'd like to have been asked! Examiners say that often students will be set a question on one aspect of the text (for example, the presentation of women) but end up writing almost as much about another (such as the presentation of men). Or they write about one aspect from the question (for example, 'nightmarish terrors') but ignore another (such as 'moral behaviour'). **Stick to the question**, and answer **all parts of it**.

3. EFFECTIVE QUOTATIONS

Do not 'bolt on' quotations to the points you make. You will get some marks for including them, but examiners will not find your writing very fluent.

The best quotations are:

- Relevant
- Not too long
- Integrated into your argument/sentence.

TARGETING A HIGH GRADE   A01

Here is an example of a quotation successfully embedded in a sentence:

Carter's warning is clear: women should fear men who are 'hairy on the inside' no matter how they may appear on the outside.

Remember – quotations can be a well-selected set of three or four single words or phrases embedded in a sentence to build a picture or explanation, or they can be longer ones that are explored and picked apart.

> **GRADE BOOSTER**   A02
>
> It's important to remember that *The Bloody Chamber* is a text created by Carter – thinking about the choices Carter makes with language and narrative will not only alert you to her methods as an author but also her intentions, i.e. the effect she seeks to create.

4. TECHNIQUES AND TERMINOLOGY

By all means mention literary terms, techniques, conventions or people (for example, '**paradox**' or '**archetype**' or 'de Sade') but make sure that you:

- Understand what they mean
- Are able to link them to what you're saying
- Spell them correctly.

5. GENERAL WRITING SKILLS

Try to write in a way that sounds professional and uses standard English. This does not mean that your writing will lack personality – just that it will be authoritative.

- Avoid **colloquial** or everyday expressions such as 'got', 'all right', 'OK' and so on.
- Use terms such as 'convey', 'suggest', 'imply', 'infer' to explain the writer's methods.
- Refer to 'we' when discussing the audience/reader.
- Avoid assertions and generalisations; don't just state a general point of view (*The Marquis is a typical Gothic villain because he's evil*), but analyse closely with clear evidence and textual detail.

TARGETING A HIGH GRADE   A01

For example, note the professional approach here:

Carter's use of the symbol of blood suggests not only the Snow Child's death but also her virginity. We may be shocked at the bluntness of this image, and at Carter's explicit description of the Duke's action, but perhaps most shocking (though entirely typical of the collection) is the absence of any explicit or indeed implied moral judgement.

QUESTIONS WITH STATEMENTS, QUOTATIONS OR VIEWPOINTS

One type of question you may come across includes a statement, quotation or viewpoint from another reader.

These questions ask you to respond to, or argue for/against, a specific point of view or critical interpretation.

For *The Bloody Chamber* these questions will typically be like this:

- **'Gothic literature is concerned with the breaking of normal moral and social codes.' To what extent do you agree?**

- **'The depiction of violence in *The Bloody Chamber* is so relentless that it soon loses its power to shock.' How far do you agree with this statement?**

- **How far do you agree with the idea that *The Bloody Chamber* shows humanity at its worst?**

- **To what extent do you agree that Gothic literature always has a moral for the reader?**

The key thing to remember is that you are being asked to **respond to a critical interpretation** of the text – in other words, to come up with **your own 'take'** on the idea or viewpoint in the task.

KEY SKILLS REQUIRED

The table below provides help and advice on answering questions about the role of women in the collection, and about contrasts between the tales:

SKILL	WHAT DOES THIS MEAN?	HOW DO I ACHIEVE THIS?
Consider different interpretations	There will be more than one way of looking at the given question. For example, critics might be divided about the presentation of women in the collection.	• Show you have considered these different interpretations in your answer. For example: *It is true that many of the women in Carter's tales show their strength by taking control of their situations. However it could equally be argued that they do this, not by empowering themselves, but by disempowering the men who control them.*
Write with a clear, personal voice	Your own 'take' on the question is made obvious to the marker. You are not just repeating other people's ideas, but offering what **you** think.	• Although you may mention different perspectives on the task, you settle on your own view. • Use language that shows careful, but confident, consideration. For example: *Although it has been said that … I feel that …*
Construct a coherent argument	The examiner or marker can follow your train of thought so that your own viewpoint is clear to him or her.	• Write in clear paragraphs that deal logically with different aspects of the question. • Support what you say with well-selected and relevant evidence. • Use a range of connectives to help 'signpost' your argument. For example: *There are clear connections between some of the tales. For example, both 'The Tiger's Bride' and 'The Courtship of Mr Lyon' draw on the same source. Yet there are significant differences, most notably in the final metamorphosis from beast to man in the former, and from woman to beast in the latter.*

ANSWERING A 'VIEWPOINT' QUESTION

Here is an example of a typical question on *The Bloody Chamber*:

'The depiction of violence in *The Bloody Chamber* is so relentless that it soon loses its power to shock.' How far do you agree with this statement?

STAGE 1: DECODE THE QUESTION

Underline/highlight the **key words**, and make sure you understand what the statement, quotation or viewpoint is saying. In this case:

Key words = *violence/relentless/loses/shock*

The viewpoint/idea expressed = *Carter's use of violence is intended to shock the reader. After a point, the reader becomes immune to the violence and is no longer surprised by it.*

STAGE 2: DECIDE WHAT YOUR VIEWPOINT IS, AND WHICH STORIES YOU'LL REFER TO

Examiners have stated that they tend to reward a strong view which is clearly put. Think about the question – can you take issue with it? Disagreeing strongly can lead to higher marks, provided you have **genuine evidence** to support your point of view. Don't disagree just for the sake of it. If you've been asked to write about more than one story from the collection, decide now which stories you will write about – it's important to choose the stories that you feel best correspond to the question.

STAGE 3: DECIDE HOW TO STRUCTURE YOUR ANSWER

Pick out the key points you wish to make, and decide on the order in which you will present them. Keep this basic plan to hand while you write your response.

STAGE 4: WRITE YOUR RESPONSE

You could start by expanding on the statement or viewpoint expressed in the question.

● For example, in **paragraph 1**:

The viewpoint expressed in the question suggests that it is Carter's intention to shock the reader and that this shock diminishes as the reader encounters frequent episodes of violence.

This could help by setting up the various ideas you will choose to explore, argue for/against, and so on. But do not just repeat what the question says or just say what you are going to do. Get straight to the point. For example:

However, Carter has, I think, a range of intentions beyond shocking the reader which her use of violent imagery, violent characters and their violent actions achieves – but which she also achieves in a variety of more subtle ways.

Then, proceed to set out the different arguments or critical perspectives, including your own. This might be done by dealing with specific aspects or elements of the stories you've chosen one by one. Consider giving 1–2 paragraphs to explore each aspect in turn. Discuss the strengths and weaknesses in each particular point of view. For example:

● **Paragraph 2**: first aspect:

*To answer whether this interpretation is valid, we need to **first of all** look at …*

It is clear from this that …/a strength of this argument is

However, I believe this suggests that …/a weakness in this argument is

● **Paragraph 3**: a new focus or aspect:

Turning our attention to the critical idea that … it could be said that …

● **Paragraphs 4, 5, etc.**: develop the argument, building a convincing set of points.

Furthermore, if we look at …

● **Last paragraph**: end with a clear statement of your view, without simply listing all the points you have made.

It is clear therefore, that to say Carter's depiction of violence loses its power to shock is not entirely convincing/close to the truth/only partly true, as I believe that …

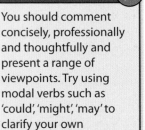

EXAMINER'S TIP

You should comment concisely, professionally and thoughtfully and present a range of viewpoints. Try using modal verbs such as 'could', 'might', 'may' to clarify your own interpretation. For additional help on **Using critical interpretations and perspectives** see pages 106 and 107.

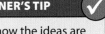

EXAMINER'S TIP

Note how the ideas are clearly signposted through a range of connectives and linking phrases, such as 'However' and 'Turning our attention to …'.

COMPARING *THE BLOODY CHAMBER* WITH OTHER TEXTS

As part of your assessment, you may have to compare *The Bloody Chamber* with or link it to other texts that you have studied. These may be plays, novels or even poetry. You may also have to link or draw in references from texts written by critics.

A typical linking or comparison question might be:

> **Compare the presentation of relationships between men and women in *The Bloody Chamber* and other text(s) you have studied.**

THE TASK

Your task is likely to be on a method, issue, viewpoint or key aspect that is common to *The Bloody Chamber* and the other text(s), so you will need to:

> **Evaluate the issue** or statement and have an **open-minded approach**. The best answers suggest meaning**s** and interpretation**s** (plural):
> - Do you agree with the statement? Is this aspect more important in one text than in another? Why? How? (Is the relationship between men and women central or not? What do you understand by the phrase anyway?)
> - What are the different ways this question or aspect can be read or viewed?
> - Can you challenge this viewpoint? If so, what evidence is there? How can you present it in a thoughtful, reflective way?

> **Express original or creative approaches** fluently:
> - This isn't about coming up with entirely new ideas, but you need to show that you're actively engaged with thinking about the question and are not just reeling off things you have learned.
> - **Synthesise** your ideas – pull ideas and points together to create something fresh.
> - This is a linking/comparison response, so ensure that you guide your reader through your ideas logically, clearly and with professional language.

> **Know what to compare/contrast**: **form**, **structure** and **language** will **always** be central to your response, even where you also have to write about characters, contexts or culture.
> - Think about standard versus more unconventional narration (use of **allusion**, flashback, **foreshadowing**, or narrative voice which leads to dislocation or difficulty in reading).
> - Consider different characteristic uses of language (lengths of sentences, formal/informal style, balance of dialogue and narration; difference between prose treatment of an idea and a poem).
> - Look at a variety of **symbols**, **images** and **motifs** (how they represent concerns of the author/time; what they are and how and where they appear; how they link to critical perspectives; their purposes, effects and impact on the collection).
> - Consider aspects of genre (to what extent do Carter and the author(s) of the other work(s) conform to/challenge/subvert particular genres or styles of writing?).

WRITING YOUR RESPONSE

The depth and extent of your answer will depend on how much you have to write, but the key will be to **explore in detail**, and **link between ideas and texts**. Let us use the example from above:

Compare the presentation of relationships between men and women in *The Bloody Chamber* and other text(s) you have studied.

INTRODUCTION TO YOUR RESPONSE

- Discuss quickly what 'relationships between men and women' means, and how well this applies to your texts.
- Mention in support the range of male/female relationships in *The Bloody Chamber* and the other text(s) – not just sexual relationships, but parent/child, master/servant and other archetypal relationships.
- You could begin with a powerful quotation that you use to launch into your response. For example:

> *"'There is a striking resemblance between the act of love and the ministrations of a torturer,"*
> *opined my husband's favourite poet.'*
>
> *The relationship between men and women is rarely conventional and, occasionally, unrecognisably distorted in Carter's collection "The Bloody Chamber". However, it is not solely presented as unresolvable 'torture', disappointment and dysfunction.*

MAIN BODY OF YOUR RESPONSE

- **Point 1**: start with a specific example of a male/female relationship in *The Bloody Chamber* and what it implies about the nature of these relationships. What is your view? Are there any similarities between the male/female relationships in the texts you are writing about? What do the critics say? Whose views will you use? Are there contextual/cultural factors to consider?
- **Point 2**: now cover a new factor or aspect through comparison or contrast of this relationship with another in a second text. How is the new relationship in this text presented **differently or similarly** by the writer according to language, form, structures used; why was this done in this way; how does it reflect the writer's interests? What do the critics say? Are there contextual/cultural factors to consider?
- **Points 3, 4, 5, etc.**: address a range of new factors and aspects, for example, other male/female relationships – e.g. father and daughter – or aspects of them, **either** just within *The Bloody Chamber* **or** in both *The Bloody Chamber* and another text. In what different ways do you respond to these (with more empathy, greater criticism, less interest?) – and why?

> *The father/daughter relationship is similarly presented as one of patriarchal domination and oppression. Although we may have some sympathy for the intentions of Miss Lamb's father in 'The Courtship of Mr Lyon', it is hard to forgive him the sacrifice of his daughter to atone for his crime of petty theft.*

CONCLUSION

- Synthesise elements of what you have said into a final paragraph that fluently, succinctly and inventively leaves the reader/examiner with the sense that you have engaged with this task and the texts. For example:

> *Carter, in keeping with the sources from which she draws her tales, places her protagonists in perilous relationships. She emphasises the idea that this peril is the result of imbalance between the sexes, of male dominance and female submission.*

EXAMINER'S TIP

Be creative with your conclusion! It's the last thing the examiner will read and your chance to make your mark.

RESPONDING TO A GENERAL QUESTION ABOUT *THE BLOODY CHAMBER*

You may also be asked to write about a specific aspect of *The Bloody Chamber* – but as it relates to either the **whole text** or to **at least two of the stories**. For example:

> Explore the use Carter makes of Gothic and fairy-tale elements in at least two of the stories from *The Bloody Chamber*.

This means you should:

- Focus on *both* the Gothic *and* the fairy-tale elements (not all 'magical' things)
- **Explain their use** – **how** they are used by Carter in terms of action, character and furthering ideas/themes. Consider the literary conventions linked to them – storytelling and suspense?
- Look at aspects of **at least two** stories, not just one

STRUCTURING YOUR RESPONSE

You need a clear, logical plan, as for all tasks that you do.

It is impossible to write about every section or part of the text, so you will need to:

- Quickly note 5–6 key points or aspects to build your essay around:
  Point a: *'Little Red Riding Hood' subverted*
  Point b: *draws on European werewolf tradition*
  Point c: *forest as typical Gothic setting – beyond civilisation*
  Point d: *wolf as Gothic monster – symbol of fear, danger, and sexual appetite*
  Point e: *subversion of metamorphosis*
- Then decide the most effective or logical order. For example, point a, then c, d, b and e.

You could begin with your key or main idea, with supporting evidence/references, followed by your further points (perhaps two paragraphs for each). For example:

Paragraph 1: first key point: *'Little Red Riding Hood' subverted*
Paragraph 2: expand out, link into other areas: *wolf not simply a symbol of danger but also of freedom, indeed truth – men who can transform to reveal true nature – 'hairy on the inside'*
Paragraph 3: change direction, introduce new aspect/point: *forest as Gothic setting*
And so on.

- For your **conclusion**, use a compelling way to finish, perhaps repeating some or all of the key words from the question. For example, either:

End with your final point, but **add a last clause** which makes it clear what you think is key to the question:

e.g. *Carter combines elements of the fairy tale and the Gothic tradition to produce not a retelling of the well known tale but a new story examining the power of transformation and the power of women.*
or:

End with a **new quotation** or an **aspect** that's **slightly different from** your main point.

Finally, as Carter draws 'The Company of Wolves' to a close, it is Christmas day: 'All silent, all still.' To the Gothic and the fairy tale, Carter adds a subversion of Christmas in a final and typically iconoclastic pagan flourish.

Or, of course, you can combine these endings.

EXAMINER'S TIP ✓

You may be asked to discuss other texts you have studied as well as *The Bloody Chamber* as part of your response. Once you have completed your response on the collection you could move on to discuss the same issues in your other texts. Begin with a simple linking phrase or sentence to launch straight into your first point about your next text, such as: *The same issue/idea is explored in a quite different way in [name of text] ... Here, ...*

WRITING ABOUT CONTEXTS

Assessment Objective 4 asks you to 'demonstrate understanding of the significance and influence of the contexts in which literary texts are written and received …'. This can mean:

- How the events, settings, politics and so on **of the time when the text was written** influenced the writer or help us to understand the collection's themes or concerns. For example, to what extent Carter might have been influenced by feminist debate in the 1970s.

or

- How events, settings, politics and so on **of the time when the text is read or seen** influences how it is understood. For example, would a reader of today still find Carter's depiction of women and society's attitude to them relevant?

THE CONTEXT FOR *THE BLOODY CHAMBER*

You might find the following table helpful for thinking about how particular aspects of the time contribute to our understanding of the collection and its themes. These are just examples – can you think of any others?

POLITICAL	LITERARY	PHILOSOPHICAL
Equality legislation of the 1970s Women leaders in political roles	Revisions of traditional tales, both feminist and other (re)versions Development of **intertextuality**	The second wave of **feminism** Theories of child development

SCIENTIFIC	CULTURAL	SOCIAL
Development of oral contraception	The sexual revolution, especially as represented in other works of art such as film, television, etc	Attitudes to marriage

> **EXAMINER'S TIP** ✓
>
> Remember that linking the historical, literary or social context to the collection itself is key to achieving the best marks for AO4.

TARGETING A HIGH GRADE (A04)

Remember that the extent to which you write about these contexts will be determined by the marks available. Some questions or tasks may have very few marks allocated for **AO4**, but where you do have to refer to context the key thing is **not** to 'bolt on' your comments, or write a long, separate chunk of text on context and then 'go back' to the collection.

For example:

Don't just write:

The development of the oral contraceptive pill gave women freedom. It allowed them the sexual freedom which had, until then, been the preserve of men. More importantly, perhaps, it gave women a sense of control over their lives and, perhaps, even a sense of power. Female empowerment is important in "The Bloody Chamber" too.

Do write:

The entire collection of "The Bloody Chamber" is dominated by representations of female empowerment. In the same way that the oral contraceptive had allowed women to take control of their bodies and their sexuality, so Carter's female characters are able to reject men who seek to shape and control their relationships and can re-create them on their own terms.

USING CRITICAL INTERPRETATIONS AND PERSPECTIVES

THE 'MEANING' OF A TEXT

There are many viewpoints and perspectives on the 'meaning' of *The Bloody Chamber* and examiners will be looking for evidence that you have considered a range of these.

Broadly speaking, these different interpretations might relate to:

1. AUTHOR'S INTENTION

Carter's **intention** in writing these stories:

- Was she seeking to update fairy tales, making them socially and psychologically relevant to a modern reader? Or do the fairy tales simply provide an accessible and familiar foundation on which Carter builds her own ideas?

- Who was she writing these stories for – and why? To reflect the experience of the female reader? As cautionary tales for men? As an expression of her own understanding of the world?

- How does Carter make her tales relevant to her reader? Are they still relevant today?

2. IDEAS AND ISSUES

What the collection tells us about **particular ideas or issues** and how we can interpret these. For example:

- How society is constructed
- The role of men/women
- What the Gothic means
- Moral and social codes, etc.

3. LINKS AND CONNECTIONS

How the collection **links with, follows or pre-echoes** other texts, ideas. For example:

- Its cultural, historic and social influences, for example fairy tale, myth, the Gothic tradition
- How its language links to other texts or modes, such as philosophical works, folk tales, etc.

4. NARRATIVE STRUCTURE

How the stories are **constructed** and how Carter **makes** her narratives. For example:

- Do the stories follow a particular narrative convention?
- What is the function of specific events, characters, devices, etc in relation to narrative?
- What are the specific moments of tension, conflict, crisis and denouement in the stories? Do any stories share similar narrative patterns – and do we agree on what they are?

> **GRADE BOOSTER** **A03**
>
> Looking at texts such as Emily Gerard's *The Land Beyond the Forest: Facts, Figures and Fancies from Translyvania* (1888), an account of Transylvanian folklore, and Bram Stoker's novel *Dracula* (1897) could help your understanding of the Dracula legend around which 'The Lady of the House of Love' is based.

WRITING ABOUT CRITICAL PERSPECTIVES

The important thing to remember is that **you** are a critic too. Your job is to evaluate what a critic or school of criticism has said about the elements above, and arrive at your own conclusions.

In essence, you need to: **consider** the views of others, **synthesise** them, then decide on **your perspective**. For example:

EXPLAIN THE VIEWPOINTS

Critical view A about metamorphosis:

> *Bettelheim argues that animals in fairy tales represent our animal nature, specifically our sexuality, and that metamorphoses imply a liberation from sexual repression.*

Critical view B about metamorphosis:

> *Gamble argues that Carter uses metamorphoses to imply liberation from sexual repression but more importantly from the 'oppression of gender' – in other words, the construction of gender identity which is 'learned' through upbringing, education, family, etc.*

THEN SYNTHESISE AND ADD YOUR PERSPECTIVE

Synthesise these views whilst adding your own:

> *The idea that the inner beast in fairy tales expresses sexuality is argued by Bettelheim in "The Uses of Enchantment" and could be considered relevant in Carter's tales. For example, in 'The Tiger's Bride', Beauty's transformation resolves the conflict between man and woman as she accepts her lover and his animal nature. On the other hand, Gamble suggests that Carter not only uses such transformations to imply liberation from sexual repression but more specifically from 'the oppression of gender': she is not trapped or restrained by her femininity or her humanity.*
>
> *However, I feel that it might be the case that, in fact, Carter's use of transformation implies …*

GRADE BOOSTER **A03**

Remember that responses to *The Bloody Chamber* have changed over time, and that readers have reacted to the collection differently according to current morals and trends in literary criticism. It is important that you are aware of context when discussing the views of others.

TARGETING A HIGH GRADE **A03**

Make sure you have thoroughly explored the different types of criticism written about *The Bloody Chamber*. Critical interpretation of short story collections can range from reviews and comments written about the text at the time that it was first published through to critical analysis by a critic or reader writing today. Bear in mind that views of texts can change over time as values and experiences themselves change, and that criticism can be written for different purposes. Here are just two examples of different kinds of responses to *The Bloody Chamber*:

Critic 1 – '[Carter] could go much further than she does.' – Patricia Duncker

Critic 2 – 'Carter's fiction is a bit extreme.' – Aidan Day

What evidence might these critics use to support their points of view?

ANNOTATED SAMPLE ANSWERS

Below are extracts from two sample answers to the same question at different grades. Bear in mind that these are examples only, covering all four Assessment Objectives – you will need to check the type of question and the weightings given for the AOs when writing your coursework essay or practising for your exam.

> Question: **With reference to at least two stories, explore the idea that men are presented by Carter as tyrants and monsters.**

CANDIDATE 1

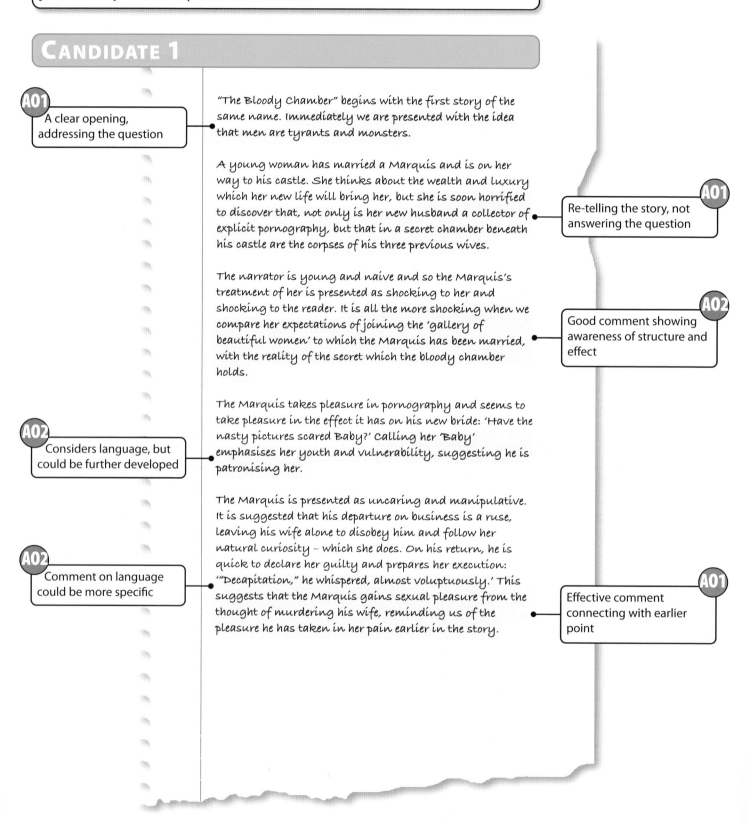

AO1 — A clear opening, addressing the question

"The Bloody Chamber" begins with the first story of the same name. Immediately we are presented with the idea that men are tyrants and monsters.

A young woman has married a Marquis and is on her way to his castle. She thinks about the wealth and luxury which her new life will bring her, but she is soon horrified to discover that, not only is her new husband a collector of explicit pornography, but that in a secret chamber beneath his castle are the corpses of his three previous wives.

AO1 — Re-telling the story, not answering the question

The narrator is young and naïve and so the Marquis's treatment of her is presented as shocking to her and shocking to the reader. It is all the more shocking when we compare her expectations of joining the 'gallery of beautiful women' to which the Marquis has been married, with the reality of the secret which the bloody chamber holds.

AO2 — Good comment showing awareness of structure and effect

AO2 — Considers language, but could be further developed

The Marquis takes pleasure in pornography and seems to take pleasure in the effect it has on his new bride: 'Have the nasty pictures scared Baby?' Calling her 'Baby' emphasises her youth and vulnerability, suggesting he is patronising her.

AO2 — Comment on language could be more specific

The Marquis is presented as uncaring and manipulative. It is suggested that his departure on business is a ruse, leaving his wife alone to disobey him and follow her natural curiosity – which she does. On his return, he is quick to declare her guilty and prepares her execution: '"Decapitation," he whispered, almost voluptuously.' This suggests that the Marquis gains sexual pleasure from the thought of murdering his wife, reminding us of the pleasure he has taken in her pain earlier in the story.

AO1 — Effective comment connecting with earlier point

A01 Not entirely relevant to the question

The Marquis presses the key to the bloody chamber on his young wife's forehead, leaving her with the bloodstain from the key on her forehead. This symbolises her disobedience and shame but could also suggest the attitudes of a patriarchal society to women who disobey their husbands. It was this attitude which Carter and other feminists wanted to change in the 1970s.

A04 Some attempt to place the text in context but could be made more specifically relevant and integrated

A03 Good comment, but rather undeveloped. What other tales/stories might 'red as blood' link with?

'The Snow Child' also presents the reader with a man who could be considered a monster. In the story, his desire for a girl as 'red as blood' immediately establishes the idea in our minds that he is bloodthirsty, and that his wishes go beyond the normal behaviour one would expect. This is backed up when he has sex with the dead girl, until she melts away. His behaviour is therefore definitely monstrous but is he a 'tyrant'? An argument against that is the fact that it is his wife's jealousy that leads her to kill the girl, not his – although he does nothing to protect the girl.

These two stories on their own therefore show that Carter does present men as tyrants and monsters but it is a bit too simplistic to say that all men in the stories are. Even the Count in 'The Snow Child' is not as evil as he might appear, otherwise why should he seem upset at the girl's death? He is a monster for what he does afterwards, but is perhaps not a 'tyrant' whereas the Marquis is both a monster and a tyrant, dominating his young wife and murdering his previous ones.

A02 Good, but needs further explanation

A01 Good linking between stories here. Could do so more often.

GRADE C

Comment

This answer clearly shows knowledge of the two texts and awareness of language and form (AO2). Initially it focuses on unnecessary retelling of the first story and would benefit from a more focused and specific exploration of language. Points are not entirely logically organised, suggesting a lack of planning. There is some undeveloped reference to AO4 context, and 'The Snow Child' is dealt with rather briefly.

For a B grade

- Keep focus throughout on 'how' the author tells the stories, not the stories themselves. (AO1)
- Unpick the layers of meaning – e.g. how does the word 'voluptuously' suggest the Marquis's pleasure? (AO2)
- Develop and integrate references to context more fully. (AO3)
- Look for opportunities to dig deeper and find links with other ideas, texts, etc. (AO4)

CANDIDATE 2

A01 Strong, well-expressed opening, focusing on the question

A first impression of a number of stories in the collection might suggest that Carter's male characters are tyrants or monsters or both. The father who gambles his daughter and loses, the husband who serially marries and murders, the werewolf that traps and beds a young girl, all suggest male traits of corruption, manipulation and appetite. However, though Carter presents us with a succession of beasts, they are not always what they seem.

A01 Clearly establishes the argument which the essay will develop

The Beast of 'The Tiger's Bride' is initially presented as an object of enigmatic fear. His very name, 'La Bestia!' strikes fear and wonder into the heart of the father's Italian landlady. His size, his painted mask, the 'growling impediment in his speech' all promise a true monster. In this, to an extent, Carter draws on and teases the reader's expectations of the fairy tale from which she has taken her inspiration.

A04 Excellent comment on literary context

To this, Carter adds a sense of sexual depravity: the Beast's 'one desire' to see the girl naked. The word 'desire' clearly emphasises his purpose which seems, at this point, to share something with the voyeurism of the Marquis in 'The Bloody Chamber'. Here Carter seems to be alluding to the feminist notion of the 'male gaze', suggesting that in his desire he seeks to control her.

A02 Close focus on language

A03 Strong comment connecting another story in the collection

A04 A partially developed comment on context

Yet here Carter introduces an element of humanity to the Beast. At the girl's refusal, the Beast indirectly presents her with a piece of jewellery magically formed from his own tears. This suggestion of forgiveness, of generosity, of emotion, instantly softens our perception of the monster. Carter continues to rehabilitate our perception of the Beast when it is he, not she, who presents himself unmasked and unclothed. This is the point at which their relationship changes, when Carter subverts the power relationship of the male gaze.

A02 Strong exploration of symbolism

A04 Further develops the earlier comment on context

A01 Key words signal relevance and keep the response on track

Ultimately the girl chooses to accept the Beast's animal nature, to be transformed by him and send her painted automaton double back to the world of men. She rejects the monstrous tyranny of her father, objectifying her as a trinket to be gambled and lost. She sheds 'the skins of a life in the world' and admires her 'beautiful fur'. She accepts, not only her lover's animal nature, but also her own.

A02 Implies awareness of language but lacks any developed comment

Indeed, the apparent tyrants and monsters of other stories may contain more contradictions than first appears. Take the Count in 'The Snow Child'. His monstrous behaviour leads not to satisfaction and fulfilment, but the death of the girl he has wished into being; it could even be said that what tyrannous behaviour there is in the story resides more in the actions of his wife, the Countess, who destroys the object of his desire rather than allowing him to have it. Yet this, too, is complicated. For having destroyed the girl using the mythic convention of rose/thorn, it is as if her own life has been drained and she is powerless as the Count commits necrophilia, and later the rose 'bites' her. The characters in the story seem to veer between tyranny and monstrosity, in a gendered power struggle.

What these tales show us is that 'tyranny' and particularly 'monstrosity' are never stable or unchanging concepts. Whilst it may be reasonably clear that the Marquis of 'The Bloody Chamber' is an unredeemable villain, many of the other stories present men who are capable of tenderness, and women who are capable of cruelty.

AO4
Good allusion to context

AO3
Opportunity to draw in critical interpretation here

GRADE A

Comment
This is a strong, well-expressed response (AO1). The candidate shows excellent knowledge and understanding of, and connections within, the text. There are several perceptive comments, particularly on how Carter shapes the reader's response, and also on the instability of one interpretation over another (AO3). There is some focus on language which could be more fully developed and explored (AO2), as could reference to critical theory, where appropriate (AO3).

For an A* grade
- Demonstrate original analysis and acknowledge a range of possible interpretations, especially critical theory. (AO3)
- Fully develop close analysis of language, its connotations and effect. (AO2)
- Consider more fully the relevance and impact of contextual factors. (AO4)
- More discussion needed of other stories to balance analysis of 'The Tiger's Bride'.

WORKING THROUGH A TASK

Now it's your turn to work through a task on *The Bloody Chamber*. The key is to:

- Read/decode the task/question
- Plan your points – then expand and link your points
- Draft your answer

TASK TITLE

'Carter has created a cruel world, filled with wicked people.' How do you respond to this view of *The Bloody Chamber*?

DECODE THE QUESTION: KEY WORDS

How do you respond ...?	= what are **my** views?
cruel	= malicious, causing pain and suffering
wicked	= morally wrong, harmful

PLAN AND EXPAND

- Key aspect: evidence of wicked people?

POINT	EXPANDED POINT	EVIDENCE
Point a *Men as monsters*	*Narrator of 'The Bloody Chamber': a victim of the Marquis or of her own naivety?* *The Tiger's bride: a victim of her father's gambling* *Relationship of Count, Countess and Snow Child*	*'Married three times within my own brief lifetime to three different graces, now ... he had invited me to join these gallery of beautiful women ...' (p. 5)* *'My father lost me to The Beast at cards.' (p. 56)*
Point b *Women as victims of circumstance*	Different aspects of this point expanded *You fill in*	Quotations 1–2 *You fill in*
Point c *Positive representations of men and women*	Different aspects of this point expanded *You fill in*	Quotations 1–2 *You fill in*

- Key aspect: evidence of cruel world?

You come up with three points, and then expand them

POINT	EXPANDED POINT	EVIDENCE
Point a *You fill in*	Different aspects of this point expanded *You fill in*	Quotations 1–2 *You fill in*
Point b *You fill in*	Different aspects of this point expanded *You fill in*	Quotations 1–2 *You fill in*
Point c *You fill in*	Different aspects of this point expanded *You fill in*	Quotations 1–2 *You fill in*

CONCLUSION

POINT	EXPANDED POINT	EVIDENCE
Key final point or overall view *You fill in*	Draw together and perhaps add a final further point to support your view *You fill in*	Final quotation to support your view *You fill in*

DEVELOP FURTHER

Now look back over your draft points and:

● Add further links or connections between the points to develop them further or synthesise what has been said, for example:

> *The characters' lives are shaped, both physically and emotionally, by the harsh winter environment. However, it is the forest setting which Carter uses to symbolise the dangers that lie beyond civilisation and lurk beneath its thin veneer.*

● Decide an order for your points/paragraphs – some may now be linked/connected and therefore **not** in the order of the table above.

Now draft your essay. If you're really stuck you can use the opening paragraph below to get you started.

> *The first tale in the collection, 'The Bloody Chamber', places a young, vulnerable, naive girl in the clutches of a sadistic misogynist with a history of murder. Isolated in a remote castle, married to a wicked man and facing a cruel execution, there seems little hope. Yet, the ability of women to escape seemingly unavoidable wickedness and inevitable cruelty runs throughout the collection …*

Once you've written your essay, turn to page 127 for a mark scheme on this question to see how well you've done.

FURTHER QUESTIONS

1. Consider the view that Gothic fiction presents the reader with a battle between good and evil.

2. 'Gothic fiction aims to create terror in the reader – but it is often a terror which has little impact on a twenty-first-century reader.' How far do you agree with this view of writing in the Gothic tradition?

3. 'Writing in the Gothic tradition evokes fear in its settings and its plot – but the real horror lies in its presentation of human nature.' In the light of this comment, consider some of the ways in which writers present human nature in the Gothic texts you have read.

4. To what extent do you agree with the view that the female characters in *The Bloody Chamber* are not afraid of men, but of themselves?

5. With reference to at least two stories from *The Bloody Chamber*, explore how Carter uses the Gothic tradition for her own purposes.

6. 'Carter's monsters are not creatures of the supernatural. They are us.' Consider at least two stories from *The Bloody Chamber* in the light of this comment.

7. Consider the significance of transformation in at least two or more stories from *The Bloody Chamber*.

8. 'The reader's fear is the objective of the ghost story – but it is not the sole intention of writing in the Gothic tradition.' Compare the intentions of the writer in the Gothic texts you have read.

ESSENTIAL STUDY TOOLS

FURTHER READING

GOTHIC TEXTS

Jane Austen, *Northanger Abbey*, 1818

Emily Brontë, *Wuthering Heights*, 1847

Geoffrey Chaucer, 'The Pardoner's Tale', in *The Canterbury Tales*, c.1387

Charles Dickens, *Great Expectations*, 1860–1

Daphne du Maurier, *Rebecca*, 1938

William Faulkner, *Sanctuary*, 1931

Joseph Sheridan le Fanu, 'Carmilla', 1872

Matthew G. Lewis, *The Monk*, 1796

Christopher Marlowe, *The Tragical History of Doctor Faustus*, 1604

John Milton, *Paradide Lost*, 1667

Toni Morrison, *Beloved*, 1987

Mervyn Peake, *Titus Groan*, 1946

Edgar Allan Poe, 'The Fall of the House of Usher', 1839

Edgar Allan Poe, 'The Raven', 1845

Ann Radcliffe, *The Mysteries of Udolpho*, 1794

William Shakespeare, *Macbeth*, 1606

Mary Shelley, *Frankenstein, or The Modern Prometheus*, 1818

Robert Louis Stevenson, *The Strange Case of Dr Jekyll and Mr Hyde*, 1886

Bram Stoker, *Dracula*, 1897

Graham Swift, *Waterland*, 1983

Horace Walpole, *The Castle of Otranto*, 1764

John Webster, *The White Devil*, 1612

H. G. Wells, *The Island of Doctor Moreau*, 1896

Oscar Wilde, *The Picture of Dorian Gray*, 1890

Sue Chaplin, *York Notes Companions: Gothic Literature*, York Press and Pearson, 2011

BIOGRAPHY

Sarah Gamble, *Angela Carter: A Literary Life*, Palgrave Macmillan, 2005

LITERARY CRITICISM ON ANGELA CARTER

Elizabeth Abel, Marianne Hirsch and Elizabeth Langland (eds.), *The Voyage In: Fictions of Female Development*, University Press of New England, 1983
Contains Ellen Cronan Rose's essay 'Through the Looking Glass: When Women Tell Fairy Tales'

Flora Alexander, *Contemporary Women Novelists*, Arnold, 1989
   Discusses *The Bloody Chamber*, as well as Carter's novels *The Magic Toyshop* and *Nights at the Circus*

Nanette Altevers, 'Gender Matters in *The Sadeian Woman*', *The Review of Contemporary Fiction*, 14:3, Fall 1994, pp. 18–23

Cristina Bacchilega, *Postmodern Fairy Tales: Gender and Narrative Strategies*, University of Pennsylvania Press, 1997
   Discusses the stories in *The Bloody Chamber* as examples of **postmodern feminist** fairy tales

Joseph Bristow and Trev Lynn Broughton (eds.), *The Infernal Desires of Angela Carter: Fiction, Femininity, Feminism*, Longman, 1997
   A collection of essays examining Carter's exploration of feminist and gender issues; includes Sally Keenan's 'Angela Carter's *The Sadeian Woman*: Feminism as Treason' and 'The Fragile Frames of *The Bloody Chamber*' by Lucie Armitt

Aidan Day, *Angela Carter: The Rational Glass*, Manchester University Press, 1998
   Examines Carter's fiction chronologically, with clear accounts of influences and theoretical interpretations

Patricia Duncker, 'Re-Imagining the Fairy Tales: Angela Carter's Bloody Chambers', *Literature and History*, 10:1, 1984, pp. 3–14
   An essay which gives a hostile reaction to *The Bloody Chamber* and *The Sadeian Woman*

Alison Easton (ed.), *Angela Carter: Contemporary Critical Essays,* Palgrave Macmillan, 2000
   Part of the New Casebook Series, this work includes Merja Makinen's essay 'Angela Carter's *The Bloody Chamber* and the Decolonization of Feminine Sexuality', first published in 1992; and Sally Keenan's essay 'Angela Carter's *The Sadeian Woman*: Feminism as Treason', first published in 1997

Sarah Gamble (ed.), *The Fiction of Angela Carter: A Reader's Guide to Essential Criticism*, Palgrave Macmillan, 2001
   This contains a useful and extensive bibliography of critical discussion of Carter's work in general, and helpfully identifies particular texts relevant to *The Bloody Chamber*

Richard J. Lane, Rod Mengham and Philip Tew (eds.), *Contemporary British Fiction,* Polity Press, 2003
   Contains Robert Eaglestone's essay 'The Fiction of Angela Carter'

Merja Makinen, 'Angela Carter's *The Bloody Chamber* and the Decolonization of Feminine Sexuality', *Feminist Review*, 42, Autumn 1992, pp. 2–15

Jago Morrison, *Contemporary Fiction*, Routledge, 2003
   Discusses significant texts by nine contemporary authors, including Carter ('Angela Carter: genealogies', Chapter 10, pp. 155–78)

Rebecca Munford (ed.), *Re Visiting Angela Carter: Texts, Contexts, Intertexts*, Palgrave Macmillan, 2006
   Contains Gina Wisker's essay 'Behind Locked Doors: Angela Carter, Horror and the Influence of Edgar Allan Poe' and Jacqueline Pearson's foreword

Linden Peach, *Angela Carter*, Palgrave Macmillan, 1997
   Looks at the magical and the **realist** elements in Carter's novels

Salman Rushdie, 'Angela Carter, 1940–92: a very good wizard, a very dear friend', *New York Times Book Review*, 8 March 1992

Lorna Sage (ed.), *Flesh and the Mirror: Essays on the Art of Angela Carter*, Virago Press, 1994
   A collection of essays on Carter's work by several contributors

John Sears, *Angela Carter's Monstrous Women*, Sheffield Hallam University Press, 1992
   Broader perspective on **feminism** in Carter's earlier works

Marina Warner, *From the Beast to the Blonde: On Fairy Tales and Their Tellers*, Chatto & Windus, 1994
   Refers to various stories from *The Bloody Chamber*

LITERARY TERMS

allegory   a story or a situation with two different meanings, where the straightforward meaning on the surface is used to **symbolise** a deeper meaning underneath. This secondary meaning is often a spiritual or moral one whose values are represented by specific figures, characters or events in the **narrative**

alliteration (alliterative)   the repetition of the same letter or sound in a stretch of language, most often at the beginnings of words or on stressed syllables

allusion   a passing reference in a work of literature to something outside the text; may include other works of literature, myth, historical facts or biographical detail

ambiguity   the capacity of words and sentences to have double, multiple or uncertain meanings

analogy   the comparison between an idea or object for the purpose of clarification or explanation; the illustration of an idea by means of a similar one; a literary parallel

anthropomorphism   the attribution of human characteristics and qualities to non-human objects or abstractions; also known as prosopopoeia (see also **personification**)

archetype   a standard character type showing typical traits, e.g. the vampire, the hero

aside   when a character in a play speaks in such a way that other characters cannot hear what is being said; or they address the audience directly. Similarly when the narrator in a story addresses the reader directly. It is a device used to reveal a character's private thoughts, emotions and intentions

caricature   a description of a person that exaggerates something about the person, often for comic effect

cliché   a widely used expression which, through overuse, has lost impact and originality

colloquial   everyday speech used by people in informal situations

commedia dell'arte   a type of comic drama evolved in sixteenth-century Italy using standard, recognisable plots usually based on love intrigues. Plot and dialogue were often improvised, and the performance would often include mimic, **farce**, slapstick buffoonery, dancing and music

conceit   an extended or elaborate concept that forges an unexpected connection between two apparently dissimilar things

couplet   a pair of rhymed lines

denouement   the point in the story where the whole plot has finally unfolded (from the French for 'untying a knot')

deus ex machina   in Greek drama a god was sometimes lowered onto the stage by a piece of machinery in order to assist the hero or untangle the plot (from the Latin for 'god out of a machine'). The phrase is often used today to indicate an unexpected and frequently improbable twist in the plot

didactic   a didactic text is one that expresses its author's intention to teach or instruct the reader in an explicit or implicit manner

epigraph   a quotation or comment placed at the beginning of a piece of work, relevant to the theme or content

eponymous   adjective describing the character who gives his or her name to the title of a play or novel

euphemism   an inoffensive word or phrase substituted for one considered offensive or hurtful

farce   a form of drama, though it can apply to any literary form, in which the comic is taken to extreme lengths of absurdity

feminism   a social perspective advocating the rights and claims of women arising in nineteenth-century Europe and re-emerging in the so-called 'second wave' of feminist writers who gained success in the 1970s. Although not a unified perspective, it had particular influence in the field of literary criticism in the latter part of the twentieth century

foreshadowing   a literary technique whereby the author mentions events which are yet to be revealed in the **narrative**, either to increase **dramatic tension**, or to provide clues for the reader to attempt to guess what will happen next

Gothic   a term originally applied to a medieval architectural style considered to be barbaric and uncivilised, in reference to the Dark Age tribe of the Goths. Later this term was taken into the identification of culture, literature or art that makes use of such stylistic reference points; though as a literary genre the term implies more than mere reference to architectural description – Gothic literature deals with passion, mystery, supernatural or horror, and usually employs a medieval setting such as a haunted castle or abbey

ideology   shared beliefs of a culture which are taken for granted and thus never questioned

imagery   descriptive language which uses images to make actions, objects and characters more vivid in the reader's mind. **Metaphors** and **similes** are examples of imagery

intertextuality   the explicit or implicit referencing of other texts within a work of literature. It is designed to put the work in the context of other literary works and traditions and implies parallels between them

irony   the humorous or sarcastic use of words to imply the opposite of what they normally mean; incongruity between what might be expected and what actually happens; the ill-timed arrival of an event that had been hoped for

magic realism   fiction or other art forms such as painting or cinema which combine **realism** with fantastic elements. It reminds the reader or observer that all art is created and invented. By the 1980s it was an established form of fiction; authors regarded as magic realists include Gabriel García Márquez (b.1928), Salman Rushdie (b.1947), Emma Tennant (b.1938) and Angela Carter

Mannerism   a term that refers to European art and architecture of *c.*1520–*c.*1600, between the Italian High Renaissance and the baroque. Mannerism is identified by its insistent use of artificial qualities: distorted forms, exaggerated postures and unnatural lighting effects; stylistically it is a rejection of the ideals of harmonious composition found in Leonardo da Vinci (1452–1519), Raphael (1483–1520) and Michelangelo (1475–1564)

Marxism   the political and economic theories of Karl Marx (1818–83) and Friedrich Engels (1820–95). In Marxism the class struggle is the basic force behind historical change. The economic conditions of a period determine or profoundly influence the political, social and cultural **ideology**. Marxist literary criticism is concerned with the relationship between the historical conditions and the ideology expressed in literature and which produces the work

materialism   in philosophy the idea that nothing exists except the material world and its shifts or changes, as opposed, for example, to religious or spiritual belief (**Marxism** is a materialist theory)

melodrama   a form of drama in which extravagant and sensational deeds and thinly drawn characters occur, with strong elements of violence, sexuality and evil and a simplistic moral or judicial code

metaphor   a figure of speech in which a word or phrase is applied to an object, a character or an action which does not literally belong to it, in order to imply a resemblance and create an unusual or striking image in the reader's mind

modernism   a movement that spanned the period from the closing years of the nineteenth century to the start of the Second World War; the term covers all the creative arts. While many artists and writers of different outlooks and achievements are categorised as 'modernist', certain principles are common, for example the rejection of established rules, traditions and conventions, and the exploration of abstract forms of expression. Authors such as T. S. Eliot (1888–1965), James Joyce (1882–1941), Virginia Woolf (1882–1941), D. H. Lawrence (1885–1930) and Samuel Beckett (1906–89) have all been called modernists

motif   a recurring subject, theme or idea

narrative   a story, tale or any recital of events, and the manner in which it is told. First person narratives ('I') are told from the character's perspective and usually require the reader to judge carefully what is being said; second person narratives ('you') suggest the reader is part of the story; in third person narratives ('he, 'she', 'they') the **narrator** may be intrusive (continually commenting on the story), impersonal or **omniscient**. More than one style of narrative may be used in a text

narrator   the voice telling the story or relating a sequence of events

omniscient narrator   a **narrator** who uses the third person **narrative** and has a godlike knowledge of events and of the thoughts and feelings of the characters

oxymoron   a figure of speech in which words with contradictory meanings are brought together for effect

paradox   a seemingly absurd or self-contradictory statement that is or may be true

parody   an imitation of a work of literature or a literary style designed to ridicule the original

pastiche   a form of imitation which uses pieces of the work of another writer either for comic effect or for acknowledgement of quality

pathetic fallacy   the attribution of human feelings to objects in nature and, commonly, weather systems, so that the mood of the **narrator** or the characters can be discerned from the behaviour of the surrounding environment

patriarchy   a social system of government in which power is held by the elder males and passed to the younger males exclusively; although the term pre-dates **feminism**, the concept of patriarchy is central to the feminist perspective

personification   the treatment or description of an object or an idea as human, with human attributes and feelings

postmodernism   a vague term, often controversial, used to refer to tendencies and developments in literature and other arts since the mid twentieth century. Characterised by a distrust of **ideologies** and theories, postmodernist literature is often non-traditional, featuring **parody**, **pastiche**, fatalism, **irony** and an eclectic approach. Forms of criticism embraced by postmodernism include **feminism**, **Marxism** and **psychoanalytic criticism**. Richard Dawkins comments on postmodernism: 'Never once have I heard anything that even remotely approaches a usable, or even faintly coherent, definition' (*A Devil's Chaplain: Reflections on Hope, Lies, Science, and Love*, 2003, p. 7)

protagonist   the principal character in a work of literature

psychoanalytic criticism   in literature, applying an approach to understanding a text by analysing the unconscious motivations of, for example, the characters

realism   literary portrayal of the 'real' world, in both physical and psychological detail, rather than an imaginary or ideal one. Victorian novels sometimes described themselves in this way

revisionism   in literature the rewriting or retelling of a well-known text or story in which characters and/or plot are changed in order to challenge the view presented in the original. These stories cover myths, folk and fairy tales, religious stories and **narratives** that have become embedded in the culture

rhetoric   structured and patterned language used in formal speech-making

satire   a type of literature in which folly, evil or topical issues are held up to scorn through ridicule, **irony** or exaggeration

semiotics   Swiss linguist Ferdinand de Saussure (1857–1913) proposed that language is made up of a system of signs. A sign is something that stands for something else (for example the word 'chair' stands for the 'thing that we sit on'). The word 'chair' is the signifier and 'thing that we sit on' is the signified. His ideas led to the development of semiotics, which examines signs in such fields as literary theory, psychology and anthropology

simile   a figure of speech which compares two things using the words 'like' or 'as'

symbol   something that represents something else by association

symbolic, symbolism   investing material objects with abstract powers and meanings greater than their own; allowing a complex idea to be represented by a single object

synonym   a word that means the same or nearly the same as another word

tragedy   in its original sense, a drama dealing with elevated actions and emotions and characters of high social standing in which a terrible outcome becomes inevitable as a result of an unstoppable sequence of events and a fatal flaw in the personality of the **protagonist**. More recently, tragedy has come to include courses of events happening to ordinary individuals that are inevitable because of social and cultural conditions or natural disasters.

TIMELINE

WORLD EVENTS	LITERARY EVENTS	ANGELA CARTER'S LIFE
1939 Second World War begins	**1939** James Joyce, *Finnegans Wake*	
1940 British Expeditionary Force rescued from Dunkirk beaches by naval and civilian fleet; assassination of Leon Trotsky	**1940** Graham Greene, *The Power and the Glory*; Edmund Wilson, *To the Finland Station*	**1940** Born 7 May in Eastbourne; evacuated to South Yorkshire
	1941 Bertolt Brecht, *Mother Courage and Her Children*	
1944 D-Day landings; Education Act raises school leaving age to fifteen		
1945 End of Second World War; welfare state in Britain introduced	**1945** George Orwell, *Animal Farm*; Tennessee Williams's *The Glass Menagerie* opens on Broadway	**1945** Family moves to Balham, south London
1946 Cold War begins	**1946** Mervyn Peake, *Titus Groan*	
1947 India gains independence from Britain	**1947** J. B. Priestley, *An Inspector Calls*	
1948 Establishment of National Health Service	**1948** T. S. Eliot awarded Nobel Prize	
	1949 Simone de Beauvoir, *The Second Sex*	
1951 Festival of Britain; Winston Churchill resigns as prime minister	**1951** J. D. Salinger, *The Catcher in the Rye*	**1951** Passes eleven plus exam; attends 'direct grant' school
1953 Coronation of Queen Elizabeth II	**1954** Kingsley Amis, *Lucky Jim*; William Golding, *Lord of the Flies*	
	1955 Samuel Beckett, *Waiting for Godot* (English translation); Vladimir Nabokov, *Lolita*	
1956 Hungarian revolution crushed by Soviet military intervention		
	1957 Jack Kerouac, *On the Road*	**1957** Anorexia affects academic performance
1958 Empire Day renamed Commonwealth Day; Campaign for Nuclear Disarmament (CND) formed	**1958** Harold Pinter, *The Birthday Party*	**1958** Works as reporter for *Croydon Advertiser*
1959 Revolution in Cuba brings Fidel Castro to power		
	1960 Penguin Books acquitted in obscenity trial for publication of D. H. Lawrence's *Lady Chatterley's Lover*	**1960** Marries Paul Carter
1961 Berlin Wall built	**1961** Joseph Heller, *Catch-22*	
1962 Cuban missile crisis	**1962** Anthony Burgess, *A Clockwork Orange*	**1962** Studies English at Bristol University
1963 President John F. Kennedy assassinated	**1963** Betty Friedan, *The Feminine Mystique*	
	1964 A. S. Byatt, *Shadow of a Sun*; Philip Larkin, *The Whitsun Weddings*	
1965 Death of Winston Churchill; abolition of death penalty; US openly enters Vietnam War		**1965** Gains BA in English

WORLD EVENTS	LITERARY EVENTS	ANGELA CARTER'S LIFE
	1966 Jean Rhys, *Wide Sargasso Sea*; Susan Sontag, *Against Interpretation*	**1966** Begins reviews for *New Society* and the *Guardian*; first novel, *Shadow Dance*, published
1967 Decriminalisation of homosexuality in Britain; The Beatles release *Sgt. Pepper's Lonely Hearts Club Band*	**1967** Gabriel García Márquez, *One Hundred Years of Solitude* (translated into English 1970); Peter Nichols, *A Day in the Death of Joe Egg*	**1967** *The Magic Toyshop* published and wins John Llewellyn Rhys Prize
1968 Student protests in Paris; Martin Luther King assassinated; Czechoslovakia invaded by Soviet troops to crush liberal reforms of Alexander Dubcek	**1968** Gore Vidal, *Myra Breckenridge*	**1968** *Several Perceptions*
1969 British troops sent into Ireland; Neil Armstrong becomes first man on moon	**1969** Maya Angelou, *I Know Why the Caged Bird Sings*; John Fowles, *The French Lieutenant's Woman*; Kurt Vonnegut, *Slaughterhouse-Five*	**1969** *Heroes and Villains*; wins Somerset Maugham Award for *Several Perceptions*; separates from husband and travels to Japan; death of mother
	1970 Germaine Greer, *The Female Eunuch*; Kate Millett, *Sexual Politics*; Dario Fo, *Accidental Death of an Anarchist* (translated into English 1979)	
1971 Women's Liberation march in London	**1971** Anne Sexton, *Transformations*	**1971** *Love*
1972 Watergate scandal; Bloody Sunday shootings in Northern Ireland		**1972** Returns to England; divorces Paul Carter; *The Infernal Desire Machines of Doctor Hoffman*
1973 Britain joins European Economic Community	**1973** Martin Amis, *The Rachel Papers*; Erica Jong, *Fear of Flying*	
	1973–5 Alexander Solzhenitsyn, *The Gulag Archipelago*	
	1974 Shere Hite, *Sexual Honesty: By Women for Women*	**1974** *Fireworks: Nine Profane Pieces*
1975 End of Vietnam War: American withdrawal is major defeat for US	**1975** Ruth Prawer Jhabvala, *Heat and Dust*	
1976 The Sex Pistols release the single 'Anarchy in the UK'	**1976** Alex Haley, *Roots*	**1976–8** Arts Council Fellow at Sheffield University
		1977 *The Passion of New Eve*; *The Fairy Tales of Charles Perrault* (translator); marries second husband, Mark Pearce; member of Virago Press advisory board
	1978 Ian McEwan, *The Cement Garden*; Iris Murdoch, *The Sea, the Sea*; Emma Tennant, *The Bad Sister*	
1979 Tories win general election; Margaret Thatcher becomes prime minister	**1979** Peter Shaffer, *Amadeus*	**1979** *The Sadeian Woman*; **The Bloody Chamber** published and wins Cheltenham Festival of Literature Award; *Martin Leman's Comic and Curious Cats*
1980 John Lennon shot	**1980** Umberto Eco, *The Name of the Rose*	**1980** *The Music People*
1981 Ronald Reagan becomes US president; mass protests at Greenham Common against nuclear weapons; first reported case of Aids	**1981** Anita Brookner, *A Start in Life*; Liz Lochhead, *The Grimm Sisters*; Salman Rushdie, *Midnight's Children*	**1980–1** Visiting professor of creative writing at Brown University, Rhode Island

WORLD EVENTS	LITERARY EVENTS	ANGELA CARTER'S LIFE
1982 Falklands War	**1982** Isabel Allende, *The House of the Spirits* (published in English 1985)	**1982** *Moonshadow*; *Nothing Sacred: Selected Writings*; *Sleeping Beauty and Other Favourite Fairy Tales* (editor and translator)
	1983 J. M. Coetzee, *The Life and Times of Michael K*; Graham Swift, *Waterland*; Fay Weldon, *The Life and Loves of a She-Devil*	**1983** Son, Alexander Pearce, born
1984 Miners' strike; IRA bomb at Conservative Party Conference; Indira Gandhi, Indian prime minister, assassinated	**1984** Pat Barker, *Blow Your House Down*; Milan Kundera, *The Unbearable Lightness of Being*	**1984** Writer in residence at University of Adelaide, South Australia; *Nights at the Circus* published and wins James Tait Black Memorial Award for Fiction; film of *The Company of Wolves* released
		1984–7 Part-time teacher at University of East Anglia
1985 Glasnost and perestroika begin in USSR	**1985** Margaret Atwood, *The Handmaid's Tale*; Gabriel García Márquez, *Love in the Time of Cholera* (translated into English 1988); Jeanette Winterson, *Oranges Are Not the Only Fruit*	**1985** *Black Venus* anthology; teaches in Austin, Texas
		1986 Teaches in Iowa City, Iowa
	1987 Toni Morrison, *Beloved*	**1987** Television film of *The Magic Toyshop*
	1988 Salman Rushdie, *The Satanic Verses*; Ayatollah Khomeini declares *fatawa* on Rushdie	**1988** Teaches in Albany, New York State; father dies
1989 Berlin Wall dismantled; Tiananmen Square protests and killings in China	**1989** Kazuo Ishiguro, *The Remains of the Day*; Emma Tennant, *Two Women of London: The Strange Case of Ms Jekyll and Mrs Hyde*	
1990 Poll tax demonstrations; Margaret Thatcher resigns; Nelson Mandela released from prison; international stock market crash known as Black Monday	**1990** Derek Walcott, *Omeros*	**1990** *The Virago Book of Fairy Tales* (editor)
1991 Collapse of Soviet Union; internet established; First Gulf War	**1991** Ben Okri, *The Famished Road*	**1991** *Wise Children*
	1992 David Mamet, *Oleanna*; Michael Ondaatje, *The English Patient*	**1992** Dies 16 February of lung cancer; *The Second Virago Book of Fairy Tales* (editor)
	1993 Vikram Seth, *A Suitable Boy*	**1993** *American Ghosts and Old World Wonders* published posthumously
1994 Nelson Mandela becomes president of South Africa	**1994** A. S. Byatt, *The Djinn in the Nightingale's Eye*	
	1995 Salman Rushdie, *The Moor's Last Sigh*	**1995** *Burning Your Boats: Collected Short Stories* published posthumously
	1999 Carol Ann Duffy, *The World's Wife*	

REVISION FOCUS TASK ANSWERS

TASK 1

The narrator's simple naivety makes it difficult for the reader to sympathise with her.

- Our sympathies are prompted from the outset of the story as it is told from her viewpoint.
- A victim, even a naive one, is likely to engender the reader's sympathy.
- If we are relieved at her escape at the end of the tale, it suggests she has our sympathy throughout.

The Marquis is to blame for the narrator's curiosity and disobedience.

- It is suggested that the Marquis traps his new bride intentionally.
- Is it in any way acceptable to blame the narrator for her actions?
- The Marquis's response suggests unquestioning obedience is the expectation of the dominant patriarch.

TASK 2

Carter's stories suggest that all human beings can change, or be changed.

- Transformation is a key element in the collection.
- Transformation and change are consistently presented as possible and positive in these stories.
- Several stories focus on the need for change, and the means by which women can achieve it.

This story is not typical of the collection; it is a straightforward retelling of a fairy tale.

- This is, perhaps, the most recognisable story in the collection.
- Carter adds layers of meaning in her use of language and symbolism.
- It shares several significant features with other stories in the collection, e.g. transformation, inadequate parenting.

TASK 3

In Carter's stories, women must become more like men if they are to become equals.

- The transformation of a woman in this story is not typical of the collection.
- It could suggest that the girl is not becoming more like a man, but acknowledging and accepting her animal nature.
- Carter rarely implies the need for equality; she emphasises escape from oppression.

Human weakness is at the heart of all these tales.

- In this tale, the father's weakness is significant to the narrative.
- It allows the girl's apparent imprisonment which, in turn, allows her liberation.
- It could be argued that weakness is at the heart of the conflicts in the stories but strength lies at the heart of their resolution.

TASK 4

'Puss-in-Boots' is so different from the other tales, it seems out of place in the collection.

- It is the only purely comic tale.

- However, like other tales it argues the ingenuity and resourcefulness of women.

- It is typical in its combination of luxuriant language and blunt vulgarity.

TASK 5

The Erl-King represents the very essence of man: selfish, unthinking, innocent and destructive.

- The image of women as song birds in cages suggests this character represents men's oppression of women.

- He is, however, presented with significant stereotypically female characteristics.

- The final lines of the story shatter and distort any clear interpretation of this tale.

TASK 6

This is the most shocking of the tales in the collection.

- There are several vivid and graphically described moments of shock in the collection.

- The incident of incestuous necrophilia combines two weighty taboos.

- It is perhaps the most vivid intrusion of taboo sexuality into the fairy-tale world.

TASK 7

This tale draws more fully on the Gothic tradition than any other in the collection.

- The setting and characters are clearly drawn from the Gothic, and specifically the vampire, tradition.

- However, Carter typically subverts the villain/victim relationship.

- Similarly subverted, the vampire is presented as a sympathetic victim of her own inescapable nature.

Carter's characters cannot help themselves: they are victims of circumstance or victims of their own nature.

- The vampire is a victim of her ancestors, her inherited vampire nature.

- Many characters in the tales find themselves in circumstances seemingly beyond their control.

- However, throughout the collection, change is always shown to be possible.

TASK 8

Many of the characters in these tales are symbols: they represent aspects of human nature or society.

- Throughout the collection, characters presented as 'real people' also carry symbolic significance.

- Some characters are undeveloped, suggesting they are purely symbolic, e.g. the grandmother in 'The Werewolf'.

- Many of the stories can be read as simple tales of conflict and resolution without any acknowledgement of their symbolic significance; in others, e.g. 'The Snow Child', the symbolism is more overt.

TASK 9

Each of Carter's tales is intentionally open to a number of different interpretations.

- Carter never explicitly provides the reader with her intended 'moral' or interpretation.

- Like the mirrors in the Marquis's bedroom, her stories create infinite reflections of human nature.

- Many stories lack full resolution, e.g. 'The Snow Child', 'The Erl-King', leaving much work for the reader to do.

TASK 10

The end of 'Wolf-Alice' – and the collection as a whole – suggests there are possibilities of harmonious and balanced relationships between men and women.

- Several of the stories end on such harmonious notes, e.g. 'The Bloody Chamber', 'The Company of Wolves', 'The Tiger's Bride'.

- These endings rely on the characters' mutual acceptance.

- The only example of a long-established relationship – 'The Snow Child' – presents a less positive picture!

TASK 11

In Angela Carter's world, all men are monsters.

- There are some sympathetic portrayals of men, e.g. the piano-tuner in 'The Bloody Chamber'.

- Few male characters are as irredeemably monstrous as the Marquis. It can be argued that Carter intends the piano-tuner's portrayal in opposition to this.

- The revelation of the man within the monster – and vice versa – is key in a number of the stories.

TASK 12

In Carter's stories, the role which society expects of women is much more complex than the role it expects of men.

- It can be argued that, in Carter's tales, men are presented simplistically; they tend to have one defining characteristic, e.g. sexual appetite.

- The repression and oppression of women and the complex consequences of this are explored extensively in these tales.

- While the stories question man's position in society, Carter presents a society which does not.

TASK 13

Every character in the collection is either a predator or a victim.

- A central concept of the fairy-tale genre is the helpless victim in danger: it insists, therefore, on predators and victims.

- Unlike fairy tales, many of Carter's stories are not resolved in the victim's escape and the predator's punishment, but in their reconciliation.

- In 'The Lady of the House of Love' Carter subverts these roles: the predator is liberated from her role in death; the young man dies in battle, a victim of 'civilisation'.

Carter's stories explore how love can transform or destroy us.

- There are several significant examples of transformation bringing emotional and physical resolution: 'The Tiger's Bride', Wolf-Alice'.

- Although transformation can be viewed as a kind of destruction – the girl in 'The Tiger's Bride' loses her humanity – the gain is presented as far outweighing the loss.

- The clearest example of threatened destruction – 'The Bloody Chamber' – is hardly a case of love, more of naivety.

TASK 14

The traditional fairy tale rewards its heroes with a happy marriage. Carter, however, presents marriage as a dark and frightening prospect.

- This is certainly true of 'The Bloody Chamber'.

- None of the other stories explore the formalisation of relationships in marriage; though 'The Courtship of Mr Lyon' ends happily with a reference to 'Mr and Mrs Lyon'.

- The majority of tales focus on the resolution of danger and reconciliation through sexuality or a variety of equilibrium between man and woman.

MARK SCHEME

Use this page to assess your answer to the **Worked task**, provided on page 112.

Aiming for an A grade? Fulfil all the criteria below and your answer should hit the mark.*

> 'Carter has created a cruel world, filled with wicked people.' How do you respond to this view of *The Bloody Chamber*?

AO1 Articulate creative, informed and relevant responses to literary texts, using appropriate terminology and concepts, and coherent, accurate written expression.

- You make a range of clear, relevant points about the cruelty of the environment and the wickedness of the characters in Carter's stories.
- You write a balanced essay covering both positions.
- You use a range of literary terms correctly, e.g. **allegory**, **protagonist**, theme, **imagery**, **symbol**, **intertextuality**, **Gothic**.
- You write a clear introduction, outlining your thesis and provide a clear conclusion.
- You signpost and link your ideas about cruelty and wickedness.

AO2 Demonstrate detailed critical understanding in analysing the ways in which structure, form and language shape meanings in literary texts.

- You explain the techniques and methods Carter uses to present cruelty and wickedness and link them to main themes of the text.
- You may discuss, for example, the ways in which the naivety of the bride in 'The Bloody Chamber' emphasises the Marquis's cruelty; or the ways in which The Beast's apparent ruthlessness in 'The Tiger's Bride' misleads the reader in their expectations of the story's denouement.
- You explain in detail how your examples affect meaning, e.g. the way in which Carter's use of graphic and explicit language in 'The Bloody Chamber' and 'The Snow Child' emphasises the savage sexuality of her characters.
- You may explore how the settings – the forest or the harsh winter landscape – contribute to the presentation of cruelty and wickedness.

AO3 Explore connections and comparisons between different literary texts, informed by interpretations of other readers.

- You make relevant links between Assef and the concept of evil, noting how the description of the former interacts with commentary on the latter.
- You make relevant links between cruelty and wickedness in two or more of Carter's stories, noting how characters' environments influence their actions and direct the reader's response to them.
- When appropriate, you compare cruelty and wickedness in the course of the stories with the presentation of cruelty and wickedness in other text(s), e.g. the creature's actions and the reader's response in *Frankenstein*.
- You incorporate and comment on critics' views of how cruelty and wickedness are presented in the stories.
- You assert your own independent view clearly.

AO4 Demonstrate understanding of the significance and influence of the contexts in which literary texts are written and received.

You explain how relevant aspects of social, literary and historical contexts of *The Bloody Chamber* are significant when interpreting depictions of cruelty and wickedness. For example, you may discuss:
- Literary context: how Carter uses, transforms and subverts the cruelty and wickedness of traditional tales.
- Historical context: the ways in which Carter's female characters reflect the sexual revolution of the 1960s and 1970s and feminist theory in challenging cruelty and wickedness.
- Social context: how the majority of Carter's male characters reflect the patriarchy of society and her stories explore the ways in which women can respond to, and escape, their dominance.

* This mark scheme gives you a broad indication of attainment, but check the specific mark scheme for your paper/task to ensure you know what to focus on.